unbreak my
HEART

unbreak my HEART

NICOLE JACQUELYN

FOREVER

New York   Boston

Copyright © 2016 by Nicole Jacquelyn
Excerpt from *Change of Heart* © 2016 by Nicole Jacquelyn
Cover design by FaceOut. Cover photography © Chris Gramly/Getty Images. Cover copyright © 2016 by Hachette Book Group, Inc.

Forever
Hachette Book Group
1290 Avenue of the Americas
New York, NY 10104
forever-romance.com
twitter.com/foreverromance

First Edition: June 2016

Forever is an imprint of Grand Central Publishing.
The Forever name and logo are trademarks of Hachette Book Group, Inc.

The publisher is not responsible for websites (or their content) that are not owned by the publisher.

The Hachette Speakers Bureau provides a wide range of authors for speaking events. To find out more, go to www.hachettespeakersbureau.com or call (866) 376-6591.

Lyrics from "Thief and a Liar" © 2012 by Jeffrey Martin. All rights reserved.

Library of Congress Cataloging-in-Publication Data
Names: Jacquelyn, Nicole.
Title: Unbreak my heart / Nicole Jacquelyn.
Description: New York : Forever, 2016.
Identifiers: LCCN 2016001579 | ISBN 9781455537969 (paperback)
Subjects: LCSH: Best friends--Fiction. | Military spouses--Fiction. | Single parents--Fiction. | Self-realization in women--Fiction. | Love stories. | BISAC: FICTION / Contemporary Women. | FICTION / Romance / Contemporary. | FICTION / Family Life.
Classification: LCC PS3610.A35684 U53 2016 | DDC 813/.6—dc23 LC record available at http://lccn.loc.gov/2016001579

ISBNs: 978-1-4555-3796-9 (trade paperback), 978-1-4555-3797-6 (ebook)

Printed in the United States of America

RRD-C

10 9 8 7 6 5 4 3 2 1

For my mother, who will cry when she reads this dedication. I love you, Mom.

Acknowledgments

Thank you to my daughters, who ate more fast food than any of us were happy about and smiled the entire time. I love you. To my parents, who made dinner and coffee and took care of my girls so that I could write, and my sister who listened to me plot: Thank you.

To Nikki, who never sugarcoated any of her feedback and loves these characters as much as I do: Thank you a million times.

To Ashley, who opened a thousand doors for me when she convinced me to send *Unbreak My Heart* to her agent, to Toni who cheered me on through every sleepless night, and to Donna who has been with me since the beginning of this journey, I can never thank you enough.

To my agent, Marisa, who was so excited the first time she read Kate and Shane's story that she was texting me as she read, and my editor, Alex, who spent hours upon hours making sure everything in *Unbreak My Heart* was just right: Thank you.

To the readers and bloggers who have gotten me this far, I owe you big, and I hope you love this story as much as I do.

unbreak my
HEART

Prologue
Shane

W hy are we going to this shit again?" I asked my wife as she messed with her makeup in the passenger-side mirror.

"Because it's important to your cousin."

"She's not my cousin," I reminded her, switching lanes.

"Fine. It's important to *Kate*," she answered, losing patience. "I don't understand why you're being a dick about it."

"How often do we get out of the house with no kids, Rach? Rarely. I'd rather not spend our one night alone at some fucking coffeehouse filled with eighteen-year-olds."

"Damn, you're on a roll tonight," she murmured in annoyance. "Kate asked me to this thing weeks ago. I didn't know you'd be home."

"Right, plans change."

"I promised I'd go! I drop everything for you every

time you come back from deployment. You know I do. I can't believe you're acting like a jackass because of *one night* that I had plans I couldn't change."

"I highly doubt Kate wants me here," I mumbled back, pulling into the little parking lot that was already filled with cars. "She's going to hate it when I see her crash and burn."

I hopped out of the car and walked around the hood to help Rachel out of the car. I never understood why she insisted on wearing high-as-fuck heels while she was pregnant—it made me nervous. She looked hot as hell, but one day she was going to fall and I was terrified I wouldn't be there to catch her.

"You really have no idea, do you?" she said, laughing, as I took her hand and pulled her gently out of her seat. "How in God's name did you grow up together and you still know so little about Kate?"

"You know I didn't grow up with her." I slammed the door shut and walked her slowly toward the small building. "I moved in when I was seventeen and left town when I was nineteen. She's not family, for Christ's sake. She's the spoiled, *weird* niece of the people who took me in for a very short period of time."

Rachel stopped short at the annoyance in my voice. "She's my *best friend*. My only friend. And she freaking introduced us, in case you've forgotten."

"Not on purpose."

"What's that supposed to mean? What wasn't on purpose?"

"She was pissed as hell when we got together."

"No, she wasn't," Rachel argued. "What are you talking about?"

"Never mind. It's not important."

"Can you please, *please*, just be nice and not act like you're being tortured when we get in there? I don't know what your deal is with her—"

"I don't have a deal with her, I just wanted to take my gorgeous wife out to dinner tonight, and instead we're going to watch her friend sing for a bunch of teenagers. Not exactly what I was hoping for."

I reached out to cup her cheek in my palm and rubbed the skin below her lips with my finger. I wanted to kiss her, but after all the lipstick she'd applied in the car, I knew she wouldn't thank me for it.

"We'll go somewhere else afterward, okay? I think she's on first, so we won't be here long," she assured me with a small smile, her eyes going soft. She knew I wanted to kiss her; my hand on her face was a familiar gesture.

"Okay, baby." I leaned in and kissed the tip of her nose gently. "You look beautiful. Did I tell you that yet?"

"Nope."

"Well, you do."

She smiled and started walking toward the building again, and I brushed my fingers through the short hair on the back of my head.

It wasn't that I disliked Kate. Quite the opposite, actually. When we were kids, we'd been friends, and I'd thought she was funny as hell. She had a quirky, sometimes weird sense of humor, and she'd been the most genuinely kind person I'd ever met. But for some reason, all those years ago, she'd suddenly focused in on me, and the attention had made me uncomfortable.

I wasn't into her, and her crush had made me feel weird, uncomfortable in my own skin. I didn't want to hurt her feelings, but shit, she just didn't do it for me. She was too clean-cut, too naive and trusting. Even then, I'd been more attracted to women who were a little harder, a little darker, than the girl who still had posters of fairies on her walls at seventeen.

So I began avoiding her as much as I could until she'd brought home a girl wearing red lipstick and covered in tattoos after her first semester in college. I'd ignored the way Kate had watched me with sad eyes as I'd monopolized her friend's time and completely disregarded her hurt feelings. I'd never liked Kate that way, and I hadn't seen anything wrong with going after her new friend.

I'd ended up married to her roommate, and from then on I'd acted like Kate and I had never been friends. It was easier that way.

"Come on, baby," Rachel called, pulling me into the darkened coffeehouse. "I see a table, and my feet are killing me."

Why the fuck did she insist on wearing those damn shoes?

"Can I get you anything to drink?" a small waitress asked us. Like, really small. She was barely taller than the bistro table we were sitting at.

"Can I get a green tea, please?" Rachel asked.

"Sure! The green we've got is incredible. When are you due?"

"Not for a while."

"Well, congratulations!"

"Black coffee," I ordered when the friendly waitress finally looked my way. Her smile fell, and I realized my words had come out shorter than I'd intended.

"Sure thing!" she chirped with a tight smile before walking away.

"Seriously, Shane?" Rachel growled in annoyance.

"What?" I knew exactly what. I'd been a jackass, but I wasn't about to explain that the crowded coffeehouse was making me sweat. People were laughing loudly, jostling and bumping into each other around the room, and I couldn't see the exits from where we sat.

"Hey, San Diego," a familiar voice called out over the speakers. "How you guys doing tonight?"

The room filled with cheers, and Rachel's face lit up as she looked past me toward the stage.

"Aren't you sweet?" Kate rasped with a short chuckle. "I dig you guys, too."

The crowd grew even louder, and my shoulders tightened in response.

"There's a coffee can being passed around, who's got it?" She paused. "Okay, Lola's got it now—back there in the purple shirt with the Mohawk. When you get it, add a couple dollars, if you can, and pass it on."

The crowd clapped, and Kate chuckled again over the sound system. "I better get started before you guys riot."

I still hadn't turned to look at her. Frankly, I didn't want to embarrass her if she sucked. I didn't—

The clear notes of a single guitar came through the speakers, and I froze as the entire room went silent. Completely silent. Even the baristas behind the counter stopped what they were doing to watch the stage as Kate began to sing.

Holy shit. My head whipped around, and I felt like I'd taken a cheap shot to the chest.

Her voice was raspy and full-bodied, and she was cradling her guitar like a baby that she'd held every day of her entire life. She was completely comfortable up there, tapping her foot and smiling at different people in the crowd as they began to sing along with her.

It was incredible. *She* was incredible. I couldn't look away. This wasn't some silly idea she'd had on the spur of the moment. She knew exactly what she was doing, and these kids knew her. They freaking loved her.

And she looked gorgeous.

Shit.

Her hair was rolled up on the sides in something Rachel had attempted a few times. I think they were called victory rolls? I'm pretty sure that's what Rach had called them when she couldn't figure them out. Her skin was smooth, and she wore deep-pink lipstick that made her teeth bright white under the spotlight. She was wearing a T-shirt that hung off her shoulder and ripped jeans that were so tight, I wasn't even sure how she'd managed to sit down.

I blinked slowly, and she was still there.

"I tried to tell you she was good," Rachel said smugly from my side.

"Did she write that song?" I asked, turning to look at my wife.

"Babe, seriously? It's a Taylor Swift song."

"Oh."

"This one's a Kenny Chesney song."

"I know this one," I murmured, looking back toward the stage. "Does she only sing country?"

"Hell no. It's mostly other stuff, but it's usually got a theme. Tonight is obviously about kids...teenagers, since the donations are going to some stop-bullying charity."

I nodded, but my eyes were on the stage again as Kate danced a little in her seat, tapping out the beat of the new song on the front of her guitar. Had Kate been bullied? I didn't remember anything like that, but like I'd told Rachel, I'd only stayed with Kate's aunt and uncle for a little over a year before I left for boot camp. Maybe I'd missed it. The thought made me grind my teeth in anger.

Kate pursed her bright lips then, blowing a kiss with a wink for the crowd.

My breath caught.

Jesus Christ.

I pushed my seat back from the table and grabbed Rachel's hand, pulling her over to sit on my lap.

"What are you doing?" she whispered with a laugh.

"If I've gotta stay here, I'm getting some perks."

"Oh yeah?"

"Yeah." I leaned in and kissed her hard, ignoring the lipstick I could feel smearing over my lips. I slid my tongue into her mouth and felt her nails dig into my shoulder as she tilted her head for a better angle. God, kissing her still felt as good as it had the first time I'd done it. I hadn't known that loving someone so much was even possible before I'd met her.

"Rain check?" she asked against my lips as she reached out blindly and grabbed a couple of napkins to clean off our faces. Her face was flushed, and I wanted nothing more than to leave that fucking coffeehouse and get her alone.

My wife was the most beautiful woman I'd ever known, and it wasn't just her looks. She'd grown up like I had, scrounged and fought for every single thing she'd needed—and I was proud of the family and the life we'd built together. We'd come a long way from our nasty upbringings.

"Can we go home yet?" I replied with a smirk as I wiped my face.

"Hey, you two in the corner!" Kate called into the mike, interrupting the incredibly sexy look Rachel was giving me. "None of that, I've got kids here."

The crowd laughed, and I glanced sharply at the stage.

Kate was smiling so brightly that she looked giddy. "That's my best friend, right there. Isn't she gorgeous?"

The crowd cheered as Rachel laughed softly in my ear and blew a kiss at Kate.

"I wanna know who the guy is!" a girl called out from across the room, making everyone laugh.

"Eh, that's just her husband," Kate answered flatly, making the crowd snicker. She met my eyes and winked, then grinned before looking away and starting in on the next song as if she hadn't just made my stomach drop.

We watched her for almost an hour as she fucking killed it on stage. Then I ushered Rachel out of the building without saying good-bye, making excuses about wanting to beat the rush of kids.

I had the distinct impression that I knew very little about the woman I'd been avoiding for the past ten years, and I wondered how I'd missed it. She wasn't the awkward girl I remembered, or the sloppy woman in sweats and tank tops that Rachel occasionally invited over to the house when I was home.

The Kate I'd seen on stage was a fucking knockout—confident and sassy. I knew then that I'd continue to avoid her, but for an entirely different reason than I had before.

Kate

Two months later

Evans Web Design," I answered my phone as I switched lanes on the freeway. God, traffic was a nightmare.

"Is this Katherine Evans?"

"Yes, who's this?"

"Sorry, this is Tiffany from Laurel Elementary School. I'm calling because you're Sage Anderson's emergency contact number—"

"Is Sage okay?" I interrupted, flipping off the car that honked at me. Why the hell would they call me and not her mother?

"Sage is fine, Ms. Evans. We were just wondering if you knew who was supposed to pick her up from school today? Class ended about thirty minutes ago, and no one was here to get her."

"Her mom picks her up," I replied, looking at the clock on my dash. "She didn't call?"

"No, ma'am. We've been trying to reach her, but haven't been able to."

"That's weird."

"It is," she agreed.

"Okay, well, I'll come get her and try to get ahold of Rachel, but it's going to take me at least half an hour." It looked like my appointment downtown was going to have to be postponed.

"That's totally fine. Sage can just hang with me in the office."

"Okay, tell her Auntie Kate will be there soon."

I hung up and pulled off the freeway so I could turn around. Shit, if I tried to go north I'd be stuck in stop-and-go traffic for the next two hours. I navigated back streets working toward Sage's school, calling Rachel over and over. The longer she didn't answer, the more my stomach tightened.

My best friend wouldn't forget to pick up her child at school. She was a second grader, for pete's sake. It wasn't like her pickup time was any different than it had been for the last two years. Something was off.

It took me less time than I thought to get to Sage's school, and I whipped into a parking space with shaky hands.

I had an awful feeling in my gut that I couldn't seem to calm.

"Hey, I'm looking for a girl, short, dark hair, goes by some ridiculous plant name..." I said in my most serious voice as I reached the front office.

"Auntie Kate! I'm right here!"

"Ah, yep. That's the one I'm looking for," I teased, smiling as my favorite girl in the whole world wrapped her arms around me.

"You just have to sign her out," the office lady said with a grin.

"No problem."

I signed Sage out and walked her to my car, popping the trunk to pull out the spare booster I kept there.

"Where's my mom?" Sage asked, bouncing around on her toes. The excitement of riding around in my car had obviously eclipsed the trauma she'd endured by being forgotten at school.

"I'm not sure, kiddo," I answered as I got her situated in the backseat.

"Daddy's at the range today!" Sage informed me as we made our way to her house.

"Oh yeah?"

"Yeah, he's been home for a long time."

"It sure seems that way, doesn't it?" I replied cheerfully. She had no idea.

I didn't mind that Rachel wanted to spend time with Shane while he was home. I totally understood it. But it sucked being the friend who was ignored when someone's significant other came home from yet another military deployment. I practically lived with Rachel while Shane was gone—she hated being alone—but the moment her husband stepped foot on American soil, I was persona non grata again.

It had been happening for years. I wasn't sure why it still bothered me.

"Mom's going to have a baby soon," Sage piped up from the backseat as I turned onto their street.

"I know, pretty exciting, right?"

"Yeah. She's having another brother, though."

"What's wrong with brothers? I have two brothers," I reminded her, pulling into their empty driveway.

I climbed out of the car as she started to answer and looked at the quiet house in confusion when no one came to greet us. Where the hell were Rachel and the boys?

Sage continued rambling on as I helped her out of her seat. "—wanted a sister. Boys stink, and they only play with boy stuff—"

"Kate?" someone called from across the street. "Where's Rachel? She was supposed to pick up the boys like two hours ago!"

I turned to see Rachel's neighbor Megan crossing the dead-end street with Gavin on her hip and Keller skipping alongside her.

"No clue," I answered quietly as she reached me. "The school called because she didn't pick Sage up. I've been trying to reach her for the last forty minutes."

"Where's my mom?" Sage asked, looking between us in confusion.

"Hey, sis, take the boys inside for me, would ya?" I handed her my keys as Megan set Gavin on the ground. "I'll be inside in a sec, and we'll make a snack. You guys want to make some cookies?"

"Yeah!" Keller yelled, throwing his fist in the air.

"No hello for your favorite aunt?" I asked him with a raised brow.

"Hi, Auntie Kate! Cookies!" he yelled, racing toward the door with Gavin and Sage trailing behind him.

I watched as Sage unlocked the door, leaving the keys hanging in the lock as she rushed inside.

"What the hell is going on?" I asked, turning to Megan.

"I have no clue. She said she was going to get her nails done and she'd be back in, like, an hour. It's been well over three now," she replied in frustration, wrapping her arms around her waist.

"That's not like her."

"No, I know it's not." She rushed to add, "I'm not mad, I'm worried. She's usually back *before* she says she'll be."

"Auntie Kate, cookies!" Keller screamed at me from the front door.

"I better get in there," I told Megan, looking over my shoulder at Keller swinging on the open door. "Thanks so much for watching them."

"No problem," she answered with a nod. "Let me know when you hear anything, okay?"

"Sure," I said, already walking toward where my little monkey was trying to climb the door frame.

"Let's go make a mess in the kitchen!" I announced loudly, picking Keller up like a football as he giggled. I forced myself not to panic in front of the kids as we pulled ingredients out of the cupboards and began trashing the kitchen. I told myself that Rachel would call soon, but the longer I was there with no word from her, the less I believed it.

* * *

We didn't hear anything, not for hours.

I tried to call Rachel at least a hundred times but she never answered, and after a while I couldn't even leave another message in her full voicemail.

It wasn't until I was making dinner for the kids that my phone rang, and I almost dropped it in my haste to answer.

"Hello?" I said, walking toward the laundry room for a bit of quiet. "Hello?"

"Can I please speak to Katherine Evans?"

"This is Katherine."

"Hello, this is Margie at Tri-City Medical Center. I'm calling about a Rachel Anderson."

My knees felt like water, and I reached out to grip the washing machine to keep me on my feet. "Is she okay?"

"Ma'am, she's been in an accident."

"Is she okay?" I could hear my voice becoming more shrill with every word, and I clenched my teeth to keep myself from yelling.

"Can you come to the hospital, ma'am?"

The woman's voice was unnaturally calm, and I knew that no matter what I said she wasn't going to give me a straight answer. Hell, it was her job to notify people that their family was in the hospital. She didn't give a shit that I was about to lose my mind.

"I'll—" I looked around the laundry room in a panic. What was I supposed to do? "I'm on my way. Tell her I'm on my way."

"Come straight to the emergency entrance when you get here."

"I will."

The minute she hung up, I bent at the waist and braced my hands on my knees, trying to get my shit together.

Rachel was fine. The baby was fine. I was freaking out over nothing. I was getting myself worked up over nothing. It was just an accident.

"Sage!" I yelled as I walked quickly through the house. "Keep an eye on your brothers. I'm walking over to Megan's real quick—I'll be right outside!"

As I reached the front porch, I began to sprint, and by the time I was at Megan's front door I was out of breath and on the verge of tears.

"Kate? What's up?" Megan asked as she swung the door open.

"Can you take care of the kids? I have to go—the hospital just called." A painful sob burst out of my throat, and I wiped my hand over my face to try to gain some control. "They said Rachel's been in an accident. I need to get over there."

"Sure, honey. No worries," she answered before I was even finished speaking. "Caleb, get your shoes on, bud! We're going over to the Andersons' for a bit."

"Woohoo!" I heard from somewhere in the back of the house.

"Did you call Shane?" she asked, sliding into some sandals by the door.

"I didn't even think to," I replied with a small shake

of my head. "He's rarely here. I forgot he was in town."
I felt like shit for not calling him, but I was so used to
taking care of things while he was gone that it hadn't
even dawned on me. I'd driven Rachel to the hospital
when she'd had Gavin, taken care of things when Keller
broke his arm, and helped with a thousand other little
events over the past few years. I stepped in every time he
was gone, and I hadn't thought about him for one second as I'd paced around the house that afternoon.

"We'll be over in a minute. I'm sure she's fine," Megan assured me with a nod. "You better go get some
shoes on and let the kids know I'm coming over for a
visit."

"I'm not telling them—" I shook my head and looked
down at my bare feet. I hadn't even noticed the hot
pavement as I'd run across it barefoot. Why didn't I put
shoes on?

"Come on," she said gently, pushing me away from
the door as her kid raced out ahead of us. "We'll walk
you over."

* * *

I'm not sure what I said to the kids about the reason I
was leaving, and I don't remember the drive to the hospital or even where I parked that afternoon. I can't recall
what the nurse looked like as she searched for Rachel's
name in their computer system or the walk toward the
room where I waited for someone to speak to me.

The first thing I remember clearly is the white-haired

doctor's kind face as he sat down across from me, and the young chaplain's small smile as he chose the chair to my left. Their words became a litany that I would hear in my dreams for years.

My Rachel was gone, but her son was alive and in the NICU.

"Is there anyone you'd like for us to call? Any family or friends that you'd like to be here?"

The question jolted me out of the fog that seemed to be getting thicker and thicker around me. *Dear God.*

"I'll make the calls," I answered, looking blankly at the wall. "Can I have some privacy please?"

"Of course. I'll be right outside if you need me," the chaplain answered, reaching out to pat my hand. "I'll take you up to the NICU when you're ready."

The room was silent after they left, and I fought the urge to scream at the top of my lungs just to hear it echo around me. I understood then why people hired mourners to wail at funerals. Sometimes the lack of sound is more painful than the anguished noise of a heart breaking.

My hands shook as I pulled my phone out of my front pocket and rested it on the table in front of me.

It only took a moment before the sound of ringing filled the room, and I rested my head in my hands as I stared at the name across the screen.

"Hello? Kate? What's wrong?"

"Shane—" I said quietly, my voice hitching.

"What? Why are you calling me?" His voice was confused, but I could hear a small thread of panic in the urgency of his words.

"I need you to come to Tri-City hospital," I answered, tears rolling down my face and landing on the glass screen of my phone, distorting the letters and numbers.

"Who?" His voice was frantic, and I could hear him moving around, his breathing heavy.

"Rachel was in an accident." I sobbed, covering my face to try to muffle the noise.

"No," he argued desperately as I heard two car doors shut almost simultaneously. "Is she okay?"

I shook my head, trying to catch my breath.

"Kate! Is she okay?" he screamed at me, his anguished voice filling the room as I'd wanted mine to just minutes before.

"No," I answered through gritted teeth, feeling snot running down my upper lip as I heard him make a noise deep in his throat. "She's gone."

He didn't say a word, and less than a second later the connection was broken.

I could barely force myself to reach across the table for a tissue as I scrolled down my contact list and pressed SEND again. I wasn't finished.

"Hello!" Her voice made me whimper in both relief and sorrow.

"Mom?" I rasped.

"Katie?"

"I—I—"

"Take a deep breath, baby. Then tell me what's wrong," she ordered.

"I need you and Aunt Ellie to come down here," I

cried, straightening my back and wiping the tears from my face. "I'm not—I don't know what to do."

"Okay, we'll find a flight," she answered immediately, like flying from Portland to San Diego was as easy as walking across the street. "Now what's going on?"

"Rachel was in an accident," I ground out, the words like gravel in my throat. "She didn't make it, and I'm worried about Shane."

"Oh, Katie. My sweet girl," she said sadly. "We'll be on the first flight down, okay, baby?" Her voice became muffled as she covered the phone and yelled shrilly for my dad.

"I just, I'm not sure what I'm supposed to be doing," I confessed with a sob. "Shane isn't here yet, and I don't think I can see her, and the baby is in ICU."

"The baby's okay?"

"Yeah, they said they were just keeping him under observation." I rubbed at my forehead, trying to convince myself that it was all just a nightmare. Where was I supposed to be? What was I supposed to do now? My best friend in the entire world was there in that hospital, but not really. I couldn't bear to see her. I couldn't help her. Where the fuck was I supposed to go? "What do I do, Mom?"

"You go see your nephew."

"What?"

"You go to the NICU, and you hold your nephew, and you tell him everything is going to be okay," she told me, tears in her voice. "You go love on that baby. Where are Sage and the boys?"

"They're with a neighbor. They're okay."

"Good. That's good."

"Yeah."

"Dad found some flights. I'm on my way, princess," she told me gently. "We'll be there soon. Now go take care of our new boy."

"I love you, Mom."

"I love you, too. I'm on my way."

I made my way to the NICU as quickly as I could, and within minutes I was holding my new nephew in my arms. The nurses told me that he'd passed all of his tests with flying colors, and I was in awe as I sat down in a rocking chair, cradling him to my chest.

"You sure got a shitty beginning, little man," I murmured against his fuzzy scalp, rocking back and forth gently. "I'm so sorry, buddy. You're probably missing your mama and that warm bubble you've been in for so long. I can't help you there."

I sniffled, closing my eyes as tears rolled down my cheeks. My whole body ached, and even though I had that little boy in my arms, the day seemed like some sort of surreal dream, foggy in some parts and crystal clear in others. I wanted to hop up and take his sleeping little form to Rachel, to tease her about the weird Mohawk thing he was sporting and make joking comments about how men always seem to sleep through the hard parts of life. I wanted to see her smile proudly at the sturdy boy she'd produced and grumble that I was hogging him.

I wanted everything to be different.

I hummed softly with my eyes closed for a long time, holding the baby close to me. It was quiet where we sat, nothing breaking up the stillness of the room until I heard someone open the door.

"There he is," the nurse murmured from the doorway.

My eyes popped open to see Shane's ravaged face just feet from me. He looked like he was barely holding on. I swallowed hard as his red-rimmed eyes took in his son carefully before rising to meet mine.

"Is he okay?" he asked thickly, searching my face. I'd never seen him so frightened.

"He's perfect," I answered, my voice throbbing with emotion. "The nurses said he's a rock star."

He nodded twice, reaching up to cover his mouth with his hand, but before he could say another word, he was stumbling and falling to his knees with an almost inaudible sob.

Chapter 1

Kate

One Year Later

Where are my monsters?" I yelled, rushing in the front door.

The house was quiet as I made my way through the living room carrying an awkwardly large gift bag. I should have just wrapped Gunner's birthday present, but I hadn't thought I had the time. I felt like I'd been running late for the past year, and that morning had been no different.

God, I couldn't believe it had been an entire year since Rachel died. Sometimes it felt like yesterday that I'd gotten that first phone call from Sage's school. Other times it felt as if I'd always had this hole in my chest where my best friend used to be.

The back door opened just as I reached it, almost smacking me in the face.

"Oh, hey. You're here," Shane said distractedly as he ushered Keller inside.

"Why wouldn't I be?"

"Go to the bathroom, bud," he ordered, giving Kell a little push before meeting my eyes. "Ellie's here. I figured you'd take a couple of days off."

"Since when did hanging out with the kids become my job?" I asked flatly as Keller tapped me on my hip in hello on his way by me.

I hated it when Shane acted like I was the freaking nanny. I wasn't the nanny. I was family, and the closest thing to a mother that those kids had left.

"You're here every fucking day, Kate. I just thought you'd want a day to yourself."

I clenched my fingers tighter around Gunner's present, ignoring the way the bag crinkled in protest. "It's Gunner's birthday—"

"I know what fucking day it is," he interrupted, moving past me to grab a beer out of the fridge.

"What the hell is your deal?"

"No deal."

"Look," I began, softening my voice, "I know today is hard—"

"Don't finish that sentence."

"Shane—"

"You have no fucking clue. None. Say one more word and I'll kick your ass out of my house."

This confrontation had been brewing. I'd felt it almost like an electric current in the air as the anniversary grew closer, but I couldn't have imagined that he'd start it in the middle of his son's birthday party.

"She was my best friend."

"She wasn't your wife," he replied stubbornly.

I wanted to scream at him. I wanted to throw Gunner's gift at his head. I wanted to tell him that I'd spent more time with Rachel in the last nine years than he had, because, while he was off playing GI Joe, *I* was the one who was holding her ass together.

But I didn't do any of those things because what would it help? He had a distorted memory of both his wife and the relationship he'd had with her, and now that she was gone, it wouldn't do anyone any good to tell him just how wrong he was.

I turned to move outside but only got a few steps.

"Party ends at three," he called out to me.

"What?"

"Party's over at three."

He wasn't looking at me, but his insinuation was clear.

I wasn't welcome at the house after the party was over.

* * *

"Auntie Kate!" Gavin yelled as he slid down the small slide into their plastic pool in the backyard.

"Hi, baby!" I called back, setting the gift I was holding on the table. "Having fun?"

"Swimming!" he yelled, splashing his arms down hard into the water.

"I see that."

"Hi, Auntie Kate," Sage murmured, wrapping her arms around my waist.

"Sage the Rage. Looking good, toots."

"I missed you," she said quietly, squeezing me tighter.

"You saw me the day before yesterday, you crazy girl," I argued, bending at the knees so I could lift her into my arms. "And your grandma came all the way from Oregon to hang with you guys."

"I don't want Grandma. I want you," she replied stubbornly.

"Well, you got me." I walked toward the bench where my aunt Ellie was sitting and plopped down next to her.

I looked around the yard and realized that there was no one else there. Keller ran out and jumped into the pool next to Gavin with a splash, but other than our family, the yard was empty. "Where's all the other kids?"

"Shane just wanted something small," Aunt Ellie murmured. "Gunner fell asleep about twenty minutes ago, so we're just going to wait until he wakes up to do cake and presents."

"What? Why is he asleep at noon? He doesn't have an afternoon nap until two." I scooted to the edge of my seat so I could stand up, but the weight of Sage's suddenly sleeping form and Aunt Ellie's hand on my arm stopped me.

"He's okay, sis," she assured me quietly, her eyes filled with understanding. "They had a hard day yesterday, and Shane didn't get a single one of them to sleep before midnight. It just messed up their schedules is all." She nodded at a sleeping Sage, and I sagged backward into the seat.

"I should have come over yesterday," I murmured, rubbing my hand softly over Sage's back. She was too old for me to carry around, and almost too big, but I didn't have the heart to stop doing it. She needed me.

"You deserve a day off."

"I don't want any days off," I snapped back, frustrated.

To the outside world, I was sure my relationship to the kids looked pretty odd. I wasn't their mother. I wasn't even legally related to them. But I'd been picking up the slack for Rachel and Shane for so long that I'd stepped in after Rachel died without thinking.

The first couple of weeks after the accident, my mom and aunt had stayed in San Diego helping Shane and me with the kids. They'd made sure everyone was fed, and someone was always with Gunner at the hospital, and a million different other things that we hadn't had the energy to deal with. But they had lives in Oregon, and once they'd left, it had been up to us to get the kids back to some kind of normalcy.

Normal. I wasn't even sure what that meant anymore.

Shane had been on bereavement leave for a little over a week and had used some time he'd had saved up for another week after that, but he'd had to go back to work. He didn't have the luxury of wallowing or making sure his kids were okay before he had to start leaving the house every day, all day.

So I'd been there.

I'd sent some of my clients to other designers that I trusted and had taken over a life that wasn't really mine. I cared for children that I loved more than myself, gave up the small semblance of a life I'd had before, and became a stand-in. And I didn't regret it. Not for a second.

But it was times like yesterday—when Shane had called me to tell me that I wouldn't be "needed" because his foster mom was in town—that I remembered how little power I had when it came to the kids.

It killed me.

"I'll take her up to bed," Shane said suddenly, coming up behind where we were sitting.

"She's fine where she is," I replied without looking at him. I could feel my chest growing tight as I imagined how yesterday must have gone. Sage couldn't have gotten much sleep if she was tired enough to fall asleep over the giddy screams of her brothers.

"She's getting too big for you to carry around—"

"She's *fine*."

Aunt Ellie looked between us, her brows furrowed, before standing up. "I'm going to check on Gunner."

I wished Shane would just walk away while my emotions were so close to the surface, but of course, he didn't.

"Sorry I snapped at you," Shane murmured, sitting down in the vacated spot next to me.

"It's fine."

"You're just here a lot. I know you had your own life before this—"

I snorted before I could stop myself, cutting off his

words. I'd barely had a life. I'd been with his wife every single day he wasn't.

"—but we need to talk," he finished.

"About what?" I asked, stomach turning.

"Deployment's coming up," he said quietly, glancing down at Sage to make sure she was still asleep.

"I thought you were going to try and get out of it?" I hissed back in surprise, looking over to find Gavin peeing in the grass. Ugh.

"I can't, Katie," he replied softly, the old endearment making me jolt. "I can't send my guys without me."

"So you're just going to leave your kids here instead?"

"You don't understand—"

"Nope, I don't."

I finally turned to look at him, and I wanted to slap the determined look off his face, but I didn't have a chance to say anything else.

"Look who's awake!" Aunt Ellie called cheerfully, carrying Gunner out the back door. Oh my God, had he grown in the day I hadn't seen him? He looked bigger.

"Sage, wake up, baby," I called, jostling her a little on my lap. "Brother's awake. It's time to do cake."

She woke with a jerk, the same way she'd been waking up for the past year, and looked around in confusion.

"Cake time, princess," Shane told her with a small smile, climbing to his feet.

When we got to the patio table, I stole Gunner from my aunt.

"Look at you, big boy," I said quietly as he stuffed his face into my neck. "Is it your birthday?"

He pulled away and smiled up at me, and my heart stuttered.

"When did the top tooth come in?" I asked Shane, glancing over to find him staring at us.

"I noticed it last night."

"Shit, I missed it," I whispered, smiling at Gunner. "Look at that chomper, dude, you're going to be asking for steak soon."

"I think we have time before that happens," Shane joked, scooting around me with a hand at my back so he could get to the table.

I closed my eyes against the small touch. It was times like these, simple conversations when he used the word *we*, that I had to steel myself against. As much as I loved them, and as much as I took care of them—those children were not mine. I had to remember that.

* * *

I left the house at three, just like Shane had asked me to.

I knew he was having a hard day, and frankly I was, too. I didn't want to get into it with him.

We'd had a sort of uneasy truce going on for the past year. While Shane was good with daddy stuff, he knew his limits, and I liked to think that he knew how much he relied on me even though he'd never acknowledged it. I wasn't the babysitter—our roles weren't that simple.

I was there while he worked, that was a given, but I'd

also stayed over all night when Keller and Sage had a stomach bug. We ate dinner together as a family at least once a week, and a few times we'd even taken the kids on day trips to the zoo and the beach.

I knew I wasn't his favorite person—that had become pretty clear when Rachel was alive and I'd been completely ignored. Hell, I'd known it the first time I brought Rachel home with me from school and he'd wooed her while acting as if I didn't exist. The friendship we'd formed as kids had deteriorated without my knowledge, and all I'd been left with was a stranger who ended up married to my best friend.

But over the past year, we'd become partners of a sort, taking care of the kids, and I figured that was probably the closest we'd ever get to being friends again.

I dreaded the day that he found someone new, which he eventually would. As the years went on, he'd want someone to spend his life with, and I knew that when that day came, I would no longer be needed.

I shook my head and stripped out of the jeans I'd been wearing. I wanted to be at the house with the kids, but I forced myself not to think of how fussy and tired they probably were. They were fine with Shane and my aunt. I just had to learn to let go a little.

A few hours later, as I was bingeing on episodes of *Call the Midwife* on Netflix, my phone started ringing next to me on the bed.

"Hello?" I answered around the large bite of chocolate in my mouth.

"Hey, sis," my aunt said with a laugh. I loved how my

family called me "sis." It reminded me of when I was a kid and things were so much simpler.

"Hey, how are the kiddos doing?"

"They're all down for the night," she answered with a sigh. "And I'm pooped."

"I bet. Where's Shane?"

"Well, that's what I was calling about."

I sat up in bed and brushed the chocolate crumbs off my chest. "What's going on?"

"He left, Katie, and I'm not sure where he was going."

"He's a big boy, Aunt Ellie, I'm sure he's fine."

"No, no, I know that," she replied before going quiet. I could picture her so clearly in my mind, biting at the cuticles on her nails anytime she was worried.

"What do you need me to do?" I asked finally, standing up and grabbing a pair of pants from the floor.

"Do you know where he'd go?" she asked. "He said he wouldn't be back until the morning."

Shit.

"I have a pretty good idea," I mumbled back, putting the phone on speaker so I could get my bra on. "I'll see if I can find him and call you back."

"Are you sure?"

"Isn't that why you called me?"

"Well...yes."

"Then, yeah. If you're worried, then I'll check on him."

We hung up a few minutes later, and I was on my way downtown shortly after that. I had a pretty good idea where he was, and the closer I got to the hotel, the more nervous I became.

Rachel and Shane had a silly tradition to meet up after every deployment at a certain hotel downtown. Before they got back to daily life, with kids and bills and taking out the garbage, they'd take one night just for themselves. And every year, I'd keep the kids for the night while they met up and had marathon sex with no interruptions.

The first time it happened and Rachel had come home bragging about it, I'd felt sick to my stomach. I knew they were having sex. They were married and had Sage by then, but knowing it and hearing the details were two very different things, and that had been the first time I'd been thankful that Rachel ignored me while Shane was home.

I'd needed to get my head on straight. They were married. *Married.* And I was just the wife's best friend. He might have been my friend first, but by that time he definitely wasn't my friend any longer. I had no right to feel anything about their sexcapades, and it had been ridiculous that I had.

I'd overcome my jealousy and hurt feelings years ago, but parking in the garage to *their* hotel had me fighting that same sick feeling in my stomach. I didn't belong there, and I so badly wanted to turn around and go back home.

I got Shane's room number from the front desk—not very safe of them to give information like that out—and strode toward the elevator.

He was going to be pissed. No doubt about it.

* * *

"The fuck are you doing here?" Shane growled as he threw open the door I'd been knocking on for a solid five minutes. I hadn't driven all the way down there for him to ignore me.

"I was in the neighborhood..." I answered, falling back into the awkward teenager I'd been trying to leave behind me for years.

"Kids okay?" he asked, walking across the room and pouring what looked like Jack Daniel's into one of the hotel coffee mugs.

"Aunt Ellie said they're already asleep."

"She called you?"

"Yep."

"I told her I'd be home in the morning."

"She worries."

"As you can see, I'm fine."

"Well, I wouldn't go that far," I replied, finally stepping into the room and letting the door swing closed behind me. "Want to share?" I asked, nodding to the bottle on the table.

"Not especially."

"*Will* you share?"

"I guess."

I sat on the edge of the bed as he poured me a mug of whiskey and nodded my thanks as he handed it over. Crap, I hated the smell of whiskey. Ever since Rachel and I had gotten wasted on some bottom-shelf shit at our first party in college, I smelled it and was reminded of whiskey-tinged vomit coming out my nose.

"You couldn't have splurged on the good stuff, huh?" I asked, taking a small sip.

His startled laugh made me smile, but I didn't look at him as he landed on the bed next to me with a small bounce.

"Figured it didn't matter if I was just using it to get shitty."

"That's your plan for the night?" I asked, eyeballing the mostly empty bottle as I felt my limbs begin to heat. Shit, it had been so long since I'd had a buzz that the feeling was almost euphoric.

"Get shitfaced, jack off, and sleep," he announced with a smirk as my eyes shot to his face. "Aw, look at you. Still blushing at the mention of masturbating."

"You're drunk," I spat back, finishing my whiskey and jumping to my feet. I was not talking about masturbation with him, for fuck's sake.

"That was the plan," he replied lazily as I stumbled a little while grabbing my purse. "I gave you three shots, Katie. You're not driving." Without any warning, he grabbed the purse from my hands and threw it across the room.

"Don't throw my shit! You probably broke my phone, you dick!" The words felt thick in my mouth, and I immediately regretted having anything to drink.

I didn't want to be stuck in a room, drunk, with an equally drunk Shane. I loved everyone when I was drunk—I knew that about myself. I was emotional, and over-the-top, and everything that I tried so hard to suppress since I'd lost my best guyfriend in my freshman year of college. Maybe the hotel had another room to rent that wouldn't completely obliterate my food budget for the week. Losing clients so I could take care of the kids had left me a little tight on cash.

"You're not going anywhere. Don't be stupid," Shane grumbled, grabbing my arm as I tried to get to my purse.

"*You're* stupid!"

"Mature, Katie."

"Don't call me Katie! Only my friends call me Katie, and you are not my friend," I argued, scrambling to move past him.

"We should have been friends," he said quietly into my ear as he caught me from behind and crossed my arms over my chest.

"We were friends, until you threw me away like garbage!" I yelled, kicking back at his legs.

"Stop fucking kicking me!"

"Let go!"

We wrestled for dominance, tripping our way around the room, and if my mind had been a little clearer, I would have stopped whatever was happening. But I was frustrated, and mad, and drunk, and wrestling around seemed like a completely rational decision then.

"You're drunk!" he yelled, finally pinning me on the bed with my arms above my head. "You're not getting into a fucking car!"

"You're not the boss of me!"

"The fuck I'm not!"

"The fuck you are!"

"What?"

"Get. Off!" I bucked my hips and pulled at my arms, but it was no use. Even drunk, Shane was still ten times stronger.

"I just wanted to get drunk in peace," he said, leaning down until we were nose-to-nose. "Why do you always have to step in like Florence fucking Nightingale? Huh?"

"Why do you always have to be such a douchebag and need saving?" I yelled back. We were breathing heavy, and I could feel sweat forming from our wrestling match.

"I don't need you to save me. I never needed you to fucking save me," he growled back, his eyes searching my face. "That's what you never understood. You just kept pushing and pushing."

I felt a lump forming in my throat as I thought about our past and turned my head to the side. I could feel tears forming in the corners of my eyes, and I couldn't stop them from rolling down the sides of my face.

"Fuck you," I whispered, my body finally going limp. "Fuck you, Shane."

"Don't fucking cry," he ordered, his hands tightening on my wrists. "Don't!"

I ignored him, keeping my eyes closed as I felt him breathing heavily above me. I was so embarrassed that I just wanted to disappear.

"Stop it!" he yelled, jostling the bed with his knees, as if shaking me would make any difference in the sob that had worked its way up my throat.

He let go of my arm then, but I left it limp above my head as I felt him grasp my jaw firmly in his long fingers and turn my face toward his. Maybe if I ignored him, he would lose interest in the fight.

"When you cry, your lips swell up," he whispered, making my eyes finally pop open in surprise.

He was so much closer than I'd realized that my breath caught in my throat as he stared at my lips.

Then his mouth was on mine.

"Pushing, always fucking pushing," he mumbled against my mouth before sucking my bottom lip between his and biting down hard enough to make me whimper.

He tugged at my lip with his teeth, and I felt my body heat in response.

"What are you doing?" I asked as his eyebrows furrowed.

"Fuck if I know."

We were silent as we stared at each other. Somewhere in the back of my mind I knew that it was a bad idea, but it wasn't enough to stop me from lifting my head and nipping his jaw hard with my teeth in retaliation.

"Harder," he ordered, groaning as he grabbed the back of my head and pressed my mouth to his throat. "Do it hard."

I followed his instructions, biting and sucking on his neck like it was my job, and his hands shook as one held me against him and the other slid down the side of my throat and ripped the strap of my bra and cami down my shoulder. He tasted salty, and the stubble under his chin rasped across my tongue.

"Jesus," Shane groaned as he leaned back on his knees and gazed at my breast that had popped free. "Your nipples are pierced."

He reached out and flicked the hoop resting against my breast, and my hips jolted involuntarily off the bed as he pulled the other strap roughly down my shoulder so both breasts were on display.

His hands were on me then, pinching and pulling on my nipples as I writhed underneath him. His nostrils were flared and his jaw tense as I reached for the athletic shorts he was wearing and pulled at them, feeling his hard erection through the silky fabric.

He was off the bed in a flash, but before I could wonder if he was going to leave me, he was back and kneeling above me—naked except for the dog tags hanging around his neck.

I reached for him immediately, but he caught my hands with his and brought them back to my breasts as he scooted up my waist. It took me a second before I realized what he was doing, but the minute his skin met mine, I couldn't help the small moan that left my mouth.

"Hold them there," Shane mumbled, looking to where his cock was nestled between my breasts. "Squeeze me tight."

I nodded dazedly as I pressed against the sides of my breasts, wrapping him up in my cleavage as he began to slide up and down. His fingers found my nipples and tortured them as he moved, and before long I was so frustrated that I let go of one breast to try to reach the waistband of my pants.

My face felt like it was on fire, and my head was cloudy as I tried to reach between Shane's thighs. My arms weren't long enough to go around him, and I needed to reach my clit. I knew it would only take a second before I went off like the Fourth of July, and then I figured he could go back to what he was doing.

I didn't think of the way my hand would slide across his balls and the inside of his thighs as I moved, but a startled yelp and then a moan had me pausing with my hand halfway to the promised land.

"Stop," Shane said, sliding off me.

"I'm really getting tired of that fucking word," I answered back, my eyes growing heavy.

He flipped me to my stomach like a sack of potatoes, and my breathing sped up as he climbed back on top of me and pulled my hips away from the bed.

"Fucking sweatpants," he grumbled, squeezing my ass with both hands as I pulled myself onto my elbows.

"They're yoga pants."

"Thank God for yoga pants."

"I'm pretty sure God didn't design these."

"I'm pretty sure he did," he retorted, making his point by pulling them down to my thighs with one swift jerk. His hands went straight between my legs from behind, and I arched my back as his fingers slid over my skin.

"So bare and slick," Shane whispered darkly, bending

over my body until his chest rested against my back. "And what is this?"

His fingers found my hood piercing, and I froze as I waited to see what he'd do. I felt one finger playing softly with the piercing as my breath grew ragged, and I was so focused on that sensation that I didn't feel him positioning behind me until he was thrusting inside.

I think I may have screamed as he came to a stop halfway inside, but my ears were ringing so loudly that I wasn't sure. Not that I would have cared either way.

"Hold on," Shane ordered roughly, nudging my hand with the wrist he'd braced by my head. "Use your nails."

I gripped his wrist the way he'd asked and turned my head to pull the skin of his arm between my teeth, making him yell out above me and increase his thrusts. He was rolling his hips, his hand moving frantically over my thighs and clit and ass, pressing and pinching and pushing deeper and deeper with every stroke. It was the most intense sex I'd ever had, and by the time he'd bottomed out inside me, we were covered in sweat and I was coming in large rolling waves.

I don't remember anything after that.

Chapter 2
Shane

*W*ake up.

The voice in my head was more familiar to me than my own, and I smiled slightly as I drifted in that hazy place between sleeping and wakefulness. Something was beeping or ringing quietly across the room, but I ignored it as I slid my bare legs against the sheets and curled deeper into the soft back that was tucked against my chest.

I slid my hand from the bed and up the smooth skin of her belly, finally reaching the bottom curve of her breast. When I reached it, it was fuller than I'd anticipated, and I groaned as I dug my fingers into her skin. *She's pregnant*, I remembered vaguely, my head pounding. *Her breasts are always larger when she's pregnant.*

When my fingertips finally reached her nipple, I felt something hard and cool there, and as she sighed and rolled her hips against my morning wood, my world crashed down around me. The woman I was holding was not my wife.

My stomach churned violently as I scrambled across the bed, and I could barely get to my feet before I tumbled off the other side. I knew that room. I'd been there a hundred times, but it took me a moment before flashes of the night before started to filter into my head.

"Oh my God," Kate whispered, curling into herself where she'd been sleeping peacefully just moments before. "Oh my God."

I stared at the curve of her back like an idiot, trying to figure out what the fuck I should do, when her head turned slowly over her shoulder and her wide eyes met mine.

"No," she whispered, squeezing her eyes tightly closed. "Oh fuck."

I was still silent. I stood there, completely nude, and stared blankly at the woman on the bed.

Kate pulled the sheet around her and sat up. Her shoulders were curved so far forward that I could see her collarbone poking sharply against the skin of her chest. Her eyes searched frantically around the room, and without warning, she lurched off the bed, falling to her knees. I stepped toward her without thought, but the sharp noise she made stopped me in my tracks.

I might have still been drunk from the night before, because I couldn't think clearly. I couldn't figure out why we were there. I remembered sliding inside her, the way her body tightened around me like a vise, and the way she'd tasted salty as I'd sucked at her skin, but I couldn't remember why we were in that hotel room to begin with.

"What are you doing here, Katie?" I asked, my voice rough. It felt like I'd swallowed gravel with the half-gallon bottle of Jack.

"I came to check on you," she answered, her voice rising as she spoke.

It came flooding back then, a barrage of scenes that I had a feeling would be burned into my memory for the rest of my life. My skin heated and prickled as I remembered her showing up at the door, and fury settled around me like a cape.

"You came here to check on me?" I asked harshly, finding my boxers on the floor and pulling them quickly up my legs. "And then what? Decided I should pay you back with some dick?"

"What?" she asked, her voice so quiet I barely heard her.

"Let's be honest here, Kate," I said conversationally. "I was drunk off my ass, and you figured, hey, I've been drooling over his dick for years and he's not picky when he's drunk. Score!"

"That's not—"

"Right," I cut in, finding my shorts and sliding my legs into them as she stood like a statue in the middle of the room. "You know—" I slid my T-shirt on over my head. "If I was a chick, you'd go to jail for this shit."

"I'd go to jail?"

"You knew I wouldn't fuck you sober, so you waited

until I was shit-housed and got what you wanted." I shook my head as I picked up my keys and wallet off the table. "You feel better now, Katie? Was it everything you'd imagined? I didn't disappoint, did I?"

She began to shake as I walked toward her, stopping just a few feet away. "I didn't want you then, I don't want you now," I said, watching detachedly as her chest heaved with silent sobs. She was staring at my chest, refusing to meet my eyes, and that pissed me off even more. "You were a lousy fuck, Kate. I won't be back for seconds."

I stumbled back a step as she fell to her knees, and I clenched my jaw as she began to vomit, her sobs no longer silent but echoing throughout the room.

She'd done this. She'd come to the hotel room I'd shared with my wife, on the anniversary of her death, and had fucked me blind when I was too drunk to know what the hell I was doing. My guilt, shame, and anger were a potent mix, and at that moment I could have thrown her out the window.

"Clean that shit up," I told her as I stepped over the mess she'd made. "I'm not paying for them to clean the carpet."

I caught sight of a pair of dirty mugs lying on her side of the bed as I passed by and vaguely remembered the two of us drinking, but I didn't stop as I made my way out of the room. *Fuck her.*

I had to get out of there. I had to get as far away from that hotel and the woman inside it as I could. I'd gone there to remember my wife—to have one night when

I could just feel it all, just take it all in. I'd wanted to remember the way she had smelled, and the way she'd looked at me, and the way we'd seemed to move together seamlessly. I'd wanted to have one night when I didn't have to keep it all together because I had four pairs of little eyes watching my every move. I'd wanted to get drunk, and be miserable, and hate the entire world for making me a widower at twenty-nine years old.

Instead, I'd made a huge fucking mistake, and now the only thing I could think about was the way Kate had moved beneath me, the way her back had arched so dramatically as I'd pressed inside her from behind. I could only feel the soreness of my throat and shoulders where she'd bit and sucked at my skin. I couldn't stop thinking about the way I'd left her on the floor of that room, sick and scared, and undoubtedly sore from the things we'd done the night before.

I hated myself, and I hated Kate, and I had no idea how I'd ever look at her again without feeling like I was going to burst out of my own skin.

She'd fucked me over, but as I pulled into my driveway and flipped the visor down in my truck to see the marks on my skin from her mouth, I knew what I had done was far worse.

* * *

"Are you sure you don't want us to drive you to the airport?" I asked my foster mom as she hugged the kids good-bye. She was so good with them, but I'd known before Sage was even born that she would be. Someone who took in troubled teenagers for no other reason than to give them some semblance of a chance at life—and never once raised her voice when they were complete assholes—was sure to be the best grandma a kid could ever ask for.

"No reason for you to drag the kids all the way to the airport just to drop me off and drive right back," she assured me, smiling at Gunner, who was in my arms. "Kate'll bring me. She's got an appointment downtown today anyway."

"On a Sunday?" My stomach clenched as Kate pulled into the driveway and I waited for her to come greet the kids. I hadn't seen her since I'd left her in that hotel room a week earlier, and I was dreading the moment we had to interact. I didn't know what to say to her. I didn't know how to apologize when I was still so angry at the part she'd played in that clusterfuck.

"Well, she's got the kids all week," Ellie said, pulling my eyes away from Kate's car. She still hadn't climbed out. "She has to take meetings sometime, and it would take her hours to get down south if she waited until you got off work at night. Traffic here is terrible."

"Thanks for coming to stay," I murmured into Ellie's hair as she wrapped her arms around me. "We love having you to visit."

"Next time, I'll bring Dad with me," she said, giving me a squeeze before wrapping a thin scarf around her neck. "I'll buy the tickets when I get home."

"What's Auntie Kate *doing*?" Sage asked in annoyance, waving her arms at Kate's car.

"I think she's on her phone," Ellie lied, glancing up at me before taking ahold of her small suitcase. "I'll carry this out myself since you've got Gunner."

Her face was sympathetic and a little questioning as she kissed my cheek, but I didn't reply as she walked out the front door. She'd known the morning I'd gotten home that something had happened between Kate and me. When Kate had never called her back the night before, Ellie had known something was up—but she'd practically swallowed her tongue when she got a glimpse of my neck.

She hadn't said a word, but she'd known.

"I'm glad Grandma's leaving," Keller announced, swinging on the front door as Kate backed out of the driveway.

"Kell, that's not a nice thing to say."

"Now we get to see Auntie Kate every day. I like it when we see her every day," he explained, grabbing the doorknob on each side and pulling his legs up through his arms so he could hang upside down. "I never wanted you to leave, though, Daddy. Even though we didn't get to see Auntie Kate," he reassured me quickly with an upside-down frown on his face. "I like it when you're here."

I had no clue what he was talking about, but nodded at him anyway. "I like being here, too, bud."

"Is Auntie Kate coming back tomorrow?" Sage asked, purposefully bumping Gavin into Keller so they'd both tumble to the porch. "I want Auntie Kate to take me to school."

"Yeah, princess. She'll be here," I answered, praying silently that I wasn't wrong. "Let's go inside and you guys can get the Play-Doh out. Gunner needs to go down for his nap."

It was going to be a long day.

* * *

I woke up anxious the next morning a full hour before my alarm was supposed to go off. I'd been sleeping like shit for days, and the night before had been the worst.

After Rachel died, it had taken everything I had just to get through the day. What with work, the house, and the kids, I'd barely had a moment to breathe, much less do anything else—and I'd been thankful for that. I'd wanted to stay busy, and I had.

At first, and unsurprisingly, my sex drive had been nonexistent. Frankly, sex hadn't been on my radar, and I hadn't missed it. But after a few months, things had started working properly again, and I began having insanely erotic dreams. The urge came back, but I'd been more than happy to take things in hand. I hadn't been able to imagine touching someone who wasn't Rachel, and I couldn't see that changing anytime soon.

Then I'd fucked up, and for the past week my dreams had contained a far different scenario than the ones before. The nipples I tasted were pierced, and the woman riding me wasn't blond. She was brunette. Suddenly, I couldn't just imagine touching someone other than my dead wife—I could remember it in vivid detail.

I hopped out of bed and ripped the clock's cord out of the wall, too keyed up to take the time to turn the alarm off. I was in the shower moments later and gritting my teeth against the urge to jerk off to the thoughts of the woman I'd see in less than an hour. For the first time that week, it didn't seem right to fantasize about Kate—and the fact that it had taken me eight days to realize that made me feel like a complete dick.

I didn't want her. Even if she hadn't been my wife's best friend and tied to me with more threads than a fucking spiderweb, I still wouldn't have wanted her. She wasn't my type. I liked women who were slender, who took the time to make sure they looked good no matter what they were doing. I wasn't into women with rounded bodies who wore sweats and yoga pants like it was their uniform.

So why couldn't I stop thinking about the way she'd felt against me? Why couldn't I stop seeing those pierced nipples and wild hair as she'd stared up at me with unfocused eyes?

It was fucking frustrating.

After everything I'd said to her, I knew she must hate me, so I wasn't sure why I was even worrying about it. I needed to get my shit straight before I saw her. I needed to move past the anger that I still felt and the guilt that sat like a weight in my belly. I needed to clear the air.

Because if I didn't, I'd be fucked when it came to the kids. I didn't think that Kate would walk away from the kids over this—it's not like we'd gotten along all that great before—but I couldn't be sure.

So when she crept silently into the house that morning, I was drinking my coffee and waiting for her on the couch.

"I wasn't sure you'd come," I said quietly, mindful of the kids sleeping upstairs.

She jerked in surprise and slowly turned toward me. "Jesus, Shane, you scared the crap out of me."

I didn't say anything. I was too busy staring at her. I'd had a thought—a stupid one, apparently—that she'd dress up when I saw her again. As I took in her sweatpants, flip-flops, and zip-up hoodie, I called myself every kind of idiot there was. Like she'd really be angling for another round after the things I'd said.

"You have to work, right?" she asked, staying close to the door.

I wondered if she was trying to stay as far away from me as possible or if she was hoping for a quick escape.

"Yeah, I have to be there at seven," I replied finally, looking at her face.

She wouldn't look at me.

"Then it looks like I have the kids." Her words were nonchalant, but she still hadn't moved a foot from the door.

My hand clenched around my coffee cup as the tension in the room seemed to pulsate between us. I'd had so much shit I'd wanted to say, but watching her cower in the doorway made every word I'd planned disappear from my memory.

She took a step back when I stood up, and I swallowed nervously when her back hit the front door.

"I still want you to keep the kids—" I started, and her eyes finally flashed up to mine.

"Why wouldn't you?" she cut me off, her voice panicked.

"No, I do." I shook my head. This wasn't going the way I'd planned. "I'm just saying, in case you were worried, you can still hang out with the kids."

I could hear her hard breaths in the quiet of the room, and for a second I wondered if she was having some sort of panic attack. Her face drained of all color, and she swayed a little.

"I wasn't worried," she whispered, her eyes wide and scared. "I didn't even think—"

"Look, I know that you didn't do it maliciously—"

"*I* didn't do it?"

"—and I shouldn't have said that shit to you. You've been a huge help with the kids, and I know you probably didn't plan all that."

"I didn't *plan* it," she whispered softly to herself.

"So I'm just saying that I'd like to forget about it, ya know? Go back to the way it was before. No drama." I nodded, finally glad that I'd gotten out what I'd wanted to say.

"You're saying I'm forgiven?" she asked, staring over my shoulder again.

I paused, something in her voice making me question our entire conversation. I'd gone over all of the points, hadn't I? I still wanted her to keep the kids, I'd known she wasn't trying to be a bitch, and I wanted to move past it . . . Yeah, I'd hit every single one.

"Yeah, Katie, you're forgiven," I answered, feeling relieved that I'd gotten the conversation over with. Everything could go back to normal. She'd stay, and I wouldn't have to worry that my kids would deal with another devastating loss so soon after their mother.

She nodded before turning and walking toward the stairs.

"I'm going to go up and crash on Sage's floor for an hour before she has to get up," she said, her back to me. "And Shane?"

"Yeah?"

"Please don't call me Katie."

Chapter 3

Kate

"Motherfucking-super-spermed-son-of-a-goat-from-Ohio!" I chanted angrily, shaking the little stick in my hand, like that would change the answer it was giving me. I wasn't even sure what I was saying, but the words rolled off my tongue easily and it felt good to swear.

I was fucking pregnant, and I didn't know who I was more pissed at—Shane for having an adequate sperm count or the doctor who must have given me a faulty fucking birth control shot.

Why? Why did I have to find myself in the most awkward position imaginable at every possible opportunity? I was always running into something, or saying something I shouldn't, or opening the door in my period underwear and a ratty tank top for the delivery service I used when I sent paperwork to my clients. And this time I was so royally fucked I couldn't even focus on the larger implications of that positive pregnancy test.

Oh no. The only thing I could think about was the fact that I'd have to tell Shane something along the lines of, *You know when I took advantage of your delicate state? Well, I also stole your sperm. I'm pregnant!*

It had been two months since the incident that should never again be brought up, and shit was finally somewhat normal when I was at the Andersons'. Shane was back to ignoring me completely, which frankly was a relief, and I was back to not worrying that I was going to show up one day and the new nanny would bar me from the house.

Gunner was finally walking. Sage was starting a dance class next week. Keller just got stitches along his hairline after he face-planted into the railing of the porch. Gavin pooped in the toilet twice that week! Success!

What the fuck was I going to do?

I threw the stick angrily into the trash and stormed into my bedroom-slash-living-room-slash-dining-room, then immediately spun back around and fished it back out again, setting it gently on the edge of the bathroom counter. So I peed on it, big deal. It was still proof, the first visible proof of my child.

My child. God, I was in so much trouble.

I quickly pulled on some clothes and grabbed my messenger bag off the floor, stuffing my laptop inside before racing out the door. I normally didn't bring my Mac when I was hanging out with the kids—it was a good way to get something spilled on it—but I knew I'd need it that day. I needed to research. I needed to plan.

My stomach rolled as I climbed into my car, and I

swallowed the extra saliva in my mouth. I was *not* going to get sick again. I'd already hacked up the chicken chow mein I'd ingested last night, and the peanut butter and jelly sandwich I'd had for lunch yesterday, and the Cheerios I'd had for breakfast. I didn't have time to get rid of the water I'd had that morning—I was already running late because of that stupid test.

I pulled into Shane's driveway two minutes late and hopped out of the car, taking a second to brace myself against the hood. Okay, no quick movements unless one of the kids was about to break their arm. Right. I just needed to take it easy.

I hadn't even made it to the front door before Shane was outside and walking past me to his truck.

"You're late," he called over his shoulder, his boots hitting the driveway at a steady clip.

"I had an emergency."

He came to an abrupt halt at my words and turned to take me in, his eyes sliding over my body. "You okay?"

"Yeah, I just—"

"I'm gonna be late for work," he cut in, turning back around. "We need to talk tonight when I get back."

"You have no idea," I grumbled as he climbed inside his truck and drove away.

Shit, I was tired. I'd been waking up to puke for the last two nights, and the lack of sleep made me feel like I was in a fog half the time. I was a person who needed a solid eight hours, and for the past few days I'd been getting less and less.

I fell onto the couch with a groan and pulled the

blanket off the back to cover myself up. I'd just rest for a little while before I had to wake Sage for school.

* * *

"Auntie Kate! Auntie Kate, wake up. It's time for school," Sage called quietly, shaking my shoulder.

"Shit!" I woke with a start and sat straight up.

"Shit!" Gavin called from across the room.

"Shit!" Gunner copied him.

"Don't say shit!"

"Shit!"

"Shit!"

"Are we late?" I asked Sage as I slid my feet into my flip-flops.

"No, but we have to leave right *now*," she answered emphatically, already walking toward the door.

"Wait! Where's Keller?"

"I think he's still asleep!"

I ran up the stairs, my stomach churning so badly I had a hard time catching my breath.

"Kell, let's go, bud," I called as I picked him up. "Gotta get sis to school."

He woke up as we made our way back downstairs, and I let him walk barefoot out of the house while I carried Gunner. We didn't have time for silly things like shoes or Gunner's increasingly nasty diaper.

"Everyone in their seats!" I called as I lifted Gavin into his seat with one arm. "Go around to the other side, Keller!"

The kids climbed into my car, Keller scrambling over the backseat to get to his place in the third row. God, I was so glad I'd traded in my smaller car for something more along the lines of an SUV last year. They'd all fit, but how the hell was I going to cart five kids around on a daily basis?

My nausea increased as I made sure all the kids were buckled in and hopped into my seat. My hands shook as I pulled the keys out of my pocket, and I took a deep breath as I fit one into the ignition.

There was no need to worry about tomorrow, I warned myself as we drove to Sage's elementary school. I just needed to worry about now. I just needed to get Sage to school on time and—

"Sage, did you eat breakfast?"

"I had a Pop-Tart."

"Okay, I forgot to make your lunch so—"

"Can I buy lunch?" she asked excitedly, bouncing in her seat.

Why did the packed-lunch kids always want to buy cafeteria food and the hot-lunch kids always dream of a packed sandwich?

"Yeah." I dug in the bottom of my purse for a few dollar bills and handed them back between the seats. "Don't lose that."

"I won't," she promised, stuffing the bills into the front pocket of her backpack.

"I'll be here to pick you up after school," I told her for what felt like the millionth time, coming to a stop in front of the sidewalk.

When she'd first started back to school after Rachel died, she'd asked me every day if I'd be there to pick her up. Every single day she'd ask, as if to make sure I wouldn't forget her. Eventually, it just became our morning routine, and before she could even ask, I'd reassure her that I'd be there.

"Okay! Love you!" she called out as she pushed her way past Gavin's legs and climbed down.

"Love you, too!"

I waited and watched her go inside the double doors even though the car behind me in the drop-off line was inching closer and closer to my bumper in impatience. They could bump the back of my car and I still wasn't going to move until I saw that Sage was safely inside.

When we got back to the house, I was sweating a little, and the boys' yelling and Gunner's dirty diaper weren't helping the situation any. I loved Kell and Gavin, but at that moment I wished I could just put on some noise-canceling headphones and zone out for two minutes while I got my stomach under control.

"Don't feel good?" Gavin asked as I changed Gunner's diaper on the living room floor.

"I'm okay, baby," I assured him, gagging. "My tummy just hurts a little."

"Frow up?"

"Maybe, dude."

"Gross."

"Tell me about it."

"Auntie Kate, I'm hungry," Keller called from where he was hanging upside down off the couch.

"Keller, why are you always upside down?"

"I like being upside down."

"Well, I don't talk to upside-down people, so you're gonna have to get down or I'm not listening," I replied calmly, pulling Gunner to his feet.

"I want pancakes," Keller ordered, coming to stand beside me. "With syrup."

I turned my head slowly and stared at the little boy, who was quickly becoming a demanding little punk. "What was that?" I asked, one eyebrow raised.

"I want pancakes." His arms crossed over his chest, and his little chin came jutting out in defiance.

"You want to rephrase that, bud?"

"I want pancakes," he said again stubbornly before lowering his eyebrows. "Now."

My jaw dropped open, and my skin flushed as I took in the little man. I couldn't believe what he was doing, though I probably should have. Keller had been getting slowly worse and worse as the weeks went by, no matter how I tried to redirect or correct his behavior.

"In your room for five minutes, Keller," I said calmly, my heart thundering in my chest as I climbed to my feet. My stomach clenched, and I was on the verge of tears, but I didn't let my impatience seep into my voice. "You know better than to talk to me like that."

"I don't wanna go to my room!" he whined as I hoisted Gunner onto my hip and led Gavin toward the kitchen.

When I didn't acknowledge Keller's whine, his voice grew louder until he was screaming.

"I don't wanna go to my room!" he yelled, his fists clenched by his sides as I strapped Gunner into his high chair and Gavin into his booster at the table.

"You guys want some oatmeal?" I asked the little boys quietly while Keller continued to yell.

"Yes please," Gavin answered while Gunner signed the word for "eat."

"Do you want brown sugar or blueberries?" I asked Gavin as I turned toward the fridge.

I didn't even make it a step before I was being pushed forward with the force of a little body slamming into the back of my legs.

"You're mean!" Keller cried, hitting at the back of my thighs. "I don't like you!"

"Keller, stop it!" I yelled over his screams, making Gunner start crying. I was trying to get ahold of his sturdy little arms without turning around, because I couldn't bear the thought of his fists hitting my nauseous stomach.

"Keller Shane Anderson, what the hell are you doing?" Shane's voice rang out over the noise of the kitchen.

Keller and I froze as Shane came stomping into the room, and the only thing that could be heard was Gunner's sniffles.

"Daddy!" Keller cried pitifully, running toward Shane and wrapping his arms around Shane's thighs.

"What's going on, bud?" he asked, looking at me in confusion.

"Auntie Kate won't make me pancakes!"

"This is about pancakes?"

Keller nodded, his face buried against Shane's side.

"You couldn't just make him pancakes?" Shane asked in exasperation, putting his hands under Keller's arms and lifting him onto his hip.

That was all she wrote.

Within a second, I was racing to the bathroom, and I made it just in time to slam the door behind me and vomit nothing but bile into the sink. I started crying, then sobbing as I braced my hand on the counter and rinsed out the sink. I hadn't even made it to the toilet.

Keller was acting like a pod person had stolen his body. Shane ignored me. Sage was still worried I wouldn't pick her up from school. I wasn't sure that Gavin was talking as much as he should be.

And I was pregnant and too sick to even make it to the toilet to vomit.

It was too much. I felt like I was slowly unraveling.

I took a deep breath as I heard Shane talking to the boys in the kitchen and pulled one of the hand towels off the rack to dry my face.

Nothing would get done if I hid in the bathroom, and I had no idea why Shane was even home. I needed to get myself together.

I walked back into the kitchen to find Gavin and Gunner just finishing up little cups of yogurt and Shane pouring himself a cup of coffee. Damn, that coffee smelled good.

"Sent Keller to his room," Shane told me softly,

handing me the cup of coffee he'd just poured. "You wanna explain what that was about?"

"Pancakes," I replied bitterly, pulling a package of wipes off the counter so I could start cleaning the boys' hands and faces.

"I didn't mean—"

"You can't do that stuff, Shane," I cut in as I helped Gavin out of his seat. "That's why Keller acts like that. I mean, we all know you're the boss, okay? We all know. But every time you bitch at me because one of the kids is throwing a fit, they think they don't have to listen to me."

"I don't—"

"You *do*." I picked Gunner up out of his high chair, and he snuggled his face into my neck, obviously still a little overwhelmed from all the noise.

"I'm their dad. They *should* come to me."

"I'm not saying they shouldn't—" Dammit, my eyes started filling with tears again, and I cursed the stupid pregnancy hormones racing through my body. "I'm saying that you keep undermining me, and now Keller thinks he can boss me around like I work for him or something."

Gunner wiggled to get down, and I set him on the ground so he could crawl into the living room where Gavin had turned on some cartoons.

"You treat me like shit, Shane."

"No I don't! I barely fucking see you."

"Exactly! You barely say a word to me unless you're asking me to do something, and anytime I'm disciplining the kids you step in—"

"They're not yours to discipline," he stated flatly, making me suck in a sharp breath.

"You're right. I absolutely had no right to send Keller to his room for being a demanding little brat."

"Don't call him a brat."

"If it looks like a brat, and talks like a brat, it's usually a brat."

"You couldn't just make him some fucking pancakes?"

"Are you shitting me right now?" I hissed, stepping forward. "I don't mind making Keller pancakes! If he'd asked, I probably would have said, *Sure, baby, you want some chocolate chips in those?* But he didn't *ask*. He *demanded* pancakes."

"He's four."

"He's *five*. And he knows better than to talk to adults like that."

"You're blowing this out of proportion," he said dismissively, turning back to the coffeepot to get his own cup.

"So it's okay for him to hit me? Is that what you're getting at? Give him what he wants so he doesn't throw a huge-ass tantrum?"

"I told him he shouldn't have hit you—that's why he's in his room right now."

I sat down heavily at the table and rested my tired eyes on the heels of my hands. Shane wasn't hearing me. He was so fucking wrapped up in his own importance, and he couldn't even see where I was coming from. "What are you even doing home?"

"Got let out early since it's Friday and there wasn't shit to do," he answered, coming to sit across from me at the table.

"Okay, well, I'm going to go say good-bye to Kell before I go." I stood wearily from the table.

"We need to talk. You got a few minutes before you leave?"

"Yeah. Let me go check on Kell first," I replied, turning toward the stairs.

I hated stairs; they seemed to mock me and my lack of energy.

When I got to Keller's room, he was passed out across the foot of his bed. Throwing the gigantic hissy fit must have worn him out—either that or the hissy fit had been because he was so tired. God, I missed the sweet little boy who thought I was God's gift to nephews.

"He's asleep, exactly what I'm going to be the second I get home," I informed Shane as I made my way back into the kitchen.

"You look like you've lost weight," he said out of the blue.

"I probably have. What did you want to talk about?"

"Can you still stay with the kids while I'm on deployment?" he asked nervously.

"It's a little late to be asking. What if I said no? You have like three weeks, Shane."

"Are you saying no?"

"Of course not, but we have some other shit to discuss."

"What other shit?" He turned his mug around and around between his palms and I couldn't seem to look away from the sight. His long fingers—nope, I wasn't going to go there. "I'll set up an allotment that goes straight to your account for bills and shit while I'm gone, groceries and stuff. I can always change—"

"I'm pregnant," I blurted without warning or buildup. If I'd had a serrated blade, I could have cut out my own tongue then.

"You're what?"

"Pregnant."

He stared at me blankly for a long time, and I was afraid to say anything else, but then his face lost the blank look and turned completely emotionless.

"Can you still keep the kids, or is it going to be a problem?"

"It's not an *it*. It's a baby."

"I need to know if you can still stay with the kids."

"Of course I can, Shane, God! Could you follow the fucking conversation?" I finally snapped, annoyed at his lack of response. "I am pregnant. The baby is yours. Now it's your turn to speak."

"I'm not sure what you want me to say here, Kate," he replied calmly, but his fingers had tightened around the coffee mug until his knuckles were white.

"Anything. At this point, I'd take anything," I replied tiredly, my heart racing.

"Are you sure it's mine?"

My body went cold then, the sweat I'd felt underneath my arms growing cool so quickly I almost shivered. "Anything but that," I whispered hoarsely, with a small shake of my head.

I rose to leave without another word, and he didn't stop me as I kissed the boys good-bye and slipped on my shoes.

"When Keller wakes up, please tell him I love him," I called out as I reached the door. "I'll pick Sage up from school today since I already told her I would."

I heard his chair skid across the linoleum and his voice calling my name, but I didn't stop. I couldn't handle any more that day.

Chapter 4

Kate

I fucked up," I announced into the phone as I lay on the bathroom floor.

"Well, hello to you, too," my foster sister Anita retorted. "Why are you echoing?"

"I'm in the bathroom—"

"I really don't want to talk to you while you shit."

"I'm not shitting, Ani. Fuck, I fucked up so bad." My voice caught on the last few words, and I couldn't hide the sob that came out of me. I was so tired, and my whole body seemed to ache from the amount of vomiting I'd done. I couldn't keep anything down—why couldn't I keep anything down?

"Crap, Katie! What's going on? Are you okay?" she asked nervously.

"I'm pregnant," I whispered, as if saying the words quietly would soften the reply.

"Didn't you get your shot? What the fuck, Kate? You can't miss a shot!"

"I didn't. I swear, I got it right when I was supposed to. I don't know what the fuck happened!"

"I hope to Christ you know what happened," she replied drily.

"It gets worse," I moaned, laying my head back on the towel beneath me. "Way worse."

"Was the guy ugly?"

"Worse."

"A gigolo?"

"Way worse."

"Oh, fuck, Katie," she whispered after a moment of complete silence. "You didn't."

"We were drunk. It was a mistake."

"That excuse stopped working when you were nineteen. It doesn't work when you're almost thirty."

"I know. I'm such an idiot. God, what was I thinking?"

"Does Shane know?"

The lights were off in the bathroom, but the sun was shining through the small window of my shower and I closed my eyes against it. Shit, even my eyeballs hurt.

"Yeah, I told him this morning."

"What did he say?"

"Not much."

"Not much?"

"He asked if I was sure it was his."

"That cocksucker!" she yelled, intensifying the pain in my head. "I hope you ripped him a new asshole!"

"No, I just left."

"What? Why? Don't let him be a dick to you,

Katherine. You've put up with far more shit than you should've from him over the years."

"No, I know. I just—" I started weeping then, feeling more pitiful than I ever had in my entire life. "I'm just tired, Ani. I'm so fucking tired, and I keep throwing up. And Keller was such a brat this morning, he actually hit me, and then Shane got home and was a complete ass about it. I just couldn't take anymore, and then I had to leave when Kell was asleep and he probably woke up and thought I was still mad at him."

"Whoa, slow down, sweetheart," she said soothingly. "Let's work this out piece by piece. You've been sick?"

"I'm so sick," I rasped, my stomach starting to churn yet again. "God, Ani. I haven't been able to keep anything down for days."

"How many days?"

"Like three, I think. God, it feels like forever."

"You're probably dehydrated, Kate. You need to go to the doctor."

"I have an appointment day after tomorrow."

"No, you need to go in now."

"I'm too exhausted. I can't even get off the bathroom floor."

I heard her rustling with something, then her voice came through the phone more clearly. "I have to call you back, sis, okay?"

"Yeah," I replied wearily. "I'll be here."

"I'll call you *right back*."

"Okay."

I hung up as my stomach revolted again, and I didn't

even bother trying to kneel up to reach the toilet. There wasn't anything in my belly to lose anyway.

By the time I was done, I was sweaty and my abs were on fire, but that didn't stop me from falling asleep curled into a ball.

* * *

"Katie?" I heard Shane call, pulling me out of the first deep sleep I'd had in days. "Kate!"

Before I could answer him, his body filled the doorway to my bathroom.

"Sorry, I must not have heard the door," I said inanely as he came to an abrupt stop. "I don't really feel like company."

"Katie," he said softly, taking a step toward me.

"Don't. I just—don't. I smell like shit, and I'm all sweaty, and just—give me a few minutes, okay?" I asked tiredly, rising slowly to my knees.

"Don't move, baby," he replied gently as he came into the bathroom. "Let's get you out of here."

The endearment made my throat feel tight, but I pushed past it. "Where are the kids?"

"I picked Sage up and brought them to the neighbors for a bit."

"Oh shit!" I tried to rise to my feet, but swayed dizzily and started crying yet again. "I was supposed to get her from school. Oh my God, she must have been so freaked out."

"Hey," he called softly, "stop. I talked to Anita, and

she told me you were sick. I got Sage right on time. She was fine. Totally fine."

"God, I'm so sorry. I fell asleep."

"I can see that. There's nothing to be sorry for."

He leaned down to pick me up, and I scrambled to try to move away. "Please don't, Shane." I sniffled. "I stink. I need a shower."

He stared at me, not replying for a long time before he leaned over my body and pushed the shower curtain back.

"What are you doing?"

"You want a shower, right?" he asked as he turned on the water. "So let's get you in the shower."

I watched in shock as he slid the curtain closed again and reached back to pull his T-shirt over his head, stepping out of his flip-flops as he did so. Next, he pushed down his khaki shorts and boxer briefs at the same time, leaving him completely naked.

"What in God's name are you doing?" I asked when my mouth finally started working again.

"Come on, let's get you up."

"Are you out of your goddamn mind?"

"If you don't stop looking at my dick, it's going to perk up and say hello," he warned.

"That's what got me into this shit show in the first place."

"Right. I'm not going to bang you against the wall. You're fucking sick, and you need to go to the hospital—so either you let me help you in the shower or I'm taking you like that—smelling like ass and looking like a homeless person."

"I'm pretty sure any sort of ego I had from sleeping with you has just shriveled up and died."

"Good, then you won't care if I see you naked."

"Oh believe me, I don't," I replied tiredly as I let him pull me off the floor. "I already know you don't want 'seconds' so I'm not worried you'll see something that turns you off."

"I was a dick."

"No worries, at least the sex was good," I answered as he pulled my T-shirt over my sore breasts. "Careful," I warned.

"I'll be careful," he promised as he slid my leggings and underwear down my legs.

"I shouldn't have said those things to you," he told me sincerely, holding my hand as we stepped into the shower. "I was so messed up that morning—"

"You think I wasn't?" I asked as he moved me slowly toward the running water. "God, I fucking threw up. I should have seen that moment for the omen it was."

"I'm sorry, Katie," he said, pulling my hands around his torso to stabilize me so he could run his fingers through my hair. "I was such a dick. I knew none of that was your fault, but fuck if I wasn't pissed anyway."

"You know that I was drunk, right?"

"It doesn't—"

"No, it does matter," I argued before he could finish his sentence, closing my eyes as he worked shampoo into my scalp. "You seem to be under some illusion that I took advantage of you or something. That's bullshit. We were both drinking, and if I recall things correctly, you fucked me while I was pinned facedown on the bed."

"Jesus Christ," he hissed, pausing as I felt his cock twitch against my stomach.

"Not that I was complaining at the time," I mumbled, making his hands tighten in my hair. "Fuck, my stomach is starting to—"

I jerked away from him and barely bent over before I was heaving. "I'm sorry," I gasped between waves. "Shit. I fucking hate—"

"Shhh," he replied calmly, bracing one of his arms across my chest and rubbing my back with the other. "You're okay. It'll pass."

"God," I groaned as my stomach finally settled again. "Why are you even here?"

"Let's get you washed up."

"Oh no, I can do this shit on my own."

"I'm not leaving you in here by yourself."

"Fine." I washed the most important areas on my body quickly, refusing to exert the extra energy for anything else, and within a few minutes I was wrapped in a towel and Shane was carrying me into my room.

"Did you really just help me take a shower?" I asked, dropping my head to his shoulder. "What the hell was that about?"

I fell asleep before he could answer, and I vaguely felt him dressing me as I faded in and out. By the time I woke up fully, Shane was once again carrying me.

"You jackass," I said, my entire body stiffening as I realized where we were.

"You need to see a doctor," he replied, marching through the waiting room of the ER.

"I don't have insurance, Shane, and it's just morning sickness."

"Rachel was never this sick."

"I'm not Rachel."

"You're getting checked out."

"When exactly did you get a say in this?"

"When Anita called and said you were sick as shit and lying on the floor of your bathroom."

"She's such a fucking drama queen."

"That's exactly where I found you."

"Semantics," I mumbled as we reached the front desk.

* * *

"I still don't understand why you're here," I called softly, rolling over gingerly in my hospital bed. The damn bed was so uncomfortable that I knew I'd be even more achy when I climbed back out of it.

"We're friends," he replied, messing with something on his phone.

He'd barely looked at me since they'd brought me back to the small room and proceeded to confirm my pregnancy. He'd left while they gave me an internal ultrasound, and had remained silent even as I caught him glancing at the images I'd conveniently left on the counter by the only chair in the room. He was restless, almost jittery, and to be honest it made my tension rise with every small movement.

"We're not friends, Shane," I told him seriously, making his head snap up in surprise. "We've got history—a shit ton of it—but we haven't been friends in a long time."

"I can't leave you here alone."

"I'll be fine. Seriously. You need to get home to the kids. Sage is probably freaking out by now."

"I just called her. She's fine."

"Well, I bet Megan is losing her mind with all those kids."

"I just talked to her. She's fine, too."

"I don't want you here," I finally said, looking away from the shock on his face. "I'm not sure what you're doing, but let's be honest here, okay?"

"I'm being honest."

"No, you're feeling guilty or something, but you're sure as fuck not being honest."

"You're being a bitch."

"Ah, there's the honesty," I replied drily to cover how his words had stung. "I know you don't want to be here, okay? You're fidgeting and sighing and looking at your watch, and frankly, it would be easier to enjoy this glorious anti-nausea medicine if I didn't feel like I was keeping you from wherever it is you want to be."

"I want to be here," he argued stubbornly.

"Why? Why would you want to be here?"

"Because you're sick and you're pregnant. I can't just leave you."

"Why is it your problem?" I stared at him, silently

pleading with him to acknowledge the child in the images next to his elbow.

"I guess it's not," he finally said, rising from the chair.

"Are you going to just keep pretending that I got myself pregnant?" I asked tiredly, looking up into his face. "The dates are on the ultrasound prints you keep staring at. I'm sure even you can do the math."

"I already have four kids," he said roughly, reaching up to scratch his jaw. "With my *wife*."

"What's that supposed to mean?" I whispered back, feeling like I was being sliced open.

"Look, you've had a couple of days to process this shit, all right?" he snapped back. "I've had hours, and most of those hours have been spent peeling you off the floor and taking you to the hospital."

"I'm sorry for being such an inconvenience."

"Can you just for one fucking second give me a little space? Fuck, Kate, just give me a minute to process the shit storm that has become my fucking life!"

I nodded once, then slowly rolled until I was facing away from him.

"Right, because this is so much easier for me," I replied flatly, refusing to look at him. "Take as much time as you want."

I could feel his eyes on the back of my head for a long time, but I clenched my teeth and controlled my breathing until I heard him open and close the door.

Then I burst into tears.

Stupid pregnancy hormones.

* * *

They only kept me for a few hours more, letting me re-hydrate with their nifty little needle in my vein, then sending me home with a prescription for anti-nausea meds and some prenatal vitamins.

Shit. Prenatal. It was really happening. I was really going to be a mom. Or was I already a mom? I sure as hell already felt protective of the little sea monkey curled up somewhere between my hip bones.

I took an expensive-as-hell cab back to my apartment and climbed the stairs, thankful that Shane had thought to bring my purse to the hospital. After losing my keys eighteen million times, I'd finally gotten into the habit of keeping an extra house key in my wallet.

When I got inside, something was off. It took a second before I realized it was the scent of lemon. What the heck?

Shane had cleaned up the bathroom.

Oh my God.

I sat down heavily on the sparkling-clean toilet and chastised myself until the tears I felt coming to the surface subsided. It was such a nice thing for him to do. But I couldn't let myself think that it was done out of anything but kindness...or guilt. Guilt was probably the reason.

I grabbed my phone out of my purse to call him, but stopped short when I saw that my mom was calling my silenced phone. Shit! Anita must have opened her big mouth.

"Hey, Ma!" I answered cheerfully, shuffling toward my bed and crawling between the—did he wash my sheets?

"Hey, baby! Whatcha doing?"

"Not much, just hanging out at home."

"Oh yeah?"

"Yeah."

I was pretty sure that she knew I was pregnant, but she wasn't going to ask. I swear, she and Aunt Ellie had perfected the whole you-know-I-know-but-I'll-wait-until-you-tell-me-as-long-as-you-tell-me-right-now routine. They'd caught many a child with that strategy as I grew up, kids who'd been impossible to understand and less trusting than an antelope surrounded by Siberian tigers.

Yes, I had a thing for exotic animals as a kid. Sue me.

My aunt and uncle had found out pretty early in their marriage that they couldn't have children and, being the awesome people they were, had immediately decided that they wanted to open their house and their lives to foster children. It couldn't have been easy—hell, I'd seen firsthand how *not* easy it was—but they'd never once faltered in what my aunt later told me they'd felt called to do. From the time I was two years old, I'd had cousins coming out of the woodwork—quiet, loud, calm, destructive, sad, and angry cousins. Some didn't last long; *most* didn't last long. But there were two that my aunt and uncle had been able to adopt—Trevor and Henry—and a few who'd stayed in touch even after they'd gone. Shane had been one of the foster kids who had seemed to hold tight to Ellie and Mike Harris's family, even though he'd been one of the oldest ever to be placed with them.

When I was five and Trevor came to stay with Aunt Ellie and Uncle Mike, my parents had some sort of epiphany. Less than a year later, our family had also started taking in kids who for one reason or another needed a place to stay. So, for the first time in my life, I had siblings. Loads of siblings. Siblings I had to say good-bye to far more often than I wanted. Then out of nowhere, in the middle of a heat wave during the long days of summer, came a pair of brothers that my parents would eventually adopt—which meant I got to keep them forever. My twin brothers, Alex and Abraham, stepped onto our front porch when I was eight and they were ten, and they never had to leave again. And thank God, because four years later my trusting and forgiving nature had trapped me into a situation that could have turned out very badly if Bram and Alex hadn't chosen that exact moment to find me outside with our newest foster brother.

After that, my parents had never again fostered any children older than me and had refused to take in any more boys. They'd let their guard down, too, and I don't know if they'll ever forgive themselves for that. My parents took in their last foster child when I was seventeen, and that's when I met Anita. She didn't want to be adopted, even though legally my parents could have, but she'd also never left. She stayed with my parents for her last two years of high school and had moved into the garage apartment so she could attend college after that.

With all those children and all their problems, my aunt and mom had become interrogators that would make the CIA look up and take notice. They'd seen everything and heard everything, and no attitude or personality could withstand them when they had their minds set on something. Unfortunately, that also meant that I'd be telling my mother whatever she wanted to know.

"Anything new happening?"

"She fuh-reaking told you!" I yelled, slamming my hand down against the bedding, making the fresh scent of Tide float up around me. Shane *had* washed my sheets!

"I have no idea what you're talking about."

"I'm pregnant," I retorted with a growl.

"What?" she asked in feigned surprise.

"I'm going to kill Anita."

"No you're not. She was worried. Don't be mad at her."

"She's nosy! I should have told you. I wanted to tell you." I began to sniffle. Nothing was how I'd imagined it. Nothing was going right.

"Oh, baby," my mom said softly. "I'm sorry. I know that kind of thing is important. I would have waited until you called me, but Ani said you were sick and I was worried..."

"I know, Ma. It's fine, I'm just—it's these stupid hormones! I can't get a handle on it. I swear I want to kill someone, and within seconds I'm crying because one of my toes has chipped nail polish."

"I remember that. If you're anything like me, you're going to be a nightmare to live with."

"Good thing I live alone then," I mumbled, wiping my face on my clean sheets. *Take that, Shane.*

"You want to talk about it?"

"Not especially."

"Are you going to anyway?"

"Yeah." I sighed, curling up into a ball and pulling the bedding over my head.

"What's going on, lovey?"

"I slept with Shane," I mumbled, sort of hoping she wouldn't understand me.

"Well...that was a long time coming."

"What?"

"Katie, you and Shane have been circling around each other for years—ever since you were kids."

"Mom, he married my best friend. I'm not sure I'd call that *circling*."

"Katiebear, I'm going to tell you something, and you can take it however you want."

"I don't think I want to hear it."

"Tough."

I snorted a laugh, and it was the first time I'd laughed since I'd found out I was pregnant. My mom could always do that—somehow make the bad seem not-so-bad with a few carefully chosen words. I hoped I could do that one day.

"Back when you were kids...Shane was running."

"What do you mean?"

"I'm not going to say he didn't love Rachel. I'd never say that, because it plain isn't true. I know he loved her—you could see it when they were together. But Katie... they never lived together for any significant period of time."

"It's his job, Mom—"

"You don't have to defend him to me, Katherine Eleanor. I know that boy, and I've loved him since he moved in with your uncle and aunt. What I'm saying is that Rachel was easy for him to love, and that's not necessarily a bad thing. She was what he needed, and I was always glad he found that in her."

"They were perfect together," I whispered, my throat growing tight.

"Well, I wouldn't say that."

"What?"

"Shane needed someone to take him at face value back then, lovey, and Rachel did that... you didn't."

"What's that supposed to mean?" My heart began to thump hard in my chest, and my hands grew clammy.

"Well, I guess Aunt Ellie and I always thought that you were too much for him."

"Gee, thanks."

"That is absolutely not a bad thing, Kate. You *saw* him, and for a while I could tell that he reveled in that. He loved that you could see straight through him. It challenged him."

"He left me, Mom. I'm not sure how you could say he loved anything about me."

"You got too close, Katie. He wasn't ready for that."

"Well, how was I supposed to know that?" I cried, sitting up in bed. "I was nineteen! I didn't know what I was doing!"

"There's those hormones."

"He dropped me, Mom. He never cared about me. You should've—" No. She didn't need to know that Shane had called me for months my freshman year of college, then had acted like he didn't want anything to do with me the minute he'd seen my best friend. It wasn't even relevant anymore. "He just...made it very clear that he wanted nothing to do with me. He's avoided me for ten years. His opinion's pretty obvious."

"I didn't mean to upset you, lovey."

"You didn't."

"Okay, new subject?"

"Yes please."

"How did Shane take the news?"

"That's the same freaking subject!"

* * *

I woke up the next morning to whispers and the smell of formula breath fanning across my face.

"Is she awake yet?"

"Not yet! Daddy said to be quiet."

"Quiet!"

"Whyet!"

"I wish she'd wake up already."

"Keller, you better zip it."

"If your daddy wanted to let me sleep, he wouldn't have left four monsters in my bed," I growled, sitting up too quickly and pulling them to me as they squealed and my stomach churned.

"Oh, Auntie Kate needs another minute, guys." I moaned, lying back against my pillow. "Want to snuggle for a little bit?"

They curled up around me, Gunner playing with my loose hair, Gavin's head resting on my sore boobs, Keller's body twisting one of my ankles in a way it didn't want to twist, and Sage holding my hand. Within seconds, I felt a million times better.

"Where's your dad?" I asked quietly, letting my eyes close as Gunner's tiny fingers ran through my hair.

"Goin' potty."

"He's taking a long time."

"I bet he's pooping! He stinks so bad!" Keller crowed, making me snicker.

"I'm not pooping, Keller," Shane mumbled from the side of the bed, making my eyes pop open. His cheeks were red with embarrassment, and I think I fell a little then.

"You stink worse, Keller," I accused, meeting Shane's eyes.

"No I don't! You do, Auntie Kate! You reek!"

"You week!" Gavin yelled right in my ear.

Shane's eyes crinkled a little at the sides as he tried to hold back a smile.

"I thought you might want to see them," Shane said

quietly as he sat on the edge of the bed. "I know you don't feel good—"

"Thank you," I cut in, letting go of Gunner for a minute to reach out and rest my hand on his knee. "This is just what I needed."

"I used the spare key." His voice grew quiet.

"I figured."

"You want it back?"

"No," I whispered.

"Okay."

"Auntie Kate, why are you sick?" Sage asked suspiciously, her voice quivering.

"Come here, Sage the Rage," I answered, pulling her toward me. "I've got news."

"Kate," Shane warned in a low tone.

"I'm going to have a baby."

My words seemed to stun the kids into silence for a moment before they all spoke up at the same time.

"Baby."

"Baby."

"What?"

"You are?"

"Yep! Growing a baby sometimes makes a mama sick, but only for a while. So that's why I'm sick. Once the baby's a little bigger, I won't be sick anymore."

"You'll be fat!" Keller yelled.

"Keller," Shane snapped.

I shook my head slightly at Shane and met Keller's eyes. He wasn't being a brat ... He was worried.

"Come here, Kell."

He crawled up and sat on my thighs.

"Careful, pal," Shane warned.

"He's okay," I said with a smile, never looking away from Keller. "I'm just growing a baby, bud. But it takes a long time—nothing's going to change for a while."

"Where is it?" he asked curiously, looking down at my relatively flat stomach.

"Right about here." I pointed, making all of the kids look closely at where my finger was.

"I don't see anything."

"That's because its really, really tiny right now."

"How tiny?" Keller asked dubiously.

"Like a little bean."

"But it's going to grow?"

"Yep."

"Cool."

"Very cool," I agreed.

"Is it going to be our cousin?" Sage asked, jolting me out of my soft conversation with Keller.

"Can you grab me a glass of water, sis?" I asked after what seemed like a really long pause. "I need to take my medicine before I get sick again."

"Ew!" Keller yelped, scooting back away from me.

As Sage climbed off the bed, I turned to meet Shane's eyes.

He looked as shell-shocked as I felt.

Chapter 5
Shane

I felt like I was spinning out of control.

As I lay there in my bed, I couldn't help but think back to when I'd sneaked the kids in to see Kate a few mornings before. She'd been sleeping so heavily that she hadn't even heard the door open or the kids' quiet conversations, and for a moment I'd felt a flash of something between protectiveness and possessiveness rush over me.

It had rattled me so badly that I'd made an excuse to use her bathroom and had locked myself in there for a few minutes to get my shit under control. Protectiveness I could handle—it wasn't a new feeling when it came to Kate. But possessiveness was wrong on so many levels that I felt like a creep for even putting a name to it. I didn't want her, and she wasn't mine.

She wasn't mine even though she was currently carrying my child.

I pushed my sheets down to my feet in irritation and rolled onto my side, trying to find a comfortable position to sleep. I had less than two weeks before I had to leave, and though I was already starting to transition into work mode and the familiar life I'd be living for the next six or seven months, my mind constantly raced with the thought of leaving my kids.

I'd left them before. Shit, I'd left over and over again...but things were different now. I wouldn't be leaving them with their mother, secure in the knowledge that everything would stay the same when I was gone. I was leaving them with Kate, and I trusted her with their lives, but I couldn't reconcile that with the place she had in mine.

She was pregnant. God, how could I have been so stupid? As if fucking Kate hadn't been enough of an epically bad decision, I'd also stormed the gates without putting on my goddamn armor.

Not that I'd had any condoms with me anyway. I hadn't had sex in a year, and I hadn't planned on having sex for a very long time after that. Then I'd made the boneheaded decision to use Kate to end my dry spell.

Kate. My wife's best friend, and the niece of the only people I'd ever called my parents. The worst mistake I'd ever made in my entire life.

I couldn't decide if I was mad about what I'd done or so fucking sad about the entire thing that I wanted to weep.

I didn't want a child with her. God, I didn't want any more children period.

I could barely keep up with shit as it was, even with Kate to take care of the kids while I worked. How the hell could I add another kid into that mix? When Rachel was alive, I'd teased her that I wanted a houseful of kids. I knew that it was a lot to place on her shoulders when I was away so much, but she'd agreed wholeheartedly with my dream, and she'd never once complained about the life we'd made.

If she hadn't died, I had a feeling that she'd probably already be pregnant by now, and I'd be ecstatic about adding to our brood.

But Rachel was dead, and Kate was the one who was pregnant. I couldn't find it in myself to be excited about that.

And as I turned to my belly and shut my eyes tightly, I finally gave in to the fear that had been niggling in the back of my mind for close to a week.

The fear that I wouldn't love Kate's child the way I loved the others.

The fear that I'd feel nothing.

* * *

"Are you sure you're okay with them?" I asked for the third time as I screwed the lid on my coffee mug.

"I'm fine, Shane. I promise. Sage doesn't have school today so I'm going to let them sleep as late as they want and then make them snuggle on the couch for a movie day."

"Are you still puking every five minutes?" I asked,

taking in her pale face and hastily tied-up hair. She still didn't look good.

"Nope. The anti-nausea stuff they gave me is like magic. I haven't puked in like—" She looked past me to the clock on the stove. "—four hours."

"You were up at two in the morning vomiting? Why the fuck would you even take that medicine if you're still puking? That's fucking bullshit. Call the doctor and see if they have anything else—another brand maybe. Did you buy generic? They say that stuff is the same as the name brand, but—"

"Whoa! Slow down there, turbo." She cut me off, raising her hands in the air between us. "It's not fool-proof, okay? It helps, but it's not a cure-all. I'd much rather puke every six to eight hours than every fifteen minutes. It's doing its job. I'm keeping my food down and can actually drink water again. It's all good."

"You're still throwing up," I replied stubbornly.

"Let's see how many different names we can think of to describe vomiting. We've used like three already. Why don't I go next?" She pursed her lips and squinted for a minute before stating, "Blowing chunks. Now you."

"What the fuck are you talking about?"

"I'm changing the subject from something you seem intent on arguing about even though it's a fruitless en-deavor. Harfing. Upchucking. Hurling."

"I'm not playing this game with you," I replied, an-noyed. If she didn't want to take care of herself, that wasn't my business. She seemed completely okay with looking and feeling like crap all the time, and who was I to argue with that?

"Yakking," she announced, following me around the kitchen as I grabbed my wallet and my keys. "Ralphing."

"Knock it off, Kate."

"Praying to the porcelain god," she retorted, with a pleased smile.

Even with her gaunt cheeks and messy hair, I wanted to kiss her so badly it hurt, and that made my frustration rise. "Does being annoying usually get you what you want?"

"If you're going to work annoyed instead of worried, then it worked."

"I'm not worried."

"You've been pacing."

"You're sick, for fuck's sake."

"I'm telling you, I'm fine. I'm excited to finally have a day off from school—just me and my monsters," she replied with a sweet, contented smile.

"They're not yours." I couldn't stop the words before they came rushing out of my mouth, but I regretted them the same second the smile fell off her face.

"I've been calling them my monsters since they were born, Shane," she said flatly. "I'm not going to stop because you've got a stick up your ass for some reason I can't quite comprehend."

"You're—"

"No," she cut in. "You don't get to be a dick to me. You don't. I haven't done anything to you, and I'm tired of feeling like I'm walking on eggshells. I've helped take care of the kids since they were born. You can't change that—it's just fact. I'm sorry that you think this is some sort of competition or whatever the fuck you think it is. They're yours. I get it. But that doesn't mean that I'm nothing, and you can't try and act like it does."

"I don't think you're nothing."

"Look, I know that you don't like me."

"That's not—"

"But for the next nineteen years, you're going to have to deal with me." Her eyes began to water, and a few tears slipped from her eyes. "I'm sorry for that. I'm so, so sorry. But we have to figure out a way to make this work because, for better or worse, I'm here, and it's exhausting trying to get along with you."

Kate turned to walk away, and my stomach clenched.

"Why do you always do that?" I asked in irritation. "You never let me say anything before you're walking away."

"I know what you have to say, Shane. You've already said it, remember? I'm just saving us both from words you can't take back."

"All you're doing is pissing me off!" I called as she started walking again.

"That's just a bonus," she called back quietly.

I scratched my head in frustration, growling deep in my throat before perching my cover on top of my head and walking out the front door.

She was so fucking irritating. She acted like I was such a dick, and though I could remember vividly the times that I had been, there were far more times over the past year that things had been just fine between us. Had we ever been best friends? Not really. But that didn't make me a dick.

And the fact that she kept saying I didn't like her pissed me off. I'd never said I didn't like her. She was fine. Likable. She just wasn't someone I wanted to hang out with in what little spare time I had. That didn't make me a dick, either.

I couldn't understand why she just kept pushing at me. Did she want me to fall on my knees and ask her to be best friends forever? Because that was never going to happen.

But I had never, not once, acted like she had to walk on eggshells.

That was complete and utter bullshit.

We had the kids in common. That was it. I wasn't going to pretend that I thought she was interesting or sexy or fun. That wouldn't be fair to her, and frankly, it would just fuck things up worse than they already were.

* * *

The house was noisy as I stepped in the front door that night after a long-ass day at work. I'd been checking and rechecking lists all day, running back and forth all over the base trying to get shit ready for the deployment that was slowly closing in. God, I was tired. Tired and in a pissy mood.

"You're doing awesome, Sage!" Kate's voice rose above the clatter of pans Gavin and Gunner were playing with on the floor. "Make sure you're cutting through all the way to the counter, okay?"

Keller was silent for the first time in a long time, building something with Legos at the kitchen table, and Kate was moving around Sage as she cut biscuits out of the dough on the counter with what looked like an empty can of corn.

"Something smells really good," I announced, setting my keys and wallet on the counter.

"We made stew, huh, Sage?" Kate said with a shy smile. "It was kind of cold out today, and I felt like some comfort food."

"Are those Ellie's biscuits?" I asked, my mouth watering at the thought.

"Yep, and my mom's beef stew recipe."

"Holy hell. When's it ready?" I asked, unbuttoning my uniform top. I wanted to peel off my uniform and get into some basketball shorts and a T-shirt that didn't smell like sweat, pronto.

"Um," Kate stuttered as she watched my fingers, and I became aware of my heart thumping hard in my chest. "Like twenty minutes," she finally answered.

"I'm gonna take a shower first then."

"Okay."

She was still staring, and I don't know if it was the stress of the day or what, but suddenly I wanted her out of the kitchen and away from the four rugrats that were making so much noise.

"Can I talk to you for a sec?" I asked, tilting my head to the side.

"Sure. Hey, Sage, hop down, would you? I'll be back in a minute."

Kate made sure Sage was away from the counter and grabbed Gunner off the floor, setting him in the playpen filled with toys between the kitchen and the living room before following me into the hall and up the stairs.

When we got to my room, I wiggled and stretched my shoulders, trying to get the tight sleeves of my uniform off my biceps. That was the trouble with having tightly rolled-up sleeves; they were so tight, they were a pain in the ass to get off.

I felt her fingers slide between my skin and the fabric of my sleeves, and stopped moving completely as she yanked first one sleeve and then the other down my arms.

Her breathing was little off, kind of heavy and shuddery at the same time, and the feel of it on my shoulder was the straw that broke the camel's back.

"Is that all you—" Kate started to ask.

My mouth was on hers before the last word was spoken, and I made an embarrassing desperate noise when her lips parted and she let me inside.

She tasted like ginger, probably from the cookies she had brought with her that morning, and for some reason it ratcheted up my desire until I was practically shaking.

My hands were shaky as they raced over her, one making its way to the ponytail at the back of her head and the other sliding down until it reached that sweet spot just below her ass. My fingers wrapped around her thigh as she whimpered into my mouth and tried to climb me, and without thought I jerked her leg high onto my hip.

Shit. She was so hot. I could feel it through her pants. For the second time in my life, I thanked God for yoga pants and slid my hand down the back of them, not stopping until I found where she was soaking wet.

Her hips tipped back, trying to get more room, and I tore my mouth from hers so I could catch my breath.

"Please don't stop," she begged as she rolled her hips against my hand.

"Lift your shirt," I ordered frantically, trying to get at everything at once. I needed it all. I needed it right that second.

Instead of lifting the tank top she had on, she slipped her arms out of the straps and carefully pulled it below her breasts. No bra. Thank fuck. I slid my hand out of the back of her pants and instantly shoved it back down the front, finding her clit and pinching it between my fingers as I bent down.

"Careful, please," she warned, jerking back as I went for her breasts.

"I'll be soft. You took out the rings," I mumbled, slowing to take her right nipple gently into my mouth.

"I thought I probably should," she replied, arching her back.

"You took out this one, too," I said, pressing two fingers deep inside her and pressing down hard with my thumb on her clit. "I liked 'em."

"Shit," she moaned, bending her knees so she could press down on my fingers inside her. "It's not enough."

"It's enough."

"No, I'm so close. God. It's not—"

I bit down on her nipple then, careful of how sensitive she seemed to be, and she came, gasping and shuddering as my hand between her legs became drenched in her.

I pulled my hand from her slowly, running my fingers over everything I could reach, then lifted it and put those two fingers in my mouth.

She tasted different than I remembered. Maybe even better.

She was going for my utility belt when the sound of little feet stomping up the stairs reached our ears.

Holy fuck.

We scrambled to get decent, her pulling her tank top back over her hard-tipped breasts, and me reaching inside my pants to pull up my painfully tight dick and hide it underneath my belt, loosening my undershirt so it would fall over everything. *Fuck, that hurt.*

"I'm hungry!" Keller yelled as he came to the doorway.

"Okay, bud. I'll be down in just a sec," Kate said awkwardly.

"I'm really hungry," he insisted.

"We'll be right down, bud," I said in my dad voice, warning him with just my tone that the conversation was finished.

"Okay." He spun on his heel and went barreling back down the stairs with all the grace of an elephant, and then there we were, standing a few feet apart and completely uncomfortable.

"Fuck," I mumbled, running my hands over my face, which just made things infinitely worse because they smelled like Kate.

"That was fun," she said with a smirk, looking anywhere but at my face.

"For you maybe," I grumbled, making her laugh a little.

"Poor baby. You need some relief?" She walked to the doorway and called down to Sage. "How's it going, sis?"

"Watching cartoons!" Sage yelled from downstairs.

"Okay, we'll be down in a minute," Kate yelled back before closing the door to my room quietly and locking it.

"What are we doing?" I asked, knowing whatever we were doing was an extremely bad idea.

"You're not doing anything," she said, reaching for my belt. "You're just going to stand there."

She dropped to her knees then, and as much as my conscience was telling me to walk the fuck out of that room, the rest of me was saying that if I stopped her, I was going to break down in tears.

She had my belt and the buttons to my trousers undone in seconds and pulled my boxers down until they were tucked under my balls at the tops of my thighs.

"My exceptionally forgiving gag reflex is on the fritz," she warned before sticking out her tongue to swipe at the head of my cock. "You'll just have to take what I can give you."

I didn't know why her words were so hot, but I didn't really care, either, because she was sucking me into her mouth and using one of her hands to slide along with her lips, and I swore it was one of the best blow jobs I'd ever had even though she didn't take me in very deep.

The way she slid her hand off my thigh and rolled my balls in her palm made my eyesight grow hazy. She was totally focused, her eyes closed and her breath puffing out of her nose against my pelvis in short pants. It didn't take long before I was pulling at her hair, eventually pulling her mouth completely off me.

She didn't swallow, but she did pull her tank top down so I could come all over her breasts and neck like I was fucking marking her or something.

When she was done, she walked toward the bathroom and I moved for the door, tucking myself back into my pants. When I looked over the railing at the top of the stairs, Gunner was still in his playpen and the older kids were still sitting quietly watching cartoons.

I'd just gotten back into my room when she came out of the bathroom, her neck and chest once again clean and covered, and her lips rosy and swollen.

Keller bursting into the room hadn't pulled me out of the fog I was in. Neither had the changes pregnancy had made to her body. I hadn't stopped when I'd realized the taste of her body had changed or when she'd gone onto her knees. But for some reason, the words that came out of her mouth as she met me in the middle of the room were like a bucket of cold water shocking me into the present.

"I'm going to go down and finish dinner," she said with a small smile.

It was way too fucking domestic. *Glad I got you off, honey. Now I need to go back to feed the kids.*

"This shouldn't have happened," I replied, erasing that smile. "What the *fuck* were we thinking?"

"Oh. Wow. Okay." She barked out a quiet derisive laugh and shook her head once. "You're totally right. Won't happen again," she assured me with a small salute.

"This isn't your house," I stubbornly continued on, the pain in my chest and the guilt in my belly feeling like they were going to burn their way out. "I'm not your husband."

"No, really?"

"I'm not going to play house with you, Kate."

"I didn't realize that's what we were doing."

"I'm grateful, so fucking grateful, that you take care of the kids the way you do. I know you do it because you love them, and they love you just as much."

She was silent as I tried to gather my thoughts, but there were so many tumbling around in my head that I couldn't make myself say what I wanted to, and everything that was coming out sounded bitter and condescending.

"You and me are never going to happen, Kate. Okay? I'm not sure what you're thinking, if you thought we'd just be one big happy family or something, but we won't. You're not Rachel. You're just not, and you're nice, but I don't feel that way about you."

She nodded, looking over my shoulder, and I watched her swallow hard before turning away from me.

"You're not going to say anything?" I asked as she reached the doorway.

"I think it's already been said, don't you?" she asked with a raised eyebrow. "I'm not chasing you, Shane. Whatever it is you're seeing isn't there. You asked me to come in here. You kissed me. You got me off, so I returned the favor. I didn't initiate any of that."

"You're right. My mistake," I ground out.

"You don't think of me that way, but you have no problem sticking your fingers in any hole you can reach, right?" She shook her head and sighed. "I don't need this shit. Don't touch me again."

I hopped in the shower as soon as I heard her walking down the stairs and grit my teeth as I washed my still painfully swollen erection. I'd just gotten some of the best head in my life, and I was still hard. When I finally got my body under control, I slipped into some shorts and an old T-shirt and headed downstairs just as the front door closed softly.

"Where's your auntie?" I asked Sage as I picked Gunner up.

"She left. She said to tell you the biscuits are on top of the stove and the stew is ready in the Crock-Pot," she replied, walking past me toward the kitchen.

When the kids were settled and food had been passed out, I finally took a deep breath in relief. This was how it was supposed to be. Just me and my kids.

Then I realized Kate had quietly left without eating any of the comfort food she'd been so excited about, and I felt like the biggest dick on the planet.

Chapter 6

Kate

Hey, big brother!" I answered my phone as cheerfully as I could while scrolling through my work email.

Only a couple of days remained until Shane left on his deployment, and I was scrambling to get as much done as I could while he had some days home with the kids. Between taking care of the little monsters and being sick as a dog still, I was having a hard time keeping up with the few clients I had left, and they were getting antsy. I was exhausted, and most nights when I walked into my tiny apartment I just wanted to crawl into my bed and sleep—but I couldn't. Work started the minute I finally put my feet up, and without the crutch of caffeine I was having a hell of a time staying awake late enough to get anything done.

"What's wrong, Katiebear?" Alex asked, suspicion in his voice.

"I guess you've heard the news then."

"What news?"

"Don't bullshit me."

"Yeah, Mom called me."

"God, will I not be able to tell anyone on my own?" I huffed, making him laugh.

"Nah, I'm sure Mom's letting you tell Bram—preferably after Shane is halfway around the world so he doesn't fly to San Diego and kill him."

"But she told you?"

"I'm stuck in Bum Fuck, Missouri. She probably figured I was the safe bet."

"How's that going? I haven't talked to you in a while," I said, reaching around to press on my aching lower back. Army life had Alex moving all over the place. Sometimes it took me a few minutes before I even remembered where he was living.

"It's fine. Boring but fine. What about you? Lots of shit happening, huh?" he said sympathetically.

"God, Alex. You have no idea."

"How the fuck did you end up sleeping with Shane of all people?" he asked.

I snorted. "I know, right? The guy can't stand me."

"Everyone likes you, Katie. Some people are just douchebags." I heard something crinkle in the background and then the sound of him chewing something crunchy. With his mouth open. God, I swear my brothers had no manners when they weren't near our mom.

"He's not a douche," I argued weakly.

"I love the guy, but he always had his head so far

up Rachel's ass it's like he couldn't see the light of day."

"That's a charming picture."

"You know what I mean. What happened?"

"You know how it goes, guy gets drunk on the anniversary of his wife's death, his foster mother asks the girl to check on him. The girl works up the courage to go to him, then proceeds to down a coffee mug of Jack with the guy, and one thing leads to another..."

"Shit, he knocked you up on the *anniversary?*"

"Impeccable timing, am I right?"

"Damn, Kate. That sucks."

I sighed, leaning back and closing my laptop. "It is what it is. Nothing I can do about it now."

"How are you feeling? Mom said you've been sick as hell."

"I'm a little better now. They gave me some meds for the nausea, so that helps. Now I'm just dealing with being tired all the freaking time."

"And Shane leaves in a few days, right?"

"Yep. I'm moving my shit into his garage tomorrow and living with the monsters full time. Shane leaves the day after that."

"Damn, I wish I was there to help you pack. You nervous?"

"About keeping the kids? Not really. I mean, I have them all day long as it is."

"About Shane deploying. Don't act like that's nothing."

"Of course I'm nervous about the deployment." I

paused, trying to formulate my words. "But I feel like it's not my right to feel like that. I mean, the guy barely acknowledges my presence, so it's not like I should be worrying about him..."

"I know you care about him, Katie. You wouldn't have slept with him if you didn't."

"But the opposite is true for him. I don't know, Al. I just feel like I'm a placeholder or something. Like our roles have never really been defined. I fill in. When he's not there, I do what needs to be done now that Rachel isn't there to do it. But now with this baby, I just...I'm more freaked out for the deployment than I ever have been before."

"That makes sense, sis. You've always cared about Shane in one capacity or another. Shit, we all do. But this is a big deal. Five children are your responsibility alone for the next six or seven months. You're it, little sis."

"I know."

"Did he get all his shit in order?"

"Yep. Allotments and life insurance and benefits are all switched over. That part made me want to vomit."

"Sounds like you're always vomiting these days."

"No shit. At least I've lost those extra few pounds I've been wanting to get rid of."

"Don't say shit like that," Alex scolded, sounding angry. "You're perfect the way you are. You shouldn't be losing weight, especially when you're supposed to be gaining it."

"It was a joke, Al."

"Stupid joke."

"I really am okay, you know," I told him softly, wishing he were there with me.

"You ready for this, Katiebear?"

"I guess I'll have to be."

"You're going to be an incredible mother."

"You think so?"

"I know so. You've been a pretty great one for the last year, haven't you?"

"You're pretty much the best brother ever, you know that?"

"I do, but make sure you tell Bram that, all right?"

I laughed, and we talked for a little longer before he had to hang up, leaving me alone with my thoughts.

My apartment was completely packed except for my bedding and my toiletries, and I couldn't say that I was sad to leave the place. I'd moved in when I'd had to scale back my business the year before, and it had never really felt like home. I missed my two-bedroom place in Carlsbad that I'd gotten for a steal. I missed being able to have people over without worrying that they wouldn't have anyplace to sit. I missed being able to leave my bras hanging from the end of my bed and not worrying that I'd show them to every person who walked in my front door.

But I couldn't say that I was excited to move to Shane's, either. The house in Oceanside wasn't mine. I was staying there, like a long-term houseguest, and even though Shane wouldn't be there to watch my every move, I was still a little on edge about it. That was Shane's house . . . *Rachel's* house. It hadn't changed much in the year since she'd died. When I was there to keep the kids, that fact hadn't really bothered me. I had my own space to come home to—my own little sanctuary that was filled with my things and decorated the way I liked.

I wouldn't have that anymore. I'd be living in someone else's home. In someone else's *life*.

At least Shane had kept his tantrums to a minimum since our little interlude in his bedroom a week or two before. God, that had turned out badly.

I'd never been good at thinking things through. Some of my earliest childhood memories were of scrapes I'd gotten myself into because I'd done something without thinking of the consequences. So when I'd seen him unbuttoning his shirt that night, I hadn't been able to think of anything beyond the way his fingers moved as he pressed the buttons through the holes. He hadn't even been paying attention to what he was doing, as if working on autopilot.

I'd let him lure me into his lair.

And even though he'd been a dick afterward, I couldn't really regret it. I'd wanted him, badly. And for a few minutes, I'd had exactly what I wanted.

I was under no illusion that Shane would magically fall in love with me. I didn't have visions of walking down the aisle or even holding hands on the sidewalk. I'd loved him from afar for most of my adult life, and while I didn't see that changing anytime soon, I also didn't expect that he'd ever return those feelings.

I was okay with that. Mostly.

I dreaded the day he'd find someone else, knowing that my life would change dramatically when that happened, but I expected it. I'd learned from an early age that sometimes people left whether they wanted to or not, and I'd much rather Shane left me because he'd found a woman who made him happy.

Once when I was nine, my parents had fostered a little boy who seemed to carry the weight of the world on his shoulders. He was a year younger than me, and quite a bit smaller. I remember that he didn't speak much, but was always unfailingly polite when he did. I swear, that kid had seemed almost like a ghost in my nine-year-old mind, but I knew even then that ghosts needed friends. So I'd tried to be friends with him, and though he tolerated me, I didn't think that he ever particularly liked me much. It wasn't until his social worker showed up one day after school that I saw the boy smile. Apparently, his mom had left his abusive dad and had been awarded custody. He'd left our house with the largest smile I'd ever seen before or since, and even though I knew I'd miss having him around, I couldn't help but be glad that he was that happy about leaving.

If Shane found someone else, that's how I wanted him to leave me behind. Joyfully. Even if it cut me to shreds.

* * *

"Megan's got the kids, so we need to make it quick," Shane informed me as he brushed by me into the apartment the next morning. "Is everything packed up?"

"Yeah," I answered, my eyes widening as two men followed in behind him. "Hi, who are you?"

"This is Eric and Miles," Shane informed me, stacking small boxes in the kitchen so he could carry three at once. "They're going to help you move."

"Wow, thanks, guys."

"No worries. Shane helped me and my wife move last year," the taller guy said, reaching down to pick up a large box in the middle of the room.

"He promised me beer," the one closest to me whispered, winking. Dang, he had that nerdy-cute thing going on.

"Hell, if you unpack when we're done, I'll bake you a cake," I shot back, smiling.

"Let's go, guys," Shane said sharply, walking out my front door with the first load of boxes.

I grabbed the garbage bags of bedding I'd packed that morning and followed the guys out of my house, huffing in annoyance as the bags went bouncing off the railing of the outdoor stairs.

"What the hell are you doing?" Shane barked, pulling the bags out of my hands before I'd made it halfway to the ground level.

"What are *you* doing?"

"You shouldn't be carrying shit down the stairs."

"They're blankets, Shane. They weigh like four pounds."

"You were about to trip."

"So the blankets would have broken my fall," I argued stubbornly. He was being an ass, and while I didn't mind sitting his moving shit out, I didn't like the tone he was using to speak to me.

"How about you just go over to the house, and we'll meet you there?"

"How about, no? How about I go back upstairs and grab some more stuff so we can get this show on the road?"

"You're not going to help us move boxes."

I went silent as Shane's friends moved up the stairs past us to grab another load, but continued glaring until they were out of earshot.

"You're being kind of a dick right now."

"Because I won't let you carry boxes?" he asked flatly.

"No, because you're speaking to me like I'm an idiot!" Oh no, the hormone-crazy was coming out.

"Shit, Katie," he said quietly, stepping down a stair. "I don't want you to get hurt. Can you please just supervise or something?"

"Whoa, complete one eighty. I'm impressed."

"Sometimes I wonder if you're deliberately trying to get a rise out of me," he said in exasperation, shifting the bags in his hands.

"Maybe I need a spanking," I replied seriously, before spinning around and moving back up the stairs while he stood there with his mouth open.

I wasn't sure if I should be mortified at my lack of belongings or impressed that the guys packed up my things so quickly because, only thirty minutes later, the trucks were loaded and we were on the road to the Anderson house.

It was time to step into shoes that were not my own.

* * *

"Auntie Kate! We got a surprise for you!" Sage called as Megan walked her and the boys across the street.

"Thanks for keeping them, Megan," I said as she handed a sleepy Gunner to me.

"No problem, neighbor. Eric was helping you guys anyway."

"Oh, is your husband the super-tall one or the super-hot one?"

"Both?"

"Okay, the super-tall one then."

We laughed, then grabbed ahold of little hands and shuffled to the lawn as the guys backed Shane's truck into the driveway.

"Come see, Auntie!" Kell whined, pulling on my hand.

"See!"

"See!"

"Okay, okay, I'm going." I turned to Megan, who was busy keeping her son from running to the back of the truck. "Thanks again, Megan."

The kids babbled excitedly as we went into the house and I was pulled and shoved toward the spare bedroom. When Sage opened the bedroom door with a flourish I couldn't stop the tears that came to my eyes.

"We thought you might need a better bed," Shane said quietly from behind my shoulder. "It's nothing great but the mattress is new, and—"

"I love it."

"Yeah?"

"It's the best bed ever in the history of beds."

"I wouldn't go that far," he replied with a small smile. "We'll put your old one in the garage in case you need it for a spare room or something later."

"You did this for me?" I called out to the kids who were bouncing on the bed. "I love it!"

"We got you new sheets, too! 'Cause Daddy said your other sheets wouldn't fit this bed," Sage yelled over the noise her brothers were making. "But Daddy forgot to wash them until this morning, so they're still in the dryer."

I glanced over my shoulder at Shane to find him laughing softly. "Whoops," he said, with a small shrug. "They're probably done by now."

"Sage and Keller," I called out, getting their attention, "can you guys go get my brand-new sheets out of the dryer so you both can help me make my bed?"

"I'll do it!" Keller announced, running past me.

"She said for both of us to do it, Keller!" Sage yelled in indignation.

I smiled at their bickering and watched as Gavin realized he no longer had anyone to play with and flopped down dramatically on the bed. By the amount of drool seeping into the shoulder of my T-shirt, I had a feeling that Gunner had already fallen asleep where I held him.

"All the boxes you need *in* the house are marked, right?" Shane asked as Keller and Sage came running back in, arguing about who could put their side of the sheets on faster.

"Yeah, they're all marked. There's eleven of them. I counted."

"Okay, I'll go grab those. You want me to take Gunner up to bed?" He reached out to slide his hand over the top of Gunner's head.

"No, but do you think you could get the rest of the monsters out of here for a while?" I asked ruefully. "I kind of want to just crawl into my new bed with Gunner and take a nap."

He smiled tenderly, the expression stealing my breath, and nodded.

"Sage! Keller! Gavin!" Shane called out. "Let's let Kate lie down with the baby for a while, and you guys can help us unload the rest of the truck."

Once everyone was out of my room, I crawled into the twisted sheets and curled around Gunner in the huge bed. My blankets and pillows hadn't made it into the house yet, but I still fell asleep almost instantly when my head hit the mattress.

I woke up a little while later under my favorite comforter, with Gunner missing.

"Gunner?" I called out in a panic.

I jumped from the bed and ran downstairs, where I could hear Shane and the kids in the kitchen.

"Where's Gun—" He was sitting in his high chair eating blueberries.

"Sorry," Shane called out sheepishly from where he'd been talking to nerdy-cute guy. "When I went up to check on you guys, he was waking up, so I brought him down here with us."

"Holy shit, I thought I'd lost him," I gasped, covering my face with one hand.

"There's a gate at the top of the stairs, Katie. He wouldn't have gone far," Shane reminded me with a laugh.

Yeah, it was funny for him, maybe. I burst into tears.

"Oh shit," nerdy-cute guy mumbled.

"Hell, Kate." Shane sighed, coming toward me so he could pull me into his chest. "Why are you crying?"

"I slept right through it! I didn't even know that he was gone."

"You were tired," Shane mumbled in my ear.

"I'm always tired! Oh God, what if I don't wake up when one of them needs me!"

"Quit it, Katie," Shane ordered firmly, sliding his hands up my back until he was gripping my head. "Stop crying. Hey! You knew I was here, right? You knew even when you were sleeping that I wouldn't let anything happen to you guys."

"I guess." I sniffled.

"Right, so you probably noticed when I grabbed Gun, but you didn't think anything of it, just turned over and went back to sleep."

"Yeah, but—"

His face was close to mine, and I could hear his quiet voice clearly even though the kids were making a ton of noise while they ate. "No more crying," he said with a small smile, wiping the tears off my cheeks.

"Auntie Kate's gonna have a baby. That's why she cries all the time!" Keller yelled over the noise, making Shane's body go completely stiff.

He let go of me and turned back to his friend, who was watching us with wide eyes. The news shouldn't even have been noteworthy to nerdy-cute guy—women my age had kids all the time when they weren't married—but the way Shane had held me and his complete change in body language after Keller's little announcement must have been a huge red flag.

"Food's on the table, Kate," Shane called without looking at me again. "You should probably eat."

I nodded even though he wasn't looking at me and moved to Gunner, whose face was covered in food. "Did you have a good nap, monkey?" I asked softly.

"*Onkey*," he replied with a huge grin.

"Jumpin' on a bed!" Gavin yelled as I passed him.

"There better not be any monkeys jumping on my new bed!" I teased, poking him in the side.

* * *

Thank God the day was finally over. The kids had been so wound up at bedtime, it had felt like they were never going to sleep. I understood it, though. Shane had to leave in the morning, and they were anxious about his departure. We'd decided that nerdy-cute guy, whose name was actually Miles, was going to drive Shane down to the drop-off point instead of bringing the kids down there. I wasn't sure what the place would be like, but I had a feeling seeing all those families saying their good-byes would probably freak them out.

I changed into a nightgown and slid between the sheets, relaxing into my familiar pillow. Shit, I was dreading the morning. I didn't know how I would sleep that night. My anxiety was building with every changed number on my alarm clock.

"Auntie Kate, can I sleep with you?" Sage whispered in the doorway, interrupting the what-if scenarios that I'd been sifting through in my brain.

"Sure, come on up," I whispered back, throwing back the covers. "This bed could probably fit twenty people."

"Me too!" Gavin called as his stubby legs raced in my door.

"I thought you guys were asleep!"

"Gavin kept kicking his wall," Sage answered with a scowl.

"Not tired," Gavin announced, crawling over Sage and me with a grunt.

"Okay, but I *am* tired. So you have to go right to sleep."

"Okay," he grumbled, laying his head on my shoulder.

I rolled toward him and pulled his body into mine as I felt Sage curl into my back.

It was quiet for a while as the kids' bodies grew heavy and Gavin started the little sniffling snore thing he always did, and I didn't realize that Keller had come into the room until he was crawling onto the foot of the bed.

"Hey, bud," I called out when he didn't say a word. "Couldn't sleep?"

"I was all alone," he said with a little sniff.

He crawled up to the other side of Gavin and lay down close, facing us.

"Aw, bud. You want to sleep in here?" After two years of sharing a room with Gavin, Keller hated to sleep alone. I wondered if he'd ever grow out of that.

"Yeah."

He was asleep within minutes, and I lay there running my fingers through his hair for a long time. Keller was going to be the one I needed to watch closely in the next few weeks.

Sage took things hard, but she tended to internalize them until she figured them out and then quietly came to terms with whatever was happening. After Rachel had died, she'd sort of shrunk into herself, but after a few months she'd become the Sage she'd always been except for the jolting way she woke up.

Gavin just went with the flow. He was so easygoing—almost too easygoing. I wondered if it was because of his age or if God had just decided that Shane and Rachel needed someone who was the exact opposite of their oldest son so they didn't lose their minds.

Keller took things hard, and when he was having trouble, everyone knew it. He was so sensitive. I think most people would have assumed that his behavior just meant that he was a brat, but I'd known him from the time he was born. The poor kid took everything to heart, and when he was feeling too much—whether it was fear or sadness or anxiety—it always came out of him as anger.

I listened to the quiet sounds of the house settling around us and prayed that I'd be able to take care of all of those little people on my own.

"Looks like a party in here," Shane said from the doorway, then walked around the bed so I could see him. "Good thing I got you a king."

"No kidding. Thank God Gunner is trapped in his crib or I'm afraid we'd be falling off the sides."

"Want me to take them into their beds?"

"Yeah, they'll probably sleep better," I replied, kissing Gavin's sweaty forehead.

Shane walked back around the bed and scooped Sage up, walking on silent feet back out the door as I stood up.

"You didn't have to get up," he whispered when he came back in.

"You should grab Gavin first. If Keller wakes up before Gavin's back in their room, he'll freak."

"Good call." He nodded, leaning over to grab Gavin. "Be right back for Keller."

I curled back into the suddenly lonely bed as Shane finally carried Keller to his room. I was kicking myself for telling him to put the kids in their beds when Shane came back in.

"Scoot over," he ordered, shutting the door behind him.

I scrambled back in the bed and swallowed hard as he pulled his T-shirt over his head before climbing in beside me and rolling until we were face-to-face.

"You couldn't sleep?" he asked.

"I wish you didn't have to go," I blurted, instantly squeezing my eyes tightly closed so I couldn't see his expression.

"Yeah, I'm not too excited about it, either," he replied with a sigh, making my eyes pop back open.

"I thought—well, Rachel always said you were anxious to go."

"Things are different now."

"That's an understatement."

"I'm not worried about you taking care of the kids. You know that, right?" he asked, grabbing one of my arms and pulling me closer until I was resting against the side of his body. "I don't trust anyone more than I trust you."

"I'm nervous."

"I would be, too. They're a shit ton of work."

"I'm nervous for you."

"That's one thing you shouldn't worry about."

"I can't help it."

"I'll be back before you know it."

"I'll be huge by the time you get back," I complained.

He laughed softly, jostling the entire bed. "Probably."

"I've missed you," I whispered softly, curling my hand into a fist on his chest.

"I'm not even gone yet."

"No, I've missed you for a long time."

He was silent for so long that I wondered if I'd messed up big by bringing up the elephant we'd been dancing around for the past year.

"I was an asshole back then."

"You were my best friend."

"I know." He sighed, pulling my body tighter against his.

"It was just a stupid crush. I would have gotten over it. I did get over it," I insisted.

"And I was twenty-one and pissed at the world," he reminded me. "It was easier to pretend you didn't exist. I knew if I had to see you watching me with those sad, big brown eyes, I'd do something stupid."

"So you hit on my roommate. God, that was such a dick move," I retorted.

"It was," he chuckled. "But shit, Rachel was hot."

"Okay, conversation over."

"Sorry."

"She was pretty hot," I grumbled. "If I was into chicks, I totally would have hit that."

He barked out a surprised laugh, and my entire body warmed.

"You're nuts."

"I miss her," I confessed, my throat tightening.

"Fuck, me too."

"Sometimes I still pick up my phone to text her."

"I used to roll over in bed in the morning and expect her to be there."

"She actually let you see her without makeup? I figured she would have jumped out of bed and put her face on before you woke up," I joked.

"She did that for the first year we were together," he said through his laughter. "I finally had to catch her before she slipped out of bed so she'd stop doing it."

"I swear she was my exact opposite," I griped. "I hate putting on makeup and doing my hair."

I tilted my head back to look at him and found him smiling at me.

"You don't need it."

"What?"

"You don't need all that shit—the makeup."

"No, I need it. I'm just too lazy."

"You don't—your skin is flawless," he said quietly, reaching up to run a finger down my cheek. "Your lips are already red, and when you smile, I swear people can't help but smile back. It's contagious."

"You don't have to say that."

"What, the truth? Kate, you're naturally self-confident. Rachel was beautiful, yes. But she worked at it, because she didn't ever feel it." He gave me a sad smile. "Don't compare yourself with her. It's like apples and oranges."

"I guess old habits die hard."

"I'm sure I didn't help with that."

"You really didn't. Dickhead," I replied with a playful scowl.

"I hate that I've seen you naked," he said, shaking his head and making me rock back in shock.

"Wow, fuck you!"

I began to push away, but he held me tighter to his chest.

"Your body is insane, Kate," he told me as he rolled over until he was leaning over me. "I look at you, and I don't see the fucking ratty clothes you wear. I see the way your breasts bounce when I pull on your nipples. I see the way you clench your jaw when you come, and the way your red lips get swollen from sucking my dick."

My mouth dropped open, and I looked at him in shock.

"You were my wife's best friend. My dead wife. Do you get that? I look at you and I don't see Katie who drove me nuts when we were kids, or Katie who was Rachel's best friend. I see Kate, the woman who can take me hard then fucking begs for more. That's not okay. What the fuck am I supposed to do with that?"

It wasn't a hypothetical question. He was asking me what to do—and I had no idea what I was supposed to say.

His arms were shaking, and his eyes were cloudy with confusion. It reminded me of the first time I'd seen him, sitting at my aunt and uncle's kitchen table for dinner—trying so hard to keep himself separate while they lured him into conversation.

I lifted my hand and laid it softly on his cheek, aching for him. It could have been my soft heart, or perhaps the pregnancy hormones that had me crying over puppy chow commercials, but I wanted to soothe him so badly.

I'd seen where this man came from. I knew his demons and his history, and I could practically feel the guilt rolling off him in waves.

"You don't have to figure it out tonight," I whispered. "You don't have to do anything."

"Yeah, I think I do," he said painfully.

Then his lips were brushing against mine, so softly I could barely feel them.

"You should tell me to leave."

"Why the hell would I do that?" I answered, sucking his bottom lip into my mouth. "It's not like you're going to get me pregnant."

He froze then, and I regretted the words I'd let slip free. I swear, sometimes I had absolutely no filter.

He moved down my body without another word and pulled my nightgown up gently from where it had been tangled around my hips. When he was finally kneeling between my knees, he leaned down and pressed his face to my belly.

"You're having my baby," he announced against my skin.

I felt my eyes well up and tears drip down my face. *Finally. He'd finally said it.*

"Sure am," I replied, my hoarse voice belying the nonchalance of my words.

"I'm going to do my best, okay?" he said nervously. "I promise. I'll be a good dad to him."

"You're already a good dad."

"But to *this* baby," he replied, lifting his face and pressing his hand to my belly. "I'm going to be a good dad to this baby."

"I never doubted that."

"I did," he confessed, his head rising to shamefully meet my eyes.

The truth of his words hit me like a ton of bricks, and

I finally understood why he'd ignored the proof of our child for so long.

I nodded once, and he nodded back, as if, without words, we were making a pact then and there to take care of this baby we hadn't planned for or wanted.

* * *

"So, I'm not going to get laid for a long time," I said tearfully after a few moments, breaking the tension that I knew must be killing him. "You know, with the whole pregnant thing happening here. And you're not going to be getting laid for a long time with the whole fighting-for-your-country thing..." I lifted my eyebrows as I wiped my hands over my cheeks and watched relief and something much softer move over his features.

"That *is* true. What're you thinking?" he asked with a sly smile.

"I'm thinking that tonight is our last night to get some sweet, sweet lovin'."

"Are you trying to seduce me, Mrs. Robinson?"

"If you have to ask, I'm obviously not doing it right," I answered as he gripped my panties and pulled them slowly down my legs.

"You're already wet," he commented in surprise as he pushed my knees wide.

I threw my arm over my face in embarrassment. "Well, your face has been very close to my downstairs!"

"Your downstairs?" he asked in amusement, his breath hitting my heated skin.

"Well, what would you call it?"

"Vagina. Cunt. Pussy . . . Clit."

"Shit," I breathed out as he licked at me. "You have a dirty mouth, Mr. Anderson."

"I can make it dirtier," he replied before sucking my clit between his lips.

Shane's hands moved over my thighs as his tongue and lips moved between them, and for the first time he was in no hurry. Every lick and suck was deliberate, pushing me gently toward the edge and then pulling me away again, until I was sweating and arching against my new sheets.

"You ready?" he asked breathlessly as he finally pulled away, pushing his shorts down his hips.

"If you don't make me come in the next thirty seconds, I'm going to hurt you," I whimpered back, making him laugh.

"When you come, your cunt practically throbs and you get so fucking wet," he whispered into my ear as he moved on top of me. "I want you around my cock when that happens."

Shane slid gently inside me with one long thrust, then pulled one of my knees up until my leg was bent between us. He watched my face closely as he pushed in slowly over and over, moving my legs around and changing the angle until he finally hit a spot that had my entire body jolting.

"There it is," he whispered with a pleased smile. "Hang on, baby."

"Holy fuck," I mumbled as he slid over that spot

again and again. My entire body was frozen as he moved. I was terrified that I'd arch and he'd lose it again, and the feeling of him rubbing against my G-spot was not one I wanted to let go of anytime soon.

"You're so cute," Shane said with a smile as I watched him with wide eyes. "You're trying so hard to keep still."

"Oh God, that feels good," I moaned back as he moved faster.

"If you don't want me to stop, you better put your hands on me," he warned, snapping his hips forward. "I know where it is now. Nothing you do is going to stop me from finding it."

"What if—"

"Hands, now," he ordered.

I lifted my hands to his torso, one wrapping around his back and the other up to wrap gently around the front of his throat.

He grunted, and I felt him swallow hard as his face dropped to mine, changing the angle of his hips so I whimpered into his mouth.

"It's okay, I've got you," he breathed, lifting both of my legs until they were bent and pressing against his chest and he was hitting my G-spot again. "There you go."

"Please," I begged hoarsely.

"Harder?" He pulled back and thrust in desperately as he kissed me hard.

"Yes. Yes. Like that."

"Jesus Christ, you're sexy," he mumbled into my mouth. "You're almost there, Kate. Take it. Fuck!"

I detonated, and he followed closely behind me with a deep groan. Our bodies were slick with sweat, and I felt like I'd run a mile by the time he pulled out of me.

"Okay?" he asked gently as he helped me straighten out my legs.

"I feel like a limp noodle," I groaned, climbing out of bed.

"Where are you going?"

"Bathroom," I mumbled, my eyes already growing heavy with exhaustion. "UTIs are no joke."

"Sexy," he teased.

"Biology," I retorted as I walked away.

When I got back to my bedroom, I was surprised to find Shane still lying in my bed.

"If you sleep close to me, we can avoid the wet spot," he informed me cautiously. "Unless you want me to go."

"No, stay," I said tiredly, crawling in beside him. "But I'm going to sleep."

"I don't know what we're doing, Katie," Shane said as he pulled me spoon-style into the curve of his body. "We probably just made shit worse."

"Regrets already?" I asked lightly, my eyes popping back open.

"No. No regrets," he assured me, giving me a squeeze.

"We don't have to figure anything out tonight," I reminded him, my stomach churning. "Right?"

"Yeah, okay," he whispered into the back of my head. I don't know what I'd been expecting, but my eyes filled with tears that I refused to let fall. I wasn't a woman who mixed sex with love—I never had been. Sexual attraction wasn't necessarily an indication of any stronger feelings. Occasionally over the years, I'd even had a couple one-night stands.

But the man lying next to me was Shane.

I wasn't sure how much longer I could hold out before old feelings started to surface again, and I knew the minute they did, he'd be gone.

And the cost would be so much larger next time.

Chapter 7
Shane

I took a shower slowly, enjoying the clean tub beneath my feet and the quiet of the morning. I didn't know how long it would be before I had the luxury of either of those things again.

Deployments weren't anything new. I'd done it all before—leaving the kids, living out of a couple of seabags, smelling like ass for six months at a time, the constant state of alertness that didn't even let me get a full night's rest.

But that morning, my chest felt tight in a way it hadn't before. I think my emotions may have been just a little too close to the surface, and that was dangerous for a man in my position. I needed to lock it all down. I needed to remember my routine, the things I could let my mind wander to, and the things I had to ignore at all costs.

When the water finally began to cool, I turned off the shower and slid the curtain back.

Kate was there in her nightgown.

I jerked in surprise. "What's wrong?"

She had her arms wrapped tightly around herself, with wide eyes and a trembling mouth. "I thought you left," she said quietly, shaking. "You—I thought you left."

I pulled my towel off the rack and dried myself quickly so I could pull her against my chest.

"I wouldn't leave without saying good-bye."

"I know. I don't know why I panicked."

"You're freezing. Come on." I gently tugged her into my bedroom, pulled a sweatshirt off the top of my dresser, and slid it over her head. "Better?" I asked as she threaded her arms through the sleeves.

"Yeah."

I steered her to the foot of the bed, and I was glad that she sat silently as I got dressed methodically in my uniform.

My routine on the day I left was important, as I'd come to realize within my first couple of deployments. It wasn't really superstition—I didn't believe in that shit—but instead a way to level out my anxiety.

First I pulled on my boxer briefs, then socks, undershirt, pants, belt, boots, boot-bands, blouse. Wallet in my pocket. Watch on my wrist. Sleeves buttoned. Photos of the kids in my chest pocket.

When I was done, I turned to see Kate watching me intently.

"Ready to wake the kids?" I asked.

"How much time do we have?" she replied hoarsely.

"A little over an hour," I answered, checking my watch.

"Can we wait a few minutes? I'm waiting for my anti-nausea medicine to kick in."

"You're still taking that?" I hadn't realized that she was still having problems, though she did look pretty tired all the time. Her pregnancy was anything but easy.

"It's not as bad anymore," she informed me as I sat down next to her.

Her hair was sticking out at all angles and matted in the back from the night before. She had dark circles under her eyes, and her lips were slightly chapped. My sweatshirt was huge on her, except where it pulled tight across her breasts, and her toenail polish was eight different colors and chipping.

Oddly enough, she still looked gorgeous.

I reached out to take her hand in mine.

"It's going to go by really quick," I told her as she nodded, looking at the wall. "Don't be scared, Katie."

"I'm not very good at this, am I?" she asked with a watery chuckle, turning her head to look me in the eye.

She wasn't. She wasn't good at this. She wasn't stoic like Rachel. She didn't assure me things would be fine or agree that the time apart would move quickly. She didn't wear a brave face or act as if she would barely no-tice my absence.

I'd been thankful that Rachel did those things. It made it infinitely easier for me to leave when the time came, knowing that she would be just fine without me.

But that wasn't Kate. Kate wasn't Rachel. She wore

her heart on her sleeve; her emotions were always out there for the world to see. If Kate had acted like she was fine with me being gone for six months, I'm not sure how I would have felt.

"You're doing just fine," I reassured her with a small smile, making her laugh again as tears ran down her cheeks. "Come here."

I pulled her onto my lap, and she pressed her face into my neck. Her nails dug into my back through my shirts as she gripped me, and I tightened my arms around her in response.

Her hair smelled like me. Shit, her entire body smelled like me.

"It's these stupid hormones," she complained, sniffling.

"Well, hopefully you get that shit under control before I get back," I replied drily, kissing the top of her head.

"Shut it, ass." She pulled away and smacked my chest, her tears finally under control. "Let's go wake the kids."

* * *

"Socks!" I called as the time grew closer for me to take off.

The kids and I were on the couch getting some last-minute cuddles. It was a tradition I'd started when Sage was just a baby and I'd had no idea how I'd leave her. I'd soaked up as much time as I could, as if that would hold me until I got to see her again.

It never had.

Each time I left, I had to deal with knowing that, by the time I returned, my children would be completely different. They'd grow, learn new things, lose teeth, and gain hair. They'd become interested in new subjects and used to my absence. It was painful.

"Here's mine!" Sage said cheerfully, handing me one of the socks off her feet.

"Mine!" Gavin handed me his.

"Here you go," Kate whispered to Gunner who was on my lap, pulling off his tiny sock and handing it to him. "What do you say?"

"My!" Gunner yelled, throwing the sock at my face.

Kate snorted, and I laughed before looking to Keller.

"Here's mine," Keller said glumly, handing his over.

"Whew!" I teased as I stuffed all of the little socks into my trouser pocket. "You have to wash your feet, man. This reeks!"

Keller laughed, looking pleased with himself, and threw his small body against my chest. "I love you, Daddy."

"I love you, too, Kell." I pressed my face into his hair and took a deep breath of little-boy sweat and baby shampoo, kissing him hard.

We all froze when the doorbell rang.

"He's early," Kate whispered with a brave smile. "That's okay, he can wait."

She walked toward the front door, leaving the kids and me on the couch. I watched her as she opened the front door, then dropped her face to her hands and started sobbing.

"Grandpa's here!" my foster dad called out as my foster mom wrapped her arms around Kate and rocked her from side to side.

Thank God they'd gotten here on time.

"Grandpa!" the kids screamed, all of them scrambling off the couch but Keller.

"Wanna help me grab my bags, bud?" I asked, standing up and placing Keller on my hip.

We walked upstairs and I grabbed my bags, handing Keller my small backpack filled with toiletries, my iPod, and an extra set of cammies. It looked huge on his tiny shoulders, and he weaved a bit before straightening and marching back downstairs ahead of me.

"Hey, son," Mike said as I dropped my bags right inside the front door. "All set?"

"Yep, all set," I answered with a nod. He shook my hand and pulled me into a tight hug.

"Thanks for coming, Dad," I said while he held on tight. "Kate's gonna have a hard time when I go."

"Nowhere else I'd rather be."

"I want some of that," Ellie interrupted, bumping Mike out of her way with her hip so she could come in for a hug. "All set?"

I laughed at the repeated question. "Yep, all set."

"We got you a present, Daddy!" Sage called out, running toward me with Keller and Gavin close behind.

"You did?"

The doorbell rang again, and I swallowed hard.

"I'll get that. You open your present," Mike said, walking away.

Kate stood holding Gunner on her hip a few feet away, and I met her eyes for a long moment before looking down at the present Keller was pushing into my hands. It was wrapped in the Sunday comics, and I couldn't help but smile at the familiar sight. Ellie had always wrapped gifts in comic paper—she said that being married to a man who owned a logging company didn't mean she had to waste paper—so she'd saved up the comics all year long to use for Christmas and birthday presents.

"A Kindle!" Keller ruined the surprise, jumping up and down as Miles and Mike made their way toward us.

"This is the best present ever," I told the kids seriously, kissing each one. "Thank you."

"Is it time for you to go?" Sage asked me in a voice too serious for an almost-eight-year-old.

"Yep. Time to go," I confirmed, reaching down to pick her up and hold her close. "I'll be back before you know it."

I did another round of hugs and kisses, and then another round, then let Ellie usher the kids toward the kitchen for breakfast.

"Walk me out?" I asked Kate quietly through the lump in my throat.

"Sure."

Mike and Miles carried my bags out to the truck ahead of us, leaving me and Kate in our own quiet little bubble. I wrapped my hand around her shoulders and rested my fingers around the side of her neck, my thumb right over her pulse-point.

"I put a bunch of books on the Kindle. Manly ones,

you know, military history and thrillers and whodunits. I wasn't sure what you—" she rambled.

I cut her words off with my mouth as we reached the back door of Miles's truck. Thank God the windows were tinted, and I knew that Mike and Miles would studiously avoid looking where we were standing . . . but it wouldn't have mattered if they hadn't.

She whimpered and gripped my head in her hands as I swept my tongue into her mouth, and I couldn't resist grabbing her ass and hoisting her up until she was braced against the truck with her legs wrapped around me.

I didn't know what I was doing. Things between us were getting so complicated. Too complicated.

But I couldn't stand the thought of leaving without the taste of her in my mouth.

"Don't let Keller talk back to you," I said when I'd finally pulled my lips away and rested my forehead on hers.

"Okay."

"Sage is going to go quiet. Make sure you watch her close."

"I will," she promised with a nod.

"I think Gavin can climb over the gate at the top of the stairs, so you should teach him how to open it so he doesn't fall when he's trying to escape."

"I can do that."

"Gunner hates bedtime, but don't let him sleep with you. You'll never get him into the crib again."

"No co-sleeping. Got it," she whispered, her thumbs sweeping back and forth at my temples.

"Make sure you take your vitamins, okay?" I asked,

rubbing my lips lightly over her cheek and jaw. "You've been too sick."

I let her legs slide slowly back down my hips, and she stiffened as her face turned scared.

"Take care of my children," I whispered, sliding my hand under her nightgown to rest it on the skin of her belly.

"I will. I promise."

I nodded, kissing her hard once before pulling her hands away from my head.

"I'll call home when I can," I promised as I held her hands tightly.

She was trying to pull away so she could reach for me, but stopped when I raised her hands to my mouth and kissed her knuckles. "Go into the house."

"No," she argued, shaking her head frantically.

"Go into the house, Kate."

"No. No." She was killing me.

"I don't want you standing out here alone. Go into the house. Right now, Katie," I ordered, giving her a little push. My stomach was in fucking knots.

She stared at me with wide eyes before finally nodding, then took a step back only to reach forward one more time to kiss me hard.

Then I watched her walk quickly to the house, her shoulders squared and head held high, and as she went through the front door I climbed in the backseat of Miles's truck.

"Cutting it close, man." Miles said, backing out of the driveway.

"Just drive," I ordered, dropping my head back against the seat as I pushed a shaking hand into my pocket to fist the four little socks that smelled like my children.

It was going to be a long deployment.

* * *

"Hello?"

I inhaled deeply at the sound of Katie's voice, the hot air almost choking me. It had been less than a week since I'd left them in California, and while I knew it would get more bearable over time, at that moment I was incredibly homesick.

"Hey, it's me."

"Shane!" she screeched, making me laugh. "I didn't think you'd get to call so soon!"

"Had a little bit of time so I wanted to check and see how things were going. How're the kids?"

"They're good. Oh my God, they're going to be so excited you called. I'll go get them—"

"Hold up," I cut her off, chuckling. "First you talk to me. How're Kell and Sage doing?"

"They're good. Well, Kell's had a few meltdowns, but nothing terrible, and Sage has been ending up with me most nights, but pretty good all around. I think having Aunt Ellie and Uncle Mike here helps."

"That's good. That's really good." I pulled my sunglasses off and pinched the bridge of my nose. "How about Gavin and Gunner?"

"Gavin's, well, Gavin. Nothing really fazes that kid, does it? And Gunner is soaking up having Aunt Ellie here to pamper him. I swear she hasn't put him down once," she said, giving a little laugh that sounded strained.

"What about you? How're you doing?"

"Oh, I'm fine," she answered breezily.

"Kate," I said warningly.

"Totally fine."

"Kate." I could tell when she was lying. I'd always been able to tell. She did this thing where the last word of her sentence would get a little higher-pitched.

"The first couple of days were hard, okay? I was upset, and I think having Aunt Ellie and Uncle Mike here gave me a bit of a free pass to lose it."

"What happened?" I sat up straighter in my chair, my stomach clenching. What the fuck did she mean?

"I was just sicker than normal," she said quietly.

"Why didn't you take your pills?" My question came out sharper than I'd intended, and I heard her let out a little huff.

"I couldn't keep them down," she mumbled.

"What the fuck, Kate?" My short fingernails dug into my palm as I felt a headache forming at my temples. "Did you go to the emergency room?"

"No, I didn't," she shot back. "I was fine at home. I think it was just the emotional overload. After a couple of days, I was back to normal."

"You can't do that shit," I growled, feeling out of control as I rubbed my hands over my face. "I left my kids with you, Kate. You can't just fucking fall apart."

"Wow. Okay, um—" She sniffled, and I felt like such an asshole. I didn't want to make her cry. *Shit.*

I couldn't get past the anger that my feeling of helplessness had stirred. I couldn't deal with this shit. Didn't she realize that? Did she realize where my focus was supposed to be, and how incredibly bad it would be if my focus was at home with her because she was losing her shit? Fuck. I needed her to keep things under control in California.

I'd never had to deal with that shit with Rachel.

"I'm going to bring Sage the phone," she said hoarsely. "Do you have enough time?"

"Yeah, I've got a few more minutes." I wanted to apologize. I could tell I'd hurt her feelings, but she could not fall apart when I was halfway around the world. She'd promised to take care of the kids. What the fuck would I do if she couldn't handle it?

"I miss you," Kate whispered, but before I could reply, she'd handed off the phone.

I knew then that I'd fucked up. Again.

"Hello?" Sage's sweet voice came through the connection.

"Hey, princess."

"Grandpa, it's Daddy!" I heard Mike chuckling in the background.

"How's it going, baby girl?"

"Gunner got into the garbage," she tattled gleefully.

"How the heck did that happen?"

"Grandma was helping Auntie Kate in the bathroom—"

"Why was Auntie Kate in the bathroom?" I asked, cutting her off.

"What?" she asked, making me repeat the question.

"Her baby was making her sick again," Sage informed me. "But she's better now. Grandpa was supposed to watch Gunner, but Kell was jumping on the couch and he had to stop him before he *busted his head open*." She made her voice deeper for the last four words as if mimicking Mike, and I couldn't help but laugh.

I didn't know how many times I'd heard that exact same phrase come out of Mike's mouth.

"Wanna talk to Keller?"

"Sure. I love you, princess."

"Love you too, Daddy!"

There was some scratching on the phone, and after a few moments I heard Keller.

"Daddy!"

"Hey, bud!"

"Whatcha doin'?" He sounded like he was eating something crunchy. A carrot? I tried to picture exactly what he was doing in my head, down to the clothes he was wearing.

"Just working. What have you been doing?"

"Playing with Grandpa. We went to the park yesterday, and I did the whole monkey bars *by myself*."

"Whoa. Your guns are going to be huge by the time I get back," I teased him, making him laugh.

"Are you coming home soon?"

My heart dropped to my stomach. "Not for a while, bud."

A guy across the room got my attention, letting me know my time was up. *Shit.*

"Hey, Kell, I have to go, buddy."

"Okay," he grumbled.

"I'll call you back soon, okay?" I said quietly, getting to my feet. "I'll have Auntie Kate set up the computer so we can talk on there."

"Okay. I love you, Daddy."

"I love you, too, Kell. Give the little boys a kiss for me, okay?"

"Okay."

"And Kell?"

"Yeah?"

"No more jumping on the couch."

"Sage!" I heard him screech before the connection was broken.

"Bye, son," I mumbled into the dead line before hanging the phone back on the receiver.

I set my cover on my head and pushed my sunglasses back on my face as I headed out of the call center. I loved calling home, but I'd have to make sure I wasn't making contact more than once or twice a week... assuming I had the time. Talking to Kate and the kids had given me a sense of relief, but I knew it would leave me in a funk for the rest of the day.

I wasn't sure how angry Kate was. I'd been a dick, but the words had poured out of me. Plain and simple? I was frustrated.

I hated that Rachel was gone. I hated that I still reached for her sometimes, especially since I'd arrived in the hot-as-hell shithole I was in. I hated that Kate had taken up any spare place in my head, leaking into everything. I hated that I'd had to ask her to take care of my kids because they didn't have a mother. I hated that I owed her for that.

I hated that I was missing school programs and new teeth and milestones.

I missed my children so fucking much.

I missed Kate, too.

The next time I called home, I decided, I'd apologize to Katie. She didn't deserve my bad mood when she already felt like shit.

And why the hell was she still sick? Wasn't that shit supposed to be almost gone?

Worry for my family settled heavy in my gut and didn't leave for a long time.

Chapter 8

Kate

The second time Shane called, I let Aunt Ellie answer the phone and pass it around to the kids.

The third time, I completely left the house.

But by the fourth time, Uncle Mike and Aunt Ellie had gone back to Oregon, and I'd had no choice but to talk to him, at least until I could hand the phone off again.

"Hello?" I answered flatly.

"Katie? It's me," he said tentatively.

"Hey, Shane. I'll get Sage."

"Wait!" he called before I could pull the phone away from my face.

"What's up?"

"How are the kids doing? How are you doing?" he asked, his voice almost desperate.

"Kids are doing good. Keller threw a huge-ass fit today because he had to share his Legos with Gavin. Sage had today off because the teachers are doing report cards. Gunner keeps putting my makeup in his mouth, and his face was covered in lipstick all day. It's the eighteen-hour stuff, and I couldn't get it off."

He laughed, and I smiled.

"And you?" he asked cautiously.

"I'm good."

"Have you been sick?"

"Nope, don't worry. I'm on top of things."

"That's not why I asked."

"Yes it is." I huffed out a small laugh. "It's fine."

"I'm really sorry, Katie."

"Nothing to be sorry about," I replied smoothly. I wasn't playing that game with him again. I was so tired of the push and pull that seemed to happen constantly. As far as I was concerned, if he was sorry, he wouldn't keep saying shitty things over and over.

I knew his background. He'd spent his entire childhood shuffled in and out of different foster homes. I knew that he'd always had a hard time thinking before he spoke, especially when he was emotional. We had that in common. However, I had never been someone who lashed out in anger like Shane did. Our histories were completely opposite, and because of that I'd forgiven him a lot. But at some point, you had to grow the fuck up and act like an adult.

"Stop acting like that," Shane said.

"Like what?"

"Like I didn't hurt your feelings!" he growled into the phone.

"You didn't. You were worried about the kids—I got it."

"Goddammit." He sighed.

We were silent for long seconds before he started speaking again.

"Do you know how hard this is for me?" he asked. "You're sick, and I can't do shit about it, because I'm fucking stuck here. It doesn't matter how sick you're feeling or what's happening back home. I'm. Stuck. Here."

"I know, that must be hard—"

"I'm sorry, okay? I shouldn't have snapped at you the last time we talked. I wasn't mad at you."

"Okeydokey."

"Knock it the fuck off."

"Shane, I don't want to go back and forth with you. You hate me, you want me, you think I'm cool then I'm irritating. I'm pregnant and taking care of four kids under eight years old. I don't have the time or energy to worry about how you feel about me."

"Katie—" He paused for a long moment. "I was frustrated that you were having a hard time, and I didn't react well. It's not because I think you aren't taking really good care of the kids...It's because I was angry I wasn't there to take care of you and the kids. Okay?"

"Well, you're chatty tonight," I replied, the joke falling flat. I didn't know what to do with the words pouring out of his mouth. I didn't know how to reply.

"Shit, Kate. It took me two weeks to talk to you. I had a lot of time to run through the apology in my head," he grumbled, making me snort.

"Just...tone it down, okay?" I asked, moving out of

the kitchen where I'd been making dinner. "You don't have to snap at me every time you're worried or whatever. It's exhausting and pisses me off."

"Yeah, and you do the silent-treatment shit like a champ."

"Damn straight."

"You're okay?" He suddenly changed the subject.

"Yeah, Shane, I'm good. Getting rounder. The doctor says that's supposed to happen."

"I bet you'll be cute as fuck. Oh, speaking of how cute you'll be—they have computers here so we can Skype. Can you set that up on your end?"

"Shane, I'm a web designer. I've got Skype."

"Awesome. Shit, my time's up," he said as I heard someone speaking in the background. "I'll call again when I can. Tell the kids I love them, okay?"

"Oh crap! You didn't even get a chance to talk to them."

"I'll email you later today with my Skype info, and we can plan out a chat sometime this week—they'll be stoked."

"Yeah, they'll freak. Be careful, okay?"

"Always."

I waited for him to hang up, but after a few moments I could still hear him breathing.

"Hey, Katie?" he called quietly.

"Yeah?"

"I'm really glad you're feeling better, beautiful. Take care of my son, okay?"

It took me a second to understand what he was

saying, and when I did, I couldn't stop the small smile that stretched my lips. "It could be a girl, you know."

"Nope. It'll be a boy," he argued, and I knew he was smiling back at me. "Bye, Katie."

"Bye, Shane."

I stood silently for a long time in the archway between the living room and the kitchen, watching the kids as they played. It was going to be a long five months.

* * *

The next few months passed slowly and quickly at the same time. It felt as if things were moving at a snail's pace when the kids and I were waiting on a Skype call from Shane, but when I had a deadline coming up, I had to race to meet it.

Work was going okay, even though I'd had to cut back yet again. I just didn't have the energy to take on as much and still do my job well, and I hated the thought of giving people mediocre work. I also hadn't anticipated that I'd still be feeling like shit almost six months into my pregnancy.

The doctors said I was still feeling the effects of morning sickness and I was anemic.

My mom said I was working too hard.

My brother Alex said that I had an alien in my belly and it was sucking the life out of me.

Shane didn't say anything because I didn't tell him that I was still sick.

Things had been good since he'd apologized for tearing my head off. Great, really. We didn't have the chance to talk very much because the kids dominated the Skype calls—with good reason—but we filled in those breaks with emails almost every day. We wrote about everything, from movies we liked—one of the guys in his room had a small DVD player and a fiancée who sent him all the new releases—to what the kids had been up to that day and websites that were driving me insane. I also posted massive amounts of photos on my Facebook page so he could scroll through them whenever he had a moment to spare, marking off every milestone the kids hit, from a lost tooth to sleeping dry all night.

We'd become friends again through our emails, and it felt really good. But it also made my anxiety rise. The closer we became, the more frightened I was that something would to happen to him—and I didn't want to worry him with things that were happening back in California.

I didn't want him to know that I was staying awake until one or two a.m. to finish projects and then rolling out of bed six hours later to get Sage ready for school. I didn't tell him that I'd begun to sit on a stool when I was making dinner because, by five o'clock in the evening, I was completely worn out. I didn't tell him that, for some ungodly reason, Gunner had started waking up at four a.m. a couple of nights a week, and we'd barely fall back asleep before my alarm went off, usually after I'd busted out my guitar and sung to him—he liked Of Monsters and Men songs.

I was handling it. Sure, I looked like shit except for the nights I knew I'd be seeing him through the computer screen—but hey, I had no one to impress.

We were three months into the deployment when Shane's birthday rolled around. He'd promised to Skype that night so I spent the whole afternoon getting the boys cleaned up and dressed for the occasion. I'd even picked up a cake on our way to grab Sage from school so it felt like an actual party.

By eight o'clock that night when my computer sounded with an incoming call, we were ready. Barely. My laptop was perched on a stool at one end of the living room, giving Shane a view of the kids as they ran around excitedly and me on the couch with Gunner and my guitar.

"Happy birthday!" the kids screamed as Shane's tanned face showed up on the screen.

"Thanks, guys!" he answered, smiling huge and fiddling with the earbuds he always wore so he could hear us.

I strummed the first chords to the birthday song, just like we'd practiced, and the kids began singing boisterously while Gunner nodded and watched wide-eyed beside me. Oddly enough, the one-year-old was the only kid with a sense of rhythm.

"We got you a cake!" Keller yelled, jumping up and down, once they'd finished singing.

"You did?" Shane replied, raising his eyebrows. "What does it look like?"

"I'll get it!"

"Wait, bud!" I yelled at Keller, imagining blue frosting covering the carpet in the living room. "Why don't you let Sage grab it?"

Sage ran out of the room while Shane chuckled softly. "What have you guys been doing today?"

"Took a bath," Gavin replied with a scowl.

"Played with my Lincoln Logs!" Keller yelled again.

"Not so loud, bud," I warned Keller as Gunner scooted onto my lap between me and the guitar I was using to hide my growing bump.

It was silly, but normally the laptop was tilted enough that Shane only saw us from the chest up and I was feeling a bit self-conscious.

"My Lincoln Logs, too!" Gavin shot at Keller.

"Mostly mine," Keller taunted back.

"Boys," Shane said sternly, quieting them both. "Enough."

God, I wished I could say two words that would stop them that fast.

"See, Daddy?" Sage called as she went to stand in front of the camera holding the small cake I'd picked up.

"That's an awesome cake!" Shane replied, nodding. "Is it chocolate?"

"Yep!"

"Why don't you guys go sit down and Auntie Kate can bring me into the kitchen while you eat it?"

"Yeah!" Keller and Gavin yelled in tandem, their screech making Shane wince and laugh. The changes in volume must have been killing his ears.

I let Gunner down so he could follow the kids into

the kitchen and stood up, holding the guitar awkwardly in front of me.

"Hey," I said before pushing my lips together and smiling slightly.

"Hey," he answered, smiling back in amusement.

It was the first time in weeks that I'd seen him without the kids crawling up and down off my lap to speak to him, and I felt shy knowing that we were relatively alone.

"Why are you carrying around the guitar?" he asked.

"Um." *Great, Katherine. Um is not an answer. Get it together.*

"I want to see you," he said quietly. "Put the guitar down."

"Um. I'm a bit bigger—"

"Let me see, Katie," he ordered gently.

I turned completely around to set the guitar back in its case on the ground and jumped in surprise when a wolf whistle played over my laptop's speakers.

I was laughing when I turned back around, but it was abruptly cut off by the look on his face.

"She's making herself known," I said sheepishly, running my hand over the curve of my belly.

"Look at you," he breathed, a small smile playing over his lips. "You're gorgeous."

"Yeah?"

"Oh, yeah." His smile grew bigger.

"Auntie Kate, come on!" Keller yelled from the kitchen, ending our quiet moment.

"Time for cake," I announced, walking toward the laptop.

"Can't wait," he replied with a smirk, and I had this odd feeling that he was staring at my boobs.

* * *

The kids were hyped up for the rest of the night, but I couldn't really blame them. A Skype date and cake all in the same night? It was like Christmas.

When I finally crawled into bed and got my laptop situated on my lap, I wasn't sure how much longer I was going to be able to keep my eyes open. I had to figure out a couple of different ideas to take to a client, and I was pretty sure they were going to be complete crap if I tried to brainstorm that night.

Instead I logged onto Facebook and began uploading photos of the night. I knew my mom and Aunt Ellie would get a kick out of seeing how excited the kids had been for the birthday party. When Shane suddenly instant-messaged me, my back straightened as if he could see me.

You awake?

I cracked my knuckles then shook my hands above the keyboard, staring at the two words. Shit, I had to answer or he was going to sign off!

Yep, just downloading some pics from tonight :)

Those should be good.

I've got one of Gunner with frosting in his hair and up his nose.

Haha How the hell did he do that?

I'm pretty sure Keller had something to do with it.

That wouldn't surprise me.

So...what are you doing online again?

I had some time.

So you decided to stalk me on Facebook?

Pretty much.

Well, stalk away then.

Hey so earlier you called the baby she...

And?

Did you already find out?

Oh! No! You just always call the baby "he" so I've been using "she." I figure that way one of us is right. Haven't had my appointment yet.

Pretty soon though, right?

Yeah, next week. The office has been completely backed up so it's a bit later than normal.

Do you think you could tell me first? I know you'll want to tell your mom.

Yes. You'll know first, I promise.

He didn't message for a while, and I watched the little green dot on the screen like a hawk, afraid that he'd signed off.

You look really good.

My stomach flipped, and I rolled my eyes at what he'd see if we were Skyping then. I'd wiped off the little eye makeup I'd had on and the concealer that covered the dark circles under my eyes. I looked like shit.

Ha! You just need to get laid.

Well, that too. LOL

No sex for you! *said in soup guy voice from Seinfeld*

You better not be getting any either.

When the hell would I have the time?

Kate.

Don't "Kate" me. You know I'm not fucking anyone.

Don't say fuck.

Fuck fuck fuck fuckity fuck fuck

…and now I'm hard.

Seriously?

Semi.

snort what are you, thirteen?

Your boobs are huge.

This conversation is over.

LOL. They are.

True that.

I miss you.

My hands shook, posed over the keyboard. I wasn't sure if I should say it back.

We miss you too.

Send me some pics

I post pics all the time! Just scroll through my Fb

You're not in any of those.

I'm the one taking the photos—so that makes sense.

I want to see you too.

Okay.

No naked pics. I swear to God there's guys looking over my shoulder every time I sit down.

I wouldn't have sent you naked ones!

Yeah you would've :)

You wish!

You. Have. No. Idea.

He was flirting with me. Flirting. With me. I didn't know what to do with that. Sure, we'd had our moments, but beyond falling into bed a couple of times, our conversations had stayed strictly platonic.

You there?

I snapped out of my fog at his newest message.

I'm here.

I better let you go—it's late there. You should be asleep.

I still had at least two more hours of work to do.

Okay. Be careful. Skype soon?

Always.
Skype week after next.

My stomach clenched. I knew not to ask any questions, but so far he'd always been able to Skype once a week. I didn't want to imagine a reason he wouldn't be able to.

Good night, Katie.

Night.

I watched the screen, waiting for him to sign off, but after a few seconds another message came through.

So beautiful.

He was gone before I could reply, which was probably a good thing.

* * *

"Keller, get back up at the table with that!" I yelled, almost in tears as I tried to clean Gunner up.

The poor kid was getting molars, which meant he had diarrhea. It had freaked me out the first time it happened, but after a frantic call to the on-call nurse, I was pretty calm about it. Apparently some kids had that reaction to new teeth, and lucky me, one of my kiddos did. Never say that Gunner did anything in half measures.

"Kell! Table! Now!" I grew increasingly frazzled as Gavin dropped his grape Popsicle down the front of his green shirt.

"Auntie Kate, I can't find the diapers," Sage told me frantically, running from the stairs.

"They're on the changing table, the same place as always," I replied, blowing my hair out of my face.

"I think they're all gone."

"Shit," I moaned as I remembered that I was supposed to go to the store that day.

"Shit," Gunner mimicked.

I ignored his words as my laptop rang on the kitchen table.

"Daddy!" Keller yelled, coming to an abrupt stop by the kitchen table.

"Keller, if you touch that laptop with Popsicle fingers I'm going to ground you off the Wii for the *week*!" I screeched, lifting a bare-assed Gunner off the floor and onto my hip as I climbed to my feet.

We hadn't talked to Shane in almost three weeks, and I'd finally gotten an email from him the night before telling me he'd be able to call us. Unfortunately, he was calling on one of the hardest days I'd had since he left.

"Can I answer it?" Sage asked, her finger posed over the keyboard.

"Go ahead, Sage." I sighed, walking toward where the big kids were gathered around the computer screen.

"Hey, guys," Shane called out cheerfully.

"Hi, Daddy!"

"I got every word right on my spelling test," Sage called over Keller's greeting.

"I got a scratch," Gavin yelled and held up his arm with the scabbed-over two-inch scratch. "I got a Band-Aid!"

"Awesome job, princess. And that looks like a gnarly scratch, Gav. How'd you do that?" Shane replied, fielding their comments like a pro.

"I got four shots," Keller announced, not to be outdone.

"Good job, bud. Now you can go to kindergarten next year.

"Hey, Katie," Shane added with a smile as I finally scooted into the group so Gunner could see his dad. "Hi, Gunner."

Gunner smiled and turned his face into my neck. He'd been increasingly shy with everyone, Shane included.

"Hey—"

"Gunner's peeing!" Keller yelled, laughing hysterically as I felt a warm, wet spot spread over the side of my belly.

"Crap," I mumbled, my eyes closing in frustration.

"Why isn't he wearing a diaper?" Shane asked through his own laughter.

"Auntie Kate forgot to buy some, and we're all out," Sage answered helpfully as my eyes filled with tears.

Gunner was half naked, Gavin looked like a ragamuffin with his shirt covered in purple slime, Keller was acting more ornery than usual, and Sage had just tattled on me. On top of all that, I looked like crap and felt even worse.

"Sage," Shane called, watching the screen intently, "did you check the diaper bag?"

"No!" She scrambled through the boys and ran toward the front door where we kept it.

"Have you been giving your auntie a hard time today?" he asked the boys after Sage ran off.

"No!"

"I been good!"

"She looks like she's not having a very good day," Shane informed them, causing them to turn their heads toward me.

They looked at me like they hadn't even seen me quietly losing it all day.

"It's okay, Shane," I said, smiling at the boys. "I'm just a little tired."

"And the baby makes her cry a bunch," Keller added seriously.

"Oh yeah? How much?"

"Not much," I answered quickly.

"Found one!" Sage called, rushing back into the room.

"Oh thank God. I didn't know how I was going to go to the store with him like this," I said, grabbing the diaper out of Sage's outstretched hand.

"Big kids, come talk to Dad so Auntie Kate can get Gunner fixed up," Shane ordered, instantly silencing the rowdy boys.

"Okay, let's go, monkey," I murmured, carrying Gunner up the stairs.

After I'd changed our clothes, I trudged back down the stairs with Gunner perched on the side of my belly. I swore I was popping out more by the day. Pretty soon he'd be able to completely sit on it.

"Okay, my time's up, guys," Shane announced to the kids, who were all crammed onto one kitchen chair. "Go get your auntie."

"I'm here," I called as I raced into the kitchen.

"Love you guys," Shane told the kids as they blew him kisses and waved. "We still on for tonight, Katie?"

"Yep."

We didn't say more than that because, if the kids knew he'd be on Skype again later, I'd never get them to bed.

"Don't forget to go to the store."

"Believe me, I won't," I groaned, making him smile.

"Bye everyone!"

The screen went blank, and he was gone.

I hated when that happened.

"Okay, Andersons! In the car. We need diapers and milk or we're going to starve covered in Gunner's pee."

* * *

I held the envelope in my palm and forced myself not to open it. I'd been holding on to it for two weeks and the anticipation was killing me. I slid my finger into the small space I'd pried open and jumped as the laptop rang.

"Hey, stranger."

"Hey yourself."

We smiled at each other for a long moment. It was so nice to finally see his face without the distraction of four little monsters screaming over one another in order to be heard.

"Bad day, huh?" he asked finally.

"You have no idea. Thankfully, we got a huge bag of diapers so we're set for a while. I even hid some around the house just in case."

"Good call." He laughed and reached up to rub his face with one hand. "You had your ultrasound?"

"Yep, everything looks great. Your monster child is measuring a bit big, but other than that, everything was normal."

"Good. That's really good."

I smiled smugly as he fidgeted. He was working up the nerve to ask me, and I'd rarely seen him so flustered.

"Well?" he finally asked.

"Well, what?"

"What are we having?"

"A baby," I answered innocently.

"Kate," he growled back, making me laugh.

"I don't know."

"What? Why didn't they tell you—" He froze as I lifted the envelope in front of the computer screen and waved it back and forth.

"I figured we could do it together," I said with a small smile.

Watching his face move from disgruntlement to awed excitement was a moment I'd never forget in my entire life.

"You waited?" he asked softly.

"I thought you might want to find out at the same time."

"Thank you, Katie."

"Yeah, well, you owe me. This thing has been burning a hole in my pocket for two weeks."

"You didn't peek?" He raised his eyebrow.

"I thought about it." I lifted the envelope and showed him the small tear. "But I wanted to surprise you, so I held out."

"Really good surprise."

"Yeah?"

"Yeah."

I slid my finger into the tear and ripped the envelope the rest of the way, pausing before I pulled the slip of paper out.

"Do you care? I mean, do you care if it's a boy or a girl?" Suddenly I was nervous. We were in unchartered territory, and frankly, nothing was solid between us. What if he was disappointed?

"I don't care, Katiebear," Shane answered softly, the endearment making my throat clog. "Now hurry up, I'm dying here."

I gave a watery chuckle and pulled the sheet out, facing it toward the screen first so I could catch Shane's reaction.

His mouth dropped open before snapping shut, and I watched him clench his jaw as his eyes rose slightly to look at me. He sniffed once and rubbed the side of his face with his palm.

"Aren't you going to look?" he asked with a little embarrassed laugh.

"No," I replied slowly, coming to a decision as I dropped the paper to my lap. "I want you to tell me."

He wiped both hands over his face before taking a breath and then smiling huge. "A princess."

My eyes widened in surprise, and he laughed at my stunned expression. I'd teased him that we were going to have a girl, but I hadn't really believed it. After he'd had so many boys, I'd figured Sage was an anomaly. "No way."

"Unless they didn't get a good ultrasound..."

"Nope, total crotch shot," I murmured distractedly, picking up the small sheet of paper and turning it over to verify. There was our little girl, with an arrow pointing and announcing her gender.

He barked out a laugh. "How could you not see that there was a penis missing?"

"I don't know what any of that looks like in the womb." I shook my head. "I can't believe we're having a little girl."

"You know what this means, right?" Shane asked with a snort.

"What?"

"None of Gunner's stuff is going to work for her. She's going to need pink and ruffles."

"Oh hell no. She can sleep in blue pajamas."

"And a blue car seat, and blue clothes and hats and onesies and socks, and—"

"Gah! I get your point!" I cut in, making him chuckle.

"Another little girl," Shane said softly.

"Yeah, do you think Sage is going to be pissed?" My mouth twitched.

"Hell, no! She'll be the only happy one in the bunch."

"You're probably right," I agreed. "Is it weird that suddenly I'm far more excited to get your spawn out of me?"

"I wish I could touch you," he announced suddenly, pulling me out of my daydream of Easter dresses and big pink bows on a tiny head.

"What?" I asked even though I'd heard him.

"I wish I could touch you right now." I watched his Adam's apple bob as he swallowed hard. "I wish I could feel her moving around in your belly. I wish I could rub your back and kiss you. I hate it that I'm missing every-thing."

"I miss you, too," I murmured back.

"Lift your shirt," he ordered quietly, glancing over his shoulder.

"Oh hell no."

"I want to see you. Give me this." I stared at him stubbornly. "Please?"

My stomach flipped as I gave in, and my heart raced as my hands went to the bottom of my nightshirt.

"That T-shirt is going to be stretched all to hell."

"Do you care?"

"Not at all."

His eyes were focused intently on the screen as I fiddled with the hem of my shirt, and they flared as I lifted it over my belly and held it against my breasts.

"Take it off," he ordered gruffly, the tendons in his neck growing taught. "All the way, Kate."

I closed my eyes as I pulled the shirt over my head and only opened them again when I heard him let out a harsh breath.

"Fuck," he groaned, his eyes dilated until they were almost black. "Do you know what we'd be doing if I was there right now?"

I nodded mutely as I watched him watching me.

"You're so fucking incredible, Kate. Jesus, those breasts—" I laughed a little as he whimpered, then slid the shirt back over my head, hiding my body from view.

However, I couldn't hide the way my nipples had pebbled as he stared, and they strained against his old T-shirt.

"I need to go take a shower," he announced, pushing back a little in his chair.

"Wait—now?"

"Right now."

I laughed hysterically as his cheekbones turned ruddy.

"Okay, well, be careful."

"Always."

"Talk to you soon?"

"I'll email you later. Go to sleep, you look exhausted."

"Gee, thanks," I grumbled.

"Sleep, Katie."

"Fine, I will. Stop worrying."

"Hey, Kate?" he called as I reached for the keyboard.

"Yeah?"

"Thank you. No one's ever done something like that for me before. Best surprise I've ever had."

The screen went black as a little smile played on my lips.

What was it with that man and his need for the last word?

Chapter 9
Shane

Clenching my fist in frustration, I forced myself not to yell as my foster father rambled on and on in my ear. I loved the guy, but I was irritated as fuck that he wouldn't put Kate on the phone. It was the third time I'd called and gotten the run-around, and I was ready to start tearing shit apart.

Kate had taken the kids up to Oregon for the end of the summer, even though I hadn't been all that happy about it. They loved it up there, and I knew our families were probably spoiling them rotten, but Kate was nearing the end of her pregnancy and I hated that she'd flown with four small kids by herself. When I'd finally talked to her on Skype less than a week after they'd arrived, I'd stopped bitching.

I hadn't realized how worn down she'd looked in the past few months, but looking at her at her parents' kitchen table—rosy-cheeked and smiling happily, the dark circles under her eyes faded to almost nothing—

I hadn't been able to ignore the change. She finally had that pregnant glow that most women got after they stopped puking up everything they ate and got a decent night's rest.

I was surprised as hell about it, but even though I hadn't seen her for months we'd grown closer over the deployment, and now that it was nearly over I was anxious to get home to her. At some point, my feelings had changed from confusion and guilt to something less identifiable. She was funny. She didn't put up with my shit, but she rarely got angry or mean. Instead, she diffused any argument with sarcasm or by changing the subject completely to some off-the-wall topic that usually had me scrambling to keep up with her. She was smarter than me, and that was sexy as hell.

She'd always been pretty. But as we spoke and bantered back and forth, it was as if I could see her with a whole new appreciation. The curves, which I never would've looked twice at before, began to fascinate me. I fucking dreamed about the roundness of her thighs and the soft skin between them, and found myself waking up embarrassed from wet dreams like a teenager.

Things were changing, and they had been for a while.

So I was irritated as hell that no one would let me talk to her. She'd answered my emails for the past two days but never agreed to a Skype date, and every time I called either her parents or mine, no one would tell me what was going on.

"Where the fuck is Kate?" I finally hissed, cutting off Mike mid-sentence. "And why the hell hasn't she brought my kids home yet? School's starting soon."

"Calm down, son."

"No, this is fucking ridiculous. Tell Kate that I'm going to Skype tonight at seven your time. I want to see my children."

I slammed the phone down and wiped sweat off my face with a paper towel I'd been carrying around in my pocket. This shit had to end soon. I needed to get home.

* * *

"Hi, Daddy!" Sage said when the call finally connected.

I breathed a sigh of relief when I saw Kate sitting in the middle of the kids, with Sage and Gavin on one side and Keller on the other. They were squished in close, and I could barely see anything beyond their faces.

"Hey, guys. Having fun at Grandma and Grandpa's?"

"Went in the big truck!" Gavin told me excitedly, waving his arms around and almost slapping Kate in the face.

"Oh yeah?"

"Uncle Bram took me on the tractor. Grandpa took us fishing!" Keller said.

"Wow, you guys have been busy." I smiled at their happy faces, and my stomach stopped churning for the first time in days. "Where's Gunner?"

"Can you bring him over, Mom?" Kate asked, looking to the side.

I saw his arms first and then the side of his head. I couldn't believe how much he'd grown since I'd been gone. His hair was so much thicker and longer than the last time I'd held him, and his body seemed so much sturdier.

I grinned as Keller's face scrunched up in disgust when Gunner blocked his view of the screen.

Then my entire body went cold.

"Mama! Mama! Mama!" Gunner whined, twisting and turning as he reached for Kate.

No. She wouldn't have.

"Shane?" Katie asked in confusion when she saw the look on my face. "What's wrong?"

I couldn't speak.

She wouldn't have done it. I *knew* Kate. I knew her. She wouldn't teach Gunner to call her "Mama." Would she?

"My time's up," I announced with a halfhearted smile for the kids. "I'll call you guys on Grandpa's phone later tonight."

"Bye, Daddy!" the kids called out, almost in unison.

"I love you guys. Talk soon."

"Shane? What—"

I clicked out of the screen quickly with shaky hands and stood abruptly.

I had shit to do. I just needed to get it done. Keep busy. I'd be home soon, and I'd take care of all of it.

The anger inside me grew as I left the computer room, and by the time I was packing up my things, I felt on the verge of losing my temper completely.

There was no way I could talk to her again before I got home.

No fucking way.

* * *

"Hey, Dad. Kids around?" I asked a couple of hours later. Shit, I'd made more phone calls in one day than I usually did in a week.

"Just Keller. Boy's having trouble sleeping."

"Shit, I waited too long to call. I got caught up," I said in disappointment. I missed my kids.

"What happened earlier? Mom said—"

"Can you put Kell on the phone?" I cut in. The argument was between Kate and me, and I didn't relish hashing it out with anyone else.

"Sure, son."

It was quiet for a few minutes before Keller's sleepy voice came through.

"Hi, Daddy."

"Hey, bud. What are you doing awake?"

"Waitin' for you."

"Aw, I'm sorry. I was working."

"That's okay. Grandpa and I were watchin' fishin' on TV."

"Well, I just wanted to say hi and tell you I loved you, bud. Go to sleep, okay?"

"Okay, Daddy. Love you."

"Bye, Keller."

"Bye." I heard him yawn loudly before the phone

disconnected, and I sat back in my chair in disappointment.

I was leaving in a few hours, finally heading home, and no one would be there to greet me.

No. Fuck that. I picked the phone back up.

"Hello?" Mike answered gruffly.

"Tell Kate to bring my kids back home."

"Well—"

"I asked her not to go to Oregon, and she went anyway. I don't give a flying fuck how much fun she's having up there. I want my kids in Oceanside when I get there."

Mike was silent for a moment before he made a harsh sound in his throat. "I didn't raise you to be an asshole."

"You didn't raise me at all," I snapped back, regretting the words as soon as they were out of my mouth.

"I'll pass along the message," he said quietly, and his lack of anger at my words made my chest ache.

"Dad—"

He hung up before I could say another word.

Christ.

Why hadn't I gotten over the need to say whatever shitty thing popped into my head the moment I got angry? I never said mean shit to my kids, no matter how frustrated I was, but that didn't seem to extend to adults. It was like my filter completely vanished the moment I got worked up. It wasn't the first time I'd hurt Mike's feelings, but that didn't mean that I felt good about it. If anything, knowing that he'd been putting up with my shit for over twelve years just made me feel worse about the comment I'd made.

I didn't have time to call him back again. Instead, I perched my cover on my head and walked toward my room to get my bags.

It was finally time to go home.

* * *

My house was closed up and silent when I arrived a few days later.

Kate hadn't brought my kids home.

I had a flight booked and was on my way to the airport two hours later.

Seven hours after I'd touched down in San Diego, I was walking through the Portland airport with nothing more than a backpack full of clothes I'd found folded in my dresser and enough rage to keep anyone from speaking to me. It must have been rolling off me in waves.

I rented a small car and headed east toward my parents' property almost an hour away. It had been quite a while since I'd driven those roads, but some things you just never forget, and I pulled up to my parents' house at seven that night without incident.

"Anyone home?" I called as I walked in the unlocked front door.

"Shane?" Mike said in confusion as he walked out of one of the guest rooms. "What in the world?"

He rushed forward, hugging me tightly when he

reached me. It was as if the conversation a few days ago had never happened. "What are you doing here?"

"Came to get the kids. Where are they?"

"Ellie took them to—" His words were cut off as the front door opened and in rushed my children.

"Mike, who's here—?"

"Daddy!"

I dropped to my knees as Keller and Sage ran to me, grasping at my shirt and wrapping their little arms around my neck.

"I missed you guys so much," I whispered into their hair, kissing them both before raising my head to see Gavin and Gunner keeping their distance. They watched us from near the front door, and Gunner had one arm wrapped tight around Ellie's jean-clad thigh.

"Hey, boys," I called gently. "I missed you."

Gavin was cautiously looking me over and took a small step forward, but there was absolutely no recognition in Gunner's eyes. He didn't remember me, not even after all the Skype chats.

That killed me.

"Have you been having fun with Grandma and Grandpa?" I asked, and suddenly Gavin was running forward and almost knocking me on my ass when he hit the tangle of small bodies already wrapped around me.

"Hey, buddy," I said with a smile, my throat thickening and making my words come out hoarse.

I closed my eyes and breathed in deeply. Finally. God, I'd missed them.

Ellie picked up Gunner as he began to fuss, and I

stood up, setting the kids down on their feet. They kept their hands on me, but all three stayed quiet. I understood their silence. I wanted to just soak it in for a minute, too.

"Where's Kate?" I asked Ellie, looking past her at the front door.

"She's at the hospital," Ellie answered slowly.

"What?" My voice echoed through the room, making the kids startle.

"Auntie Kate has to stay in bed all the time," Keller piped up, tipping his head back to look at me. "So the baby doesn't come out."

"Explain," I ordered, panic starting to flutter in my stomach.

"She's been on bed rest, what, three weeks now?" Ellie asked Mike.

"Yeah. About three weeks."

"She was having contractions last week, and they admitted her overnight so they could stop them. They let her go home the next day, but the contractions started up again yesterday. Looks like they'll be keeping her in there for a while now."

My anger faded, and confusion set in.

"Why didn't anyone tell me?"

"Kate didn't want you to worry—"

"That's bullshit."

"It's what she wanted."

"What hospital?" I was already lifting my hand off Keller's head to reach in my pocket for the keys to the rental car.

"OHSU," Mike said as I leaned down to kiss the kids again.

"They won't let you in tonight," Ellie informed me, walking forward as she switched Gunner from one hip to the other. "Visiting hours are over, and they're strict about that stuff. Kate needs to rest."

"They'll make an exception," I argued as the kids began to chatter, trying to get my attention.

"They won't." Ellie shook her head. "Kate's exhausted, Shane. This is the only way they know she'll rest."

My whole body felt wired, and I fidgeted as I tried to figure out what I was supposed to do.

"Take tonight with the kids, son," Mike ordered, reaching out to squeeze my shoulder. "They've missed you like crazy. You can see Katie in the morning."

"Daddy, look!" Sage yelled, pointing to a space in her mouth where she'd lost a tooth. "I got four bucks for it!" She did a little, excited dance.

I felt torn between rushing to the hospital to see Kate and spending some much-needed time with my children. I didn't want to leave them. We had months to make up for.

"Whoa! The Tooth Fairy must be having a good year," I replied, poking Sage in the side until she giggled.

Ellie came closer, and I reached out to rub Gunner's back gently, my decision made. "Hey, Gunner," I said softly. "How you doin', bud?"

He watched me with curious eyes.

"Want to say hi, Gunner?" Ellie asked.

"Hi." His voice was raspier than I remembered from the few words he'd said before I left, and my chest tightened. I'd missed so much.

"Hi!" I smiled. "Want to come hang out with me and the other kids?"

I stuck my hands out and waited for what felt like forever before he finally leaned away from Ellie and reached for me.

He was smaller than Keller and Gavin had been at that age. Both my older boys had been built like tanks from the very beginning, but Gunner was more streamlined. Tall and lanky. I clenched my jaw and kissed his forehead as he watched me closely.

I remembered this moment with Sage and Gavin. They'd both been so little when I left on deployments that they hadn't remembered me when I got home, but thankfully little kids seemed to adapt pretty fast. I didn't think Gunner would be any different. It would just take a few days for him to grow used to me.

I don't think I'd ever been as happy to be home as I was in that moment.

"Okay, kiddos," I announced, looking between the little bodies jumping around the entryway. "Tell me what you've been up to while I've been gone."

Chapter 10

Kate

I sat back down in my hospital bed and started brushing out my wet hair. God, I hated the hospital.

I missed the kids. I missed sleeping deeply. I missed my mom's cooking and the smell of summer outside.

I hadn't been in the hospital very long, and the doctors said they only wanted me to stay one more day, since I was almost full term, but I was going stir-crazy. Shane was coming home soon, and my anxiety was building as I prepared for the day he'd get home and realize that we were still in Oregon.

When we'd first arrived at my parents' house, I'd cried in relief. I'd just been so unbelievably *tired*. And for the first couple of weeks after that, I'd felt like a new person. With our families around, I'd had far less to do and more time to do it. Everyone pitched in with the kids so I could work during the day instead of late at night. I hadn't had to bend over the bathtub anymore to give the kids baths because my mom or Aunt Ellie did it, which meant my back wasn't killing me when I crawled into bed at night.

It had felt like for the first time since Shane had left, I'd been able to relax.

I'd needed that break.

But as I'd slowly prepared myself to go back to California with my little monsters, taking over their day-to-day needs from the other women, my body had begun to protest. It was as if, once I slowed down and my body realized it was possible, it wouldn't let me go back to the way things had been.

I began to have contractions, and the doctors put me on bed rest.

The window for making it back to California before I had the baby was closed, but I couldn't tell Shane that. Instead, I'd ignored the questions in his emails and avoided that conversation when he called.

I didn't want him to worry when he was halfway around the world, especially when that worry could distract him...I also didn't want to make him angry. We'd grown so close over the last six months that I dreaded anything that would upset the fragile balance we'd found.

He hadn't told me not to go to Oregon, but he also hadn't been happy about it. If he'd known that we were stuck there, I wasn't sure how he'd react.

I was setting my brush down on the bedside table when the door to my room slowly opened but no one greeted me.

"What's—Shane?"

I couldn't believe my eyes.

There he was. Tan and healthy and strong, standing in the doorway to my hospital room. My heart raced.

"How're you feeling?" he asked as he finally stepped inside and let the door swing shut behind him.

"I feel fine," I answered with a surprised smile and a roll of my eyes. "No contractions for the last twelve hours, but they want to be careful. How are you here?"

I knew better than to hop from the bed and run to him, but I could barely hold myself back as he froze inside the doorway. The longer he stood there, the more awkward things became, until finally I felt my hands begin to tremble.

I thought I'd have time to prepare before I saw him, and now that the time had come, I felt out of place in my own hospital room. I was extremely aware of my ugly hospital gown and swollen feet. My stomach felt rounder and more conspicuous, and I hated that my hair was wet and brushed haphazardly away from my face.

"You should have told me," he suddenly stated.

"Why, so you could just worry? I'm fine." I shook my head. "The baby is fine, the kids are fine, everything was handled."

"I left you in charge," he said quietly. His tone making me freeze. "You didn't think I deserved to know that they weren't with the person I'd left them with, but that Ellie and Mike were taking care of *my* kids while I was gone?"

"I—I didn't—"

"You don't get to make unilateral decisions about my children, Kate. That's above your pay grade."

He was calm, and his voice never rose, but I felt like I'd been slapped.

"I apologize," I replied. "The decision was made with the best intentions. I didn't want you to worry, and I've seen the kids every day I've been here. Either my mom or Ellie drives them in."

I squirmed on the bed, a sense of dread filling me as I felt my abdomen grow tight. Time to lie down on my side like the doctors advised.

I didn't meet his eyes as I pulled my legs up and under the blankets, but I saw him come closer out of the corner of my eye as I shoved a pillow between my knees and finally relaxed my head into the pillow.

"I knew you did what you thought was best, Kate," Shane finally said, coming to sit on the edge of the bed. "You sure everything's okay with the baby?"

"Yeah. They're going to let me go home tomorrow."

"That's good."

"I missed you," I whispered, trying to call forth the Shane I'd been speaking to for the last few months. He wasn't acting like my Shane, and that scared me, because I remembered how Rachel's Shane treated me. Like I was invisible.

"Sage and Keller's school starts next week," he informed me, ignoring my words.

"I know." I grimaced. I didn't know what the hell I was going to do—

"So I'm going to take the kids back with me to San

Diego." Suddenly I felt like I couldn't breathe. "I know you can't fly right now, and I'm sorry you can't come with us."

"What?" He had to be kidding.

"They need to get back into their normal routine before school starts up again. Especially Keller."

His voice was kind, so kind, but his eyes were blank. I didn't move as he watched me, but I couldn't speak, either. I didn't think I could say anything without yelling or, worse, bawling my eyes out.

What was he doing? And why the fuck did he think he knew anything about the kids' routine? I was the one who knew their routine. I was the one who knew what they needed to fall asleep. *Me.*

My worst fear had been realized. He was taking them away from me, and there was nothing I could do about it.

"Why?" I asked when I could finally speak. "You're that mad about me not telling you I was in the hospital?"

"No." He rubbed his hand over his face. "I have to go back, Kate. I have the next couple of days off, but my CO doesn't even know I flew to Oregon."

"Okay, well, when can you get leave? Can't you just—"

"They belong with me, Katie. I'm their dad."

"And I'm nothing?"

"I didn't say that."

"That's what you're insinuating."

"Don't put words in my mouth. I know you're

important to them!" he finally exploded, losing his control and standing from the bed. "But you're not their parent!"

My eyes slammed shut, and I jerked backward at the venom in his words.

"Hey, what's all the yelling about?" my brother Bram called out, walking into the room. "I could hear you guys all the way outside."

"It's nothing," I answered immediately, not willing to let my overprotective big brother into the middle of it.

"Hey, Bram," Shane said, his voice again calm.

"Dickhead," Bram answered with a nod. "Glad you made it back."

"Bram, don't be an ass," I hissed. God, he got on my nerves sometimes.

"It's fine. I'm gonna go," Shane said.

"Wait, you just got here!"

"I should probably go get the kids."

"Our mom's already on her way up here with the kids," Bram cut in with a nasty smile. "You'll pass her on the highway."

"Then I'm going to go grab a cup of coffee," Shane mumbled before leaving the room.

I stared at my brother in irritation as he watched Shane walk away.

"Did you really have to be an ass? You couldn't have just behaved like a normal person?" I asked, trying to control the tears of panic that I could feel building behind my eyes.

"I was willing to let the fucker keep his head, that is until I heard him yelling at you from down the hall."

"He wasn't yelling."

"You're too forgiving."

"You don't forgive anyone!"

"And no one takes advantage of me, do they?" he asked, raising an eyebrow. "Brought you a donut from Joe's."

"Thanks."

"You want to talk about it?" He handed me a small paper sack holding what I knew would be a maple bar from our favorite donut shop.

"He's taking the kids back to California," I said, my voice reed-thin.

"What the fuck?" He looked as shocked as I felt. "Don't let him!"

"There's nothing I can do, Bram."

"Fuck that. I'll—"

"Don't," I warned, placing my donut on the table next to me. "It's not your fight."

"It's been my fight since I was ten years old."

"And I love you for it, but there's nothing you can do this time. Not without making everything worse."

My mom shuffled through the door a few minutes later, a little gaggle of Andersons following in her wake like ducklings, and I had to clench my jaw against the urge to cry.

"Annie!" Gunner yelled as my mom set him on the bed. He hadn't yet mastered the *t* sound in *Auntie*. "An-nie. Annie. Annie." He lay down next to me and curled

around my belly, tucking his head into the space between my drawn-down chin and my chest.

"He's been asking for you all morning," my mom informed me with a smile. "How you feeling?"

"Fine," I whispered shakily, pulling Gunner toward
me as I watched Keller and Sage fight over the only
chair in the room while Gavin showed something in his
hands to Bram.

What the hell was I going to do?

* * *

Shane picked me up the next morning after I'd been dis-
charged, and we made the silent and strained trip back
to my parents' house. I wasn't sure why he was silent. *He*
was the one who'd pulled the rug out from under *me*. I
also wasn't sure why he'd offered to pick me up, instead
of my mom like we'd planned.

"We're leaving at four," Shane said, finally breaking
the silence between us as he turned the car onto my parents' driveway. "Our flight leaves at six thirty."

"Seriously?"

"I have to be home in case I get called in. I've been
lucky so far," he replied quietly.

"So, that's it?" I huffed out a derisive laugh. "What
are you going to do with the kids while you work?"

"Megan said she can keep them until I find a daycare."

"You're putting them in daycare instead of leaving
them with their family who loves them," I said flatly

as we rolled to a stop in front of the house. "Good move."

"They belong with me, and I live in California."

"There's nothing I can do to change your mind, is there?" I asked desperately.

Shane shook his head once, his jaw flexing.

"Fine." I stared out the windshield for a long moment after he put the car in park. I didn't know what to do with myself. It felt like there was a hole in my chest that was spreading, leaving a path of destruction in its wake.

"Thank you so much for taking care of them for me—" I threw my door open and climbed out of the car so I didn't have to listen to his bullshit.

"I've got it," I hissed as Shane rushed around the car to grip my elbow. "Don't."

"Kate—" he said, his voice strained.

"No. You don't get to do this and then act like everything's fine."

"You're on bed rest! It's not like you can take care—"

"Sis?" Bram called out from the front door, walking toward us. "You need some help?"

I turned to my brother, who was practically vibrating with tension. He was trying, I knew he was, but it was taking a toll on him to sit back and do nothing when he knew I was hurting. *My protector.*

When Alex and Bram had come to our family, I'd been curious to see how two boys who looked so incredibly similar would compare. We hadn't known then that my parents would adopt them—that came two years later—but as far as I'd been concerned, they were my brothers as soon as they stepped foot in the house—and I'd been almost giddy that I had two for the proverbial price of one.

I soon came to realize that, though the boys were twins, they were as different as chalk and cheese. Alex became my confidant. He was understanding, and calm, and willing to listen to anything I said. Bram? Well, he didn't care what an eight-year-old girl had to say. He hadn't really wanted to bother with me at all. I'd been convinced that he just didn't like me until one day when I'd accidentally walked into a blackberry bush and scratched a deep groove into my eyelid. I'd been scream- ing, stumbling around as blood ran into my eye and partially blinded me, when Bram came running. He'd been bigger than me, even then, and had picked me up and carried me all the way home.

I'd known then that, though Bram wasn't interested in my day-to-day drama, he wouldn't hesitate if he thought I'd needed him. He was the most solid man I knew. Stalwart. Loyal. And he wanted to beat the hell out of the man standing next to me.

"Help me inside?" I asked tremulously. Shane made a small sound of protest in the back of his throat.

"Yeah, no problem," Bram said, hopping down off the porch and scooping me into his arms to carry me bridal-style. "Kids are waiting for you inside."

* * *

"You guys are going to go back to San Diego with your dad," I tried to explain to the older kids for what felt like the twentieth time that afternoon. The only one who seemed completely okay with the situation was Gunner, who sat oblivious, snacking on a small bowl of marshmallows. I swear it was the only way I could keep the kid still for more than a few minutes at a time. I'd figured it out months ago and had used the trick to keep him quiet and happy during Shane's Skype calls.

"What are you going to do?" Sage asked in confusion.

"I have to stay here, Sage the Rage. I can't fly. I'm not even supposed to get out of bed."

"We should stay too then," Keller said, a small scowl on his face. "We shouldn't leave you here by yourself."

"I'll be okay. I have my mom and your grandma to take care of me," I told him, my eyes watering.

"I don't wanna go back."

"You start kindergarten next week, bud. You don't want to start later than everyone else, do you?"

"We could go to school here," Sage interrupted excitedly. "We could ride the bus."

I glanced up to where Shane stood in the doorway to my room and flinched at the misery in his eyes.

"You have to go with your daddy, sweetheart," I told her gently. "He's missed you guys."

"But you'll miss us!" Keller said, turning to his dad. "She'll miss us if we leave her."

"I know, bud," Shane said consolingly, "but she'll come—"

"She can't move or Iris will come out!" Keller yelled back, his whole body shaking with sudden fury. "She has to stay in bed!"

"It's not forever, baby," I tried to calm him down.

"Iris?" Shane asked.

"That's the baby's name," Sage informed him. "It's a flower, and it only has four letters, like mine!"

"Awesome." Shane smiled.

"I'm not going," Keller announced, his voice trembling. "I'm staying here with Auntie Kate."

Gavin had been sitting quietly, watching everything unfold, but at Keller's announcement he started crying.

"Oh, monkey," I cooed, sitting up to pull him onto what was left of my lap. "It's okay."

He mumbled something back that I couldn't understand then began to sob as I rocked him back and forth.

"Son, it's time to go, if you're going," I heard Mike say from the hallway, making my body go cold.

"Give Auntie Kate a kiss, guys. It's time to go," Shane called out as he stepped toward the bed.

"No," Keller replied as Sage's face grew terrified. She looked between me and Shane, her lower lip quivering.

"Give me a smooch, sweet thing," I teased, my voice hitching. "Time to go."

As she leaned over and gave me a quick kiss, wrapping her arms around where I held Gavin, I closed my eyes and tried to get my emotions under control. Sobbing would only make their departure harder for them, and I couldn't let that happen.

Sage crawled off the bed and walked to the door

without looking back, dodging the hand that Shane held out to her.

"Give me a kiss, monkey," I said into Gavin's ear as he hiccuped. "You get to ride on an airplane!"

"Don't wanna."

"You love to fly! I bet the flight attendants will even give you some pretzels if you use your manners."

Ellie came into the room then, and I widened my eyes at her strained face. "Come on, Gavie," she called, picking Gavin up off my lap after another quick kiss. "Grandma will help you buckle your seat."

"Mama!" Gunner yelled as I watched Ellie carry Gavin out the door. "Annie! Mama! Mama!"

"No more, bud," I told him with a small sniffle, setting the small bowl of marshmallows to the side as I kept Keller in the corner of my eyesight. He'd climbed off the bed and was standing rigidly across from Shane.

"Can I have a kiss?" I asked Gunner, pulling him toward me.

"No! Mama!" He twisted and turned, pissed at me for not giving him more marshmallows. Before I could get him settled, he was plucked out of my arms.

"Mamas are marshmallows?" Shane asked, a weird look on his face.

I nodded. I couldn't even speak to him.

"We'll get you some mamas for the car, bud," Shane mumbled, rubbing Gunner's back as he met my eyes. "I'll take him to the car. Come on, Kell," he ordered, his voice absent of any emotion.

"No. I'm staying with Auntie Kate," Keller argued mutinously.

"Keller," Shane warned with a stern look before walking out the door with my baby.

"Mama! Annie! Annie! Mama!" Gunner yelled fearfully, trying to pull away from Shane. He still wasn't quite comfortable with his daddy, and my stomach turned as he began to cry.

When they disappeared from view, I turned to Keller, tears rolling down my face.

"I'm going to stay with you," he said, reaching out to wipe at my face with his grubby fingers. "Don't cry."

His words only made the tears come faster.

"You gotta go, baby," I argued. "Your dad wants you with him. He's missed you like crazy."

"He can take Sage and Gavie and Gunner." He straightened as we heard Shane's footsteps thudding back down the hallway. "And I'll just stay with you."

"Let's go, bud," Shane said resolutely as he stopped in the doorway.

"I'm staying here."

"No, you're not. Get in the car, Keller."

"No."

Shane started toward us, his jaw flexing, and Keller scrambled up behind me on the bed.

"No!" he screamed, cleaving my heart in two. "Don't!"

Shane gently but firmly pulled Keller away as he grasped at me, pulling at my shirt and arms.

"Don't let him take me!" he shouted, his eyes dry but

his voice filled with panic. "Auntie Kate! Auntie Kate! Please! Please!"

He fought Shane. God, he fought hard. But he was no match for a full-grown man.

I dug my fingernails into my thighs as I called back to him, trying to calm him in the only way I could. "It's okay, baby. It's okay. I'll call you tonight. I love you! You're okay."

They left the room, and I sat silently listening as Keller screamed the entire way to the car. I had no choice.

I was almost thirty years old, and I'd never hated anyone until that moment.

Chapter 11

Kate

I knew that time had passed since Shane had taken my kids away, but I wasn't sure how long it had been. It felt like an eternity. The light beyond my closed eyelids slowly disappeared as the sun fell out of the sky, and at some point someone had turned on the lamp sitting on the nightstand next to my bed, but I didn't open my eyes to find out who had done it. I didn't care.

I couldn't move. I could barely breathe. My limbs were so heavy that I wasn't even sure that I'd be able to roll over. I wondered if this was what it felt like to be dead.

Family came in and out of the bedroom, checking on me and talking in low whispers that they thought I couldn't hear. Maybe they thought I was asleep, but I wasn't. Not at any point. I didn't know if I'd ever be able to sleep again.

Keller's screams replayed over and over in my ears

until I dragged my arm over the side of my head, pushing my biceps hard against my ear. It didn't help. I could still hear him. I could see the way his frantic eyes had met mine as he'd kicked and screamed.

Finally, blessedly, the sounds melted away until there was only white noise. Everything was blank, almost like I was floating between sleep and wakefulness.

"I'm just gonna keep you company, sis," my dad's voice said, floating past the emptiness. The sounds of something heavy hitting the carpet were followed by rustling and the sigh of relief my dad always made as he sat down.

Then there was nothing again.

Voices came and went. Someone brushed my hair back from my face, but I still didn't move.

Iris squirmed restlessly then must have gone to sleep. My belly tightened on and off, but it didn't hurt, so I ignored it.

"I wish Alex was here," Ani said softly, lying down on the bed next to me.

I wasn't sure if she was talking to me or not, but I didn't reply. I didn't want Alex. I didn't want my dad who wouldn't leave the room or my mom who sat at the foot of the bed rubbing my feet. I didn't want Ani or Bram or my uncle and aunt, who'd stopped by for a while but hadn't stayed. It had to have been weird for them, knowing that a man they considered their son had done this to me.

Our family dynamics were so odd; I wondered sometimes how the outside world saw us.

Me, Bram, Alex, Trevor, and Ellie and Mike's other son Henry had all grown up together since we were kids. We acted, looked, and felt like cousins even though our appearances were so different. Over the years, we'd even picked up facial expressions from our parents that strengthened the similarities. Shane and Anita, though, had come in when most of us were almost grown. They were considered ours, but they didn't share our history or have the same type of bond—which was probably a good thing considering the fact that Shane had gotten me pregnant, and Anita and Bram...I didn't even know what the hell to say about them. Something was going on between them, just below the surface, but neither of them talked about it.

Anita shifted beside me, and I wanted to scream at her to leave me alone. I didn't want to feel her moving or hear her murmuring to Bram. I wanted to be nothing. I wanted to find my blank spot and stay there so that my chest didn't feel like it was breaking open each time I inhaled. If not for the baby nestled below my heart, I'm not sure what I would have done to find that place.

"What the fuck do you want?" Bram's voice rumbled from somewhere below the bed. He must have been sitting on the floor, but I didn't bother to open my eyes to check. It didn't matter. None of it mattered. "Fuck you, douchebag," Bram said. He needed to go away if he was going to talk on the phone.

"Not as easy as you thought to take a kid from the only mother he's ever known, huh?" Bram said nastily.

"Bram, is that Shane?" my mom asked in confusion.

Bile rose in my throat, and I tried valiantly to swallow it back down. Oh God, I couldn't breathe. Bram nodded, and my throat closed up.

"Hold on," Bram ordered into the phone. "Katiebear, Shane's on the phone."

"What's wrong?" I choked out, uncovering my head. I'd been lying there so long that my arm was completely numb and I could barely move it.

"He said Gunner's upset, and he can't get him calmed down," Bram said, pushing himself up off the floor.

I didn't even realize I was crying until I nodded and the air hit the wet spots on my cheeks. "Hey, Dad," I said, my voice hoarse, "can you grab my guitar for me?"

I pushed awkwardly against the mattress and sat up with Ani's help as my dad opened up my guitar case in the corner. I only knew of one way that Gunner would settle down so late at night. Inhaling a shaky breath, I dug my fingertips into my eyes, trying to control the feeling of helplessness. My baby was crying for me, and I couldn't hold him or rub his back—but this, I could do this.

"Ask him to put the phone on speaker, okay?" I said to Bram, my voice catching on the last word. My belly went hard as a rock and pain hit me with the force of a sledgehammer as I took the guitar from my dad and rested it on my thighs. I breathed through my nose for a minute as I pretended to get situated. I could barely reach the strings with my massive belly in the way. "Put yours on speaker, too, brother," I said, watching as Bram nodded and hit the SPEAKERPHONE button before setting his phone on the bed.

An involuntary whimper left my throat as the sound of my crying boys filled the room. It wasn't just Gunner. Gavin was crying, too.

"Hey, monkey," I called out above the noise, my voice breaking. "Gunner? Gavin? Where are my monkeys?"

Slowly the noise through the speaker decreased.

"Annie?" Gunner cried. Oh God, he sounded scared.

"Hey, baby," I said, lifting my hand to cover my eyes. If I didn't see the room I was in, maybe I could pretend they were right there with me. "Why are you crying, huh?"

"Annie," Gunner whined.

"You have to sit quiet, okay?" I called, my hands shaking. "Gavin, you ready?"

"Yeah." Gavin's voice came through shrill.

"Are Keller and Sage there?"

"Yeah."

I began strumming Gunner's favorite song and shuddered as the little voices went silent. I almost stopped again just so I could hear them. Closing my eyes again, I started to sing. My voice was deeper than normal, raspy and breaking, but it didn't matter. My stomach tightened and my breath caught at the sharp pain that seemed to be pulsing between my hips, making my shoulders curve inward as my body began to shake, but I still didn't stop singing.

Those were contractions, I thought as the pain started to ebb. *I'm going into labor.*

All of a sudden, Sage's voice came through the speaker, high and clear, singing along with the chorus. My chin hit my chest as I tried not to sob. Labor could wait.

I shuddered in pain when another contraction hit, and I felt a gush of liquid between my legs just as the song came to a close, but my fingers didn't stop moving along the strings of the guitar as I segued into a new one. I wasn't ready to stop even though the kids seemed to have settled down. I couldn't bear to hang up the phone and cut the only connection I had with them.

Bram staggered back against the wall as my voice cracked, but I ignored him. I just kept playing, until suddenly, Shane was speaking into the phone.

I grit my teeth as my fingers suddenly went numb.

"They're asleep," he said quietly. "Thanks, Ka—"

Bram grabbed his phone from where it was lying on the bed and threw it hard against the wall, cutting off Shane's words and shattering it into a million little pieces.

"You're probably going to need that," I said, letting my guitar fall forward as I reached for Bram's hand.

"I'll get a new one," he replied.

"That's good, because my water just broke and someone needs to call Alex," I said quietly, my lips trembling as a mix of excitement and terror warred with my devastation. I hadn't been able to say good-bye.

"You're an idiot," he said with a smile, shaking his head as our dad rounded the bed and picked me up, cradling me in his arms.

"*You're* an idiot," I taunted back weakly over Dad's shoulder as my mom said something about getting me in the shower.

My stomach cramped again, and my dad's arms tightened around me as my entire body froze in agony. "You're all right, Katiebear," he said softly, setting me on my feet in the bathroom. "She's coming a bit early, but everything's gonna be just fine."

He was wrong. I didn't think anything would ever be fine again.

Chapter 12
Shane

I fucked up. Bad.

I finally dropped to the couch with a sigh and rubbed my hands over my face. I had no idea what to do.

When I'd decided to take the kids home with me, I hadn't done it out of spite. Fuck, if anything I'd thought I was doing the right thing.

My children belonged with me, end of story. And I hated that Kate had to stay in Oregon, but that wasn't my fucking fault. I'd warned her, I'd made it clear that I didn't think she should take the kids there in the first place, and now look what had happened.

I'd had to take four heartbroken kids back to California while we left her behind.

I'd known that it would be an adjustment for the little ones. Kate had been taking care of them for as long as they could remember, and I felt like a stranger. I got that. I did. But I hadn't anticipated that my oldest two would completely hate me. Sage wasn't talking—not to anyone—and Keller was as rabid as a junkyard dog.

The baby would be born soon, and Kate would be able to come back home. I'd *planned* on her coming back when I'd made the decision to bring the kids with me— but I hadn't planned for the shit show I'd just participated in.

It was as if I'd stolen my own children.

A knock on the front door startled me, and I shot to my feet to see who it was. Midnight was pretty late to be showing up on someone's doorstep.

"Alex?" I asked in surprise. "What the hell are you doing in Oceanside?"

"Lots to talk about, champ. Can I come in?"

"Yeah, yeah, come on in."

I watched in confusion as he dropped a duffel by the front door and shuffled toward the kitchen.

"You have beer?" he called back quietly.

"I have no idea. I just got here."

"Yeah I heard," he answered, coming back toward me with two beers in his hands.

"What's going on?" I asked as he tossed one to me.

"Oh, I'm pretty sure you know why I'm here."

"Kate," I replied, dropping back down onto the couch.

"What the fuck is going on, Shane? This seems low, even for you."

"What the fuck does that mean?"

"You've never been crazy about Kate—we've all seen that. So why the hell did you sleep with her?"

"We were drunk," I sputtered.

"Try again. You're not eighteen, and you weren't at a frat party."

"I don't see how this is any of your business."

"Well, see, that's the thing." Alex sat forward and rested his elbows against his knees. "Bram and I have been watching out for sis since she was eight years old. We've patched her up and defended her honor more times than you could count. Hell, we almost went to jail for her when that little fucker of a foster kid tried to rape her—"

"What?" I shouted, coming off the couch.

"Oh calm down, idiot. He didn't get far, and that was years ago."

"When?"

"Well, let's see . . . she was about twelve, I think. Long before you came around."

"Christ."

"We're getting off topic," Alex said with a shake of his head.

"Why the fuck would no one ever tell me that?" I asked, furious.

"What the hell is it to you? Up until about nine months ago, you didn't care if Kate dropped dead in the middle of the street."

"That's bullshit."

"No, that's the truth," he shot back, his fists clenching. "Oh, I know all about that shit when we were kids—you hanging out with Kate, taking what you wanted from her and giving nothing back. Hell, we *all* saw that. But Kate is Kate, and she begged us not to step in. For some unknown reason she continued to trust blindly even after what that little shit had done years before... and for that you fucked her right the hell over, didn't you?"

"It wasn't like that," I argued, my face heating.

"Oh, it was exactly like that. You didn't want sweet Kate. She wasn't cool enough for you. Hot enough for you. Whatever, man, that was your deal. But you strung her along for years before she finally got rid of you... but she didn't, not really."

I crushed the beer can in my hand, making beer pour out all over the floor.

"Oh, no. You had to twist the knife a little farther, right? Had to have your last coup de grâce. So instead of walking the fuck away, you went for her best friend. Hell, her only friend back then. The one that finally made her feel cool. The only girl she'd ever met who took her at face value and didn't see anything wrong with her."

"I fell in love with her!" I hissed. "What the fuck was I supposed to do, just drop Rachel because *Kate* didn't like it?"

"Yes," he answered simply, taking the breath from my lungs. "You should have never started that shit in the first place, but hey, we were all young and stupid once, right? It's the shit you've done since then that makes you a fucking loser."

"I haven't done anything to Kate. What the fuck are you talking about?"

"You have no idea." He shook his head and leaned back against the chair, staring at the ceiling. "Jesus, I didn't realize you were that stupid."

"Stop calling me stupid before I beat your ass."

"You can try, jarhead. Not sure you'd succeed."

"Get the fuck out of my house. I don't have to deal with this shit."

"Oh, I'm not done." Alex's body never moved from his relaxed position on the chair even though mine was practically vibrating with suppressed anger.

"I'm done," I announced.

"Did you know that Kate practically lived with Rachel while you were on deployment?" he asked conversationally.

"What?"

"Yeah, the moment you stepped foot out the door, Rachel was calling Katie to come over and help her."

"No she wasn't." I tried to remember the phone calls and emails from Rachel on my previous deployments, but they'd already started to fade from my memory.

"Yeah, man, she was," Alex said softly. "Rachel wasn't good at being alone, you know? Not sure if you're oblivious or she just hid that shit really well, but Rachel— she was a good girl, don't get me wrong—but she used Kate for years."

"You're wrong," I argued, shaking my head.

"I'm right, man, and if you think back, you'll know exactly what I'm talking about. Kate moved here for *Rachel*. She could do her job anywhere, so why wouldn't she stay in Oregon with her family? She set things aside, and moved things around, and was at your wife's side for years while you were off on deployment after deployment. She didn't keep a boyfriend beyond a month or two because they saw that shit and either couldn't deal or tried to talk to Kate about it and she dropped them. She practically raised your kids, man."

"Oh my God."

"Don't get me wrong, Kate loved it." He sighed tiredly and shook his head. "She'd do anything for her friends, and she fell in love with Sage the first moment she saw her. Hell, I think she was the first one to ever even hold Gavin. She loves those kids, and if I asked her, I think she'd say that she wouldn't change one minute of the last nine years. Which is crazy fucked up because when you were home? She lost all that. See, Rachel didn't need her anymore. She had you, right?"

"Stop," I ordered, holding up my hand. I was trying to remember something Keller had said to me last year. *What had he said?*

"In one way or another you've been controlling her life and happiness for almost half her life, you self-important prick. It's always been you. She fucking revolves around you, like you're the sun or some shit," Alex growled in frustration. "And now, when she's pregnant with your child, you take her kids and leave her?"

"They're not her—"

"You finish that sentence and I'll knock you the fuck out," he cut in before finishing his beer and setting the can down on the coffee table. "I guess she should be used to it by now, right? You're home from deployment, only makes sense that she's out on her ass again."

"*Now we get to see Auntie Kate every day. I like it when we see her every day...I never wanted you to leave though, Daddy. Even though we didn't get to see Auntie Kate...I like it when you're here.*"

Keller's words finally came back to me, and I dropped my head to my hands. "Jesus Christ."

"Look, man, Kate wouldn't thank me for coming here and telling you all of this—"

"Then why are you here?" I asked in frustration, looking up to meet his eyes.

"Because she's at the hospital, about to give birth to your daughter, and since I was already on my way west, I thought someone should tell you in person."

"Fuck!" I stood from my seat and looked around the room in a panic. "She's not due for weeks."

"I can stay here with the kids, if you want. Drive them up in the morning—I came out to visit a couple of months ago, so they know who I am." He stood and stretched his lanky body. "If not, I'll just grab a flight and head up myself."

"No! No, I'll just—" I looked around the room in confusion. "I just need to call my CO and make sure I can get my time, and, um..."

"Go get it done, man. I'll find you a flight."

He walked toward his bag and pulled out a laptop as I raced quietly up the stairs. I needed to get to Kate. I should have never left her up there.

My mind raced and so did my heart as I emptied the

bag on my bed and began to repack it while dialing my commanding officer.

There had been too many revelations in one night. I couldn't keep up or reconcile Alex's memories with my own.

Had Rachel really treated Kate like that? How had I never noticed? How had I missed something so huge? Had Sage and Keller talked about Kate more than I'd realized? By the way Alex had explained it, she'd been like another parent to them, and I'd never known.

I couldn't think about all of that then. I needed to get to Oregon. I could figure everything else out after I got to Kate.

* * *

I'd barely made it a few feet into the waiting room when I got knocked on my ass by a sucker punch to the jaw.

"What the fuck?"

"Get the fuck out of here," Bram ordered, pointing toward the door.

"Abraham, knock it off!" Kate's dad, Dan, ordered in a gruff voice. "This is not the time or the place, son."

"I'll fucking kill you," Bram said quietly as his dad stood up from his seat. "Watch your back."

"Is she okay?" I asked the room as Bram stalked away and I climbed to my feet.

"Everything went really well," Ellie assured me as she walked toward me. "Mom and baby are doing good."

"She's already here?" I asked, my voice cracking as disappointment filled me.

"About an hour ago, sweetheart," Ellie said sympathetically, reaching up to give me a hug.

"Fuck."

"You want to go see them?"

"Yeah."

I followed Ellie down the hall but stopped short when we reached the door for Kate's room. My palms were sweating, and it felt like I had a boulder pressing on my chest. I didn't know if I could go in there.

But when Ellie opened up the door, my feet moved forward without conscious thought, bringing me toward the two figures lying quietly on the bed.

"Katie?" I called softly as her mom stood up from her place next to the bed and followed Ellie back out of the room. "I'm here, baby."

Her eyes were closed as I reached out and rubbed my fingertips over her hair. She looked so worn out. Her eyes and lips were swollen, and she had little red dots all over her cheeks where the capillaries must have burst during labor. So beautiful.

It had always been Kate. My hands shook as the truth seeped into my pores. It had been her since I was just a stupid kid.

"Don't touch me," she said shakily, finally opening her eyes. "Get out."

"Katie, I—"

"Where are my children?" she asked, her eyes foggy from medication.

"They're in Calif—"

Her arms tightened around our daughter as if she was afraid I was going to snatch her away. "Get out."

"Katiebear, I'm so sorry."

"I hate you," she whispered, her eyes filling with tears. "I wish you were dead because then I could have my children back."

I stumbled away from the bed, horrified, and watched as she fell asleep as if I'd never even been there.

Jesus Christ, what had I done?

Chapter 13

Kate

"Time to get you dressed, sweet girl," I cooed into Iris's sleeping face as I lay her on my hospital bed. "We don't have our own house yet, but you're going to like Grandma's house. Your brothers and sister *love* it there."

Dressing a newborn is a lot like dressing an octopus: Their little limbs are so bendy that trying to push them through the tiny holes is a test in patience—not to mention the floppy neck and the head that's completely out of proportion.

"Don't worry, Iris, you'll grow into that head just like Keller did," I mumbled, pulling her little stocking cap on gently. "I can't say I would have complained if your head was a little smaller, but hey, we got through it, didn't we?"

My labor had gone fast. I'd been almost fully dilated by the time my parents had gotten me to the hospital, but I'd pushed for hours before she finally slid into the world. I'd lost my mind halfway through it, and my face heated as I remembered the things I'd shouted at my poor family when I'd reached my breaking point.

I would have thought that I'd be embarrassed that my dad and Bram stayed in the room while I was giving birth, but I'd been oddly okay with it. The room had been freaking packed. Mom, Ani, and Aunt Ellie had been in the thick of things, but Dad and Bram had stayed in the room . . . near my head. I don't think they wanted to see my downstairs any more than I'd wanted them to.

They just hadn't wanted to leave me, no matter how messy things got. I couldn't fault them for that, though I think Bram would have dealt with things much better if he'd stayed in the waiting room. At times, I'd thought he was going to burst out of his clothes like the Hulk and tear the room apart.

I smiled as I picked Iris up and shuffled over to her car seat. I'd planned on using Gunner's old infant seat, but that plan had been obviously nixed since it was still in the garage in California. My breath hitched.

I missed Sage, Keller, Gavin, and Gunner more than I'd ever thought possible. It didn't feel like I'd only seen them the afternoon before. It felt like I hadn't seen them in weeks. Maybe it was the distance between us. It wasn't as if I could just drive to them, especially with the little bean I was currently buckling into her seat.

"Hey, sis. You almost ready to go?" Bram asked as he walked into our room.

"What are you doing here? I thought Mom was picking me up," I said with a wide smile. My brother looked like he hadn't slept or showered since the night before, his beard and hair wild around his face like a mountain man.

"Yeah, well, I thought it would be better if I got you guys. How's my girl?"

"She's just fine. They had to poke and prod at her earlier—which she was pissed about—but after a little food, she passed out. It reminded me of Dad."

Bram scoffed. "She's too pretty to remind anyone of that wrinkly old man."

"Don't let him hear you say that!"

"I'll deny it," he replied with a smile, lifting Iris's seat. "All set?"

"Yep. Let me grab my bag."

"I'll get it," he argued, pulling it from my hands and slinging it over his shoulder. "You're moving like an old woman. I'm guessing you're, ah, sore." His face reddened, and I laughed.

"Yep. *Sore* is one word for it."

"I'd imagine stitches, ah—"

"Let's just leave it at that, shall we?" I cut in, chuckling.

"Yep. Let's go. I brought my truck; I figured that way we could see her while we drive. Plus, you know, it's big as a tank."

"Mom's car would have worked fine," I snorted. "But the truck works, too."

The drive back to my parents felt like it took forever, especially when Iris began to scream about twenty minutes from home.

"What's wrong?" Bram yelled frantically over the noise.

"I think she's just hungry," I called back, between shushing noises. "Just keep going. We're almost there, and then I can feed her."

Iris's face turned beet red, and the screaming continued. By the time we reached the long driveway to the house, Bram and I were wound so tightly it felt like both of us would snap at the slightest provocation.

The minute he stopped the car, I was unbuckling Iris from her seat and pulling her against my chest.

"Shhh. Good grief, sis, you're going to lose your voice at this rate," I said quietly into her ear while she sobbed.

"I'll get the stuff. You just take her inside," Bram said, opening my door and helping me out of the truck.

"Thanks for picking me up, brother."

"Of course."

I smiled at the sight of the front porch. There were pink and purple balloons tied to every single post and even the railings of the porch swing.

My mom was standing in the doorway with an odd look on her face, but I didn't pause as I moved toward her. I needed to change Iris and get a nipple in her mouth, pronto.

"Katiebear—"

"Talk while we walk, Ma. She's been screaming for the last twenty minutes."

"You have a visitor—" she began as I stopped short at the entry to the living room.

My heart began to race and I smiled gleefully. "Are the kids here?" I asked, looking between Shane and my dad, who seemed to be facing off across the room from each other. "Where are they?"

"No," Shane rasped, his eyes on Iris. "I didn't—"

"Get the fuck out," I cut in flatly, my heart sinking.

"Katie—"

"Don't call me Katie," I ordered before turning to my mom. "I'm going to feed her in my room."

I walked away.

"Kate!"

"She doesn't want to see you," I heard Bram growl behind me.

"We need to talk!"

I ignored Shane and continued to my room at the back of the house as tears fell down my face. I just wanted my kids.

* * *

"You can't ignore him forever," Anita chastised, rocking Iris back and forth while I got dressed. God, I was still swollen and tender from giving birth, and the stitches the doctor had given me itched like crazy.

"I don't want to see him."

"He should be able to see Iris, at least."

"He's seen her."

"He hasn't even held her yet."

"Yeah, well, he's a dick, and I don't want her contaminated."

"Look, I'm the first one who'd string him up in a tree out back...but shit, sis. This isn't you."

"What isn't?" I asked while gently pulling on a nursing bra. My boobs had grown even more massive, and they felt almost hot to the touch. My milk still hadn't come in, but the nurses told me that it should only be a couple of days. I hoped the girls would feel a little less like bowling balls when that happened; that shit was getting ridiculous.

"You, ignoring Shane. I know you're mad, but nothing is going to get settled if you won't even talk to him. You have no idea what he wants to say. Maybe he wants to let the kids live up here with you, but you'll have no idea if you won't even be in the same room with him."

"I highly doubt he'll let his children live with their *aunt* in another state. Get real."

"You have no idea what he wants, Katiebear. That's what I'm saying. If he sinceriously wants to work something out, don't you want to?"

"Sinceriously?"

"What?"

"That isn't even a word."

"Yes it is."

"Since when?"

"Since the hot guy from *Arrow* said it was. Stop changing the subject. He's been here for two days. You need to talk to him."

"Fine," I grumbled. "But I'm taking Iris with me."

I walked gingerly to Ani and grabbed my daughter from her aunt.

"How dare you steal that baby from her aunt!" Ani scolded.

"Really?" I asked, aghast.

"Too soon?"

"Yeah, way too soon. Asshole."

I left the room as she snickered, and I hid my smile. Anita had always been a bit rough around the edges, but she'd be the first person to have your back in a fight, whether it was physical or verbal. She came to our family so late in our childhoods that I knew she felt a little out of the loop, but I'd always considered her my sister... even when she made completely inappropriate jokes. Eventually, she'd figure that out, too.

"Kate," Shane said, standing from my parents' kitchen table.

"Et tu, Brute?" I asked my dad, who was still seated. "I didn't know you shared a table with douchebags."

"That's disgusting, Katie," my dad replied.

"Not actual douche—oh forget it." I shook my head. "What do you want, Shane?"

"I wanted to talk to you," Shane said hesitantly, his gaze darting between me and my dad.

"I'll just go find your mother," my dad announced, using his hands braced on the table to rise from his seat. "Gimme my granddaughter."

"I just got her back," I protested as he gently took her from me.

"You need to have this out," he whispered back, kissing my cheek before walking away.

"Well?" I asked, crossing my arms. "Talk."

"Kate—" Shane rubbed his hands over his scruffy face. "I thought I was doing the right thing—"

"Yeah, we're done here," I mumbled, shaking my head.

"Listen!" he snapped, jerking to his feet. "God, just listen for a second, would you?"

"What the hell else is there to say? I've given you everything, Shane," I yelled back, my hands fisting. "I took your shit like I was thankful for the fertilizer! I took care of everything so you wouldn't worry. Even when you were gone, even when you acted like you'd never known me. What the hell else could you want from me at this point?"

"I just want another chance," he answered quietly. "I just want to make things right."

"You want to make things right?" Bram scoffed from the doorway to the kitchen, startling me. I turned to find him fiddling with his phone.

He walked toward us and slid his phone across the table as my mom's voice started to play from the speakers.

"*You're doing so good, sis. Just a couple more pushes!*"

"*I can't,*" I sobbed. "*Where's Shane?*"

"*Baby, we went over this. You know Shane's not here.*"

"*I want Shane,*" I begged desperately. "*Please. Go get Shane, I want Shane. Go get him. Bram, where's Shane?*"

My mom's voice murmured something unintelligible, but it didn't seem to have an effect.

"*Please. I don't want to. I'm too tired. I want Shane. Get Shane, Mama. Please.*"

I'd closed my eyes as soon as I'd heard my pleading words, but finally opened them when the recording shut off and the kitchen was silent.

Shane was frozen, staring down at Bram's phone like it was about to explode. His face was slack and his eyes wide and filled with tears.

"Goddammit, Bram," I yelled, turning to shove him backward. "What the *fuck* is the matter with you!"

"How the fuck are you going to make that *right?*" Bram said contemptuously, stepping out of my reach to glare at Shane.

Bram looked back to me, but there was no apology in his expression. "You deserve better."

Bram reached out to touch me, but I pulled away sharply. I was so angry and embarrassed I could have hit him. He shook his head before turning on his heel and storming out of the room.

"Kate, I—" Shane's voice shook, but at that moment, I heard someone pull up in front of the house. I raised my hand to stop his words and listened carefully before walking quickly to the front door.

There was a silver mini van that I didn't recognize parked in the driveway, but the glare on the windshield hid the driver from my view. They turned off the engine but didn't climb out. Then suddenly the back door slid open and a little body was tumbling out and running for me.

"Auntie Kate!" Keller screamed. "I'm here! Auntie Kate!"

I ran across the porch, ignoring the ache between my legs, and met him at the bottom of the steps, crouching as tears rolled down my face.

"I missed you," I cried as his body hit mine—his

arms and legs wrapping around me like a vise. "Oh, buddy, I missed you so much."

"I came back," he said quietly into my ear. "I missed you too much."

"This is the best day ever," I replied, reaching out behind me to steady myself as I sat down on the bottom stair.

I looked up as my brother Alex stepped out of the car with a small smile, then walked back to the other door and opened it wide. It took a few moments before anything happened, and then first Gavin, then Sage, and finally Gunner were racing for me, rubbing their eyes and looking tired.

"Hi!" I called, laughing as I cried.

"Annie!" Gunner shouted, tripping on the gravel and climbing right up again to run, only this time sobbing from the small scratches he'd gotten on his palms. "Annie! Annie!"

Gavin and Sage reached me first, hugging me tightly, their little hands pulling at my shirt.

"Hey, hey," I crooned as they held me tight, reaching out to pull Gunner onto my lap. "It's okay, guys."

"Gavin peed in his car seat, and Uncle Alex had to cover it with a garbage bag!" Keller announced.

"It was an *anccident*!" Gavin cried back, his face turning red. "*Anccindents* happen, Keller!"

"He's right, bud," I told Keller sternly. "You wouldn't want Gavin making fun of you."

"I made you a bracelet," Sage said quietly, reaching in her pocket and pulling out a jumble of embroidery thread.

"Thanks, princess!" I reached out so she could tie it on my wrist.

"Baby?" Gunner asked abruptly in confusion, pushing on my still-squishy belly.

"Where's Iris?" Keller yelled, his head snapping back.

My face ached, I was smiling so hard, as I answered in a stage whisper, "She's in the house with Uncle Mike and Auntie Liz."

"She came out?" Gavin asked, eyes wide.

"Yep!"

The kids scrambled off me, and we turned to head toward the house—then froze.

Shane was standing outside the closed front door, completely wrecked. "You guys going to go in to see Iris?" he asked softly, looking between us, but never meeting my eyes. "You have to be really calm and quiet so you don't scare her, okay? She's really small."

The kids gave their agreement, and he pushed the door open so we could pass him. I let the children go first, but when I tried to move past, he halted me with a hand gripping my hip.

"I'm sorry, Katiebear," he leaned down and whispered in my ear. "I won't ever do it again." I stood frozen as his breath fanned over my cheek and jolted as his lips brushed over mine.

Before I could pull away, he was moving farther onto the porch and pulling the door closed between us.

"That guy loves you," Alex told me from a few feet away.

"Hey, brother," I greeted, hugging him tight. "Thank you for bringing the kids up."

"He does, you know."

"Have you seen the baby yet?" I asked, ignoring his words.

"Nah, I was waiting for you," he answered with a cheeky smile.

"She's gorgeous," I gushed, pulling him toward the family room where I was pretty sure my parents were hiding. "Bald, but I've heard that goes away at some point..."

I was giddy as I reached the family room and found my mom holding Iris while the kids crowded around, staring at her and pointing out different things. Gavin wanted to know why she was wrapped so tight, Keller wanted to take her hat off, Sage wanted to hold her, and Gunner poked gently at her face over and over again, saying "nose."

It was like Christmas and Halloween and every birthday I'd ever had all rolled together. It may have been the best moment of my life.

* * *

"If you sleep in here, Iris will wake you up," I warned Keller as the kids and I looked down at Iris, who was lying on my bed. "She has to eat a lot."

"I can make her bottles," he replied stubbornly.

There was a movie playing on the TV across the room, and while Sage and Gavin had been in and out all day, Keller and Gunner had barely left my side.

"Bedtime," Shane called, making Keller stiffen as he walked into the room. "You guys have fifteen more minutes."

"I'm sleeping in here," Keller told him mutinously. "I'm going to make Iris her bottles."

"Uh, I don't think Iris has any bottles, bud," Shane said, glancing quickly at my breasts.

"Then what does she eat?" Gavin asked me curiously, never looking away from his baby sister.

"Well, she's breast-fed," I told the kids calmly, trying to keep a straight face. I'd sneaked away during the day to feed Iris since there was no way to really do it discreetly when we were still working on her latch. I hadn't wanted to flash Alex and Dad my boobs.

"What?" Keller asked in confusion.

"Auntie Kate feeds her with her boobs!" Sage answered before I could, snickering.

"Gross!"

"Ew!"

"Goss!"

The boys' faces showed varying levels of disgust, and I couldn't stop the laughter that poured from my mouth. "It's just like animals, guys."

"That's so weird. I think she wants a bottle instead," Keller told me seriously.

"Breast-feeding is good for her, buddy," I assured him.

"Okay, time for bed," Shane called in amusement from the foot of the bed.

Gunner immediately began to cry like his heart was

breaking and scrambled into my lap, startling Iris awake and causing her to accompany his howls with her own. Suddenly my breasts felt funny.

"You wet," Gunner hiccuped after a moment, leaning against my chest. "Wet, Annie."

I looked down and felt my face flush. What an awesome time for my milk to freaking come in.

"Shit," I hissed.

"Shit," Gunner repeated.

"Come on, guys," Shane called out, trying to keep the laughter out of his voice. "Let's go."

Gavin, Sage, and Keller moved slowly off the bed, grumbling. I smiled when both boys crossed their arms over their chests in annoyance.

"I'll be right here when you wake up," I assured them over Iris's cries. "Go to sleep, and tomorrow you guys can help me give Iris a bath."

Shane herded them out of the room while I sat Gunner down next to me and reached for a tiny diaper on the bedside table.

"She's probably wet," I told him as I started pulling up her little nightgown. "She doesn't like getting her pants changed, though."

"Peen?" he asked as I whipped Iris's wet diaper off and slid the dry one under her.

"Yeah, she doesn't have one, does she? Girls don't have a penis like boys. You're a boy, and Iris is a girl."

"I didn't realize we'd be having a birds-and-bees talk with Gunner at twenty-one months old," Shane said softly from the doorway.

"Yeah, well, the little man is curious," I retorted, lifting Iris and rubbing her back.

"Want me to take him?"

Gunner was lying down by that point with the pointer and middle fingers of one hand in his mouth and his eyes drooping.

"No, he can stay in here," I answered, lying down beside him and placing Iris between us. "I still need to feed the baby, and it'll be easier for him to fall asleep if he's in here with us."

Iris began turning her face toward my chest, and my face heated as I realized Shane wasn't planning on going anywhere.

"Do you mind?" I asked in irritation, pulling at the nursing tank top I was wearing.

"Not at all," he answered with a smile, walking farther into the room.

I blocked him out as I pulled down my wet tank top and moved Iris's head toward my nipple. We weren't pros at getting her to latch right yet, but I thought she may be getting the hang of it.

The room went silent as she finally started to nurse, and I felt my entire body relax into the bed.

"Baby," Gunner murmured around his fingers, reaching out to touch Iris's head.

"You're getting to be such a big boy," I whispered back, running the tips of my fingers down his arm. "Time to sleep, monkey."

After a few minutes, he pulled his hand back and curled it into his chest, falling asleep. When it was time to put Iris on my other breast, I slid my finger into her mouth and unlatched her before sitting up.

I glanced to my side to find Shane taking a photo with his phone, which had me scrambling to cover my bare breast. I'd known he was there, but I had kind of ignored it as I'd snuggled with the babies.

"I just wanted one of Gunner and Iris," he said softly before putting the phone back in his pocket. "Here, let's get you out of that wet shirt."

He grabbed one of my camisoles off the end of the bed and moved toward me, throwing the shirt over his shoulder. "Come on, I'll help you. I know you're sore."

"I can do it," I replied, reaching for the shirt on his shoulder.

"Just—please, Kate? Just let me help you."

"Turn around," I ordered, making his shoulders slump in defeat.

"I've already seen everything," Shane mumbled once his back was turned. "So this is kind of ridiculous."

"Yeah, well, that's when I was being your doormat. No more tits for you."

He barked out a quiet laugh, and I rolled my eyes, peeling my tank top down over my hips so I didn't have to try to pull it up and over my sore breasts.

"You were never a doormat, Katie," he said seriously, turning around before I was ready. "You were—you just loved me."

I opened my mouth to reply when Iris squawked on the bed.

"I need to finish feeding her," I said, turning away

and climbing onto the bed. Iris and I seemed to work best if I was lying down and she was pulled in against me, so I lifted her up and lay between her and Gunner. When we were situated, Shane took a few steps closer to the bed and climbed in behind Iris.

"What the *fuck* do you think you're doing?" I asked in astonishment. The man must have brass balls.

"I'm not going to touch you," he assured me, his face reddening. "I just—I wanted to be close for a minute, okay? I haven't really got to see her much..."

Shane's eyes left mine and landed on the small baby lying between us. He reached out and ran his finger over the back of her neck, making her startle a little.

"She's really beautiful," he commented, his voice almost a whisper. "Some babies, well, remember Keller? Some babies are cute just because they're so small even though they look like a gremlin."

I laughed a little. Keller had been such a homely baby.

"But she's really gorgeous. She could model for baby food or something."

"Our daughter isn't modeling for anything."

"Oh hell no. I just meant, well you know, she could." His eyes met mine again. "Katie, I—"

"Don't, Shane," I cut in. "Just leave it for right now."

"I want you to come home with us."

"Shut up, Shane."

"You belong at home with us. We're your family."

"Oh, you just decided this now?" I argued, clenching

my jaw. "Kids weren't so easy when you didn't have help?"

"That's got nothing to do with—"

"Sure it does. You couldn't do it on your own, so now you're hoping that I'll come back and play nanny for you again. Fuck you." I hissed as Iris's mouth went slack and she slid off my nipple.

He reached out and grabbed my jaw firmly but gently when I tried to move away.

"I—" His words faltered as he stared at me, and his mouth opened and closed a few times before he shut his eyes in defeat. "I want you with us in San Diego," he told me as I pulled away and scooped Iris up against my chest before crawling off the bed. "The kids and I want you with us."

"Low blow," I murmured as I set Iris down in her bassinet.

"It wasn't meant to be a low blow. Christ, Kate. You want to be there, too."

"I can't go back to how it was before, Shane. You—" I closed my eyes and swallowed down the lump forming in my throat. "I had to just let you drag them away kicking and screaming."

"I won't ever do it again," he assured me, taking a step forward. "I promise."

"Yeah, well your promises mean very little to me," I replied flatly. "Can you bring Gunner into the playpen in the kids' room?"

"Yeah." He sighed and picked Gunner's limp-as-a-noodle body off the bed. "Just think about it, okay?"

I nodded and watched as he walked Gunner into the hallway. Then, overwhelmed, I crawled into bed and brought my hand to my mouth to cover my sobs.

I didn't have to think about anything. I'd follow my children to California.

I was just terrified that I'd lose what little was left of me once I was there.

Chapter 14

Kate

Do you think this is the best idea?" my mom asked as she helped me pack up Iris's clothes. "Why don't you wait a couple of weeks and then Dad and I can drive you down—"

"I don't want to be away from the kids that long," I murmured back, zipping up the diaper bag.

"Well, why don't they stay here with you? Then all of us can go—"

"Mom," I cut in, "Sage and Keller start school in four days. They need to get back to Oceanside."

"I don't see why you can't at least fly back. You're not ready for a drive that long. You just gave birth, for goodness' sake."

"Iris can't be around so many people yet. Her immune system isn't ready for that."

"Well, this is just ridiculous," she huffed, zipping one of the suitcases closed.

"Hello, hello, hello!" Anita called, walking into the room. "So you're really going, huh?"

"Yeah, we're going to leave in the morning. Early. Hopefully the kids will sleep the first couple of hours," I replied, wrapping my arms around her and dropping my forehead to her shoulder. "I'm already exhausted."

"I bet. How's my baby doing today?"

"Awesome. Dad's got her in the living room. I think he and the kids are watching a movie."

"Uh, Dad and the big kids were walking toward the creek when I got here."

I looked at her in confusion and moved around her, making my way out of the room and down the short hallway to the living room. When I got there, my heart thumped hard in my chest.

"I would have stolen her from Dad," Anita murmured, patting me on the back as she passed me.

Shane was sitting in my dad's recliner, and on his lap was Iris—completely unwrapped from her blanket and partially stripped of her clothes.

"I'm sorry," Shane blurted as I moved closer. "I was trying to follow your lead, but I—I just wanted to hold her."

"Is there a reason she's half naked?" I asked quietly as I reached them.

His face reddened as he began to clumsily press her feet back into her pajamas. "I just wanted to check things out. Count toes and all that. I hadn't really had the chance to . . . Well, I hadn't gotten a good look at her yet."

I watched but made no move to help him as he

buttoned her back up, misaligning the little snaps and having to redo them twice. He wrapped her up like a pro when he was finished, and as he pulled her close to his chest, I sat down wearily on the couch behind me.

"You hadn't held her?" I asked softly, watching him gently rub her back.

"I didn't think you wanted me to—"

"I don't mind."

"Thank you. I just miss so much with the kids, you know?" He glanced at me, and I nodded. "I don't want to miss anything else if I can help it. She's been right here, and I didn't want to piss you off, but I wanted—I needed to hold her. She probably doesn't even know who I am."

"She doesn't know who anyone is. She's four days old."

"She knows who you are," he argued.

"That's because I have the goods," I said, gesturing at my chest.

"No, she knows your voice and your smell. She instantly calms down when you have her. It's the coolest thing I've ever seen."

"You have four other children, that's not a new phenomenon."

"I know," he said softly, meeting my eyes. "Gunner did the same thing. The minute you had him, he was happy."

"Sage, Keller, and Gavin were that way with Rachel, too."

"I guess I wasn't paying attention." He gave me a sad smile and shook his head. "I didn't pay attention to a lot of shit I should have."

"You had a lot going on."

"I've had more going on in the last two years than I'd ever had before, and I still know the exact moment you walk into a room. I saw every time you blew a raspberry on Gavin's belly or helped Sage do her homework."

"You were just more aware of things because—"

"I can't keep my eyes off you," he filled in before I could say another word.

"Auntie Kate!" Sage yelled as she burst in the front door. "Keller fell in the creek!"

"Son of a bitch," I mumbled under my breath, standing up. "Where is he?"

"Grandpa's taking off his clothes outside since he's all muddy."

"Okay." I turned to Shane. "You've got her?" I asked, nodding to Iris.

"Yeah."

"Then I'm going to run a bath for Keller. He probably has mud everywhere."

Shane gave me a tender smile and a nod before turning toward Sage, who was trying to get a good look at Iris. I didn't know what that smile meant, but I didn't have time to mull it over. Keller ran into the room in his underwear, his face and arms covered in green slime and a huge smile on his face.

* * *

Late that night, I sat nursing Iris while Bram paced the floor and Alex kicked back in our dad's recliner.

"This is bullshit, Katie," Bram hissed. "You shouldn't be driving all the way to California—especially with that prick."

"He'll be careful," Alex drawled, taking a drink of his beer.

"Yeah, because he's been so careful in the past," Bram argued, turning to look at me. "You've got nothing to add?"

"You two seem like you've got it covered," I replied with a wry smile. My brothers had been having the same conversation for almost an hour, Bram getting more worked up and Alex more relaxed as time passed.

"Why are you doing this?" Bram asked, coming to a stop. "He treats you like shit, Katherine."

"Ooh, he's using your full name," Alex said in amusement.

"Shut the fuck up, Alexander."

"Calm it on down, Abraham."

"Are you guys kidding right now?" I huffed in annoyance. "You're thirty years old. Grow up."

"We're thirty-one," they both replied before turning to glare at each other.

"Exactly. Shut it already."

"You're being an idiot, Kate," Bram growled, taking a step forward.

"Leave her be, Bram," Shane said, moving into the room in nothing but a pair of sweats.

"You shut the fuck up," Bram said, pointing at Shane. "You're not a part of this conversation."

"Interesting. Sounds like I'm the *topic* of the conversation."

"I didn't beat your ass because my dad asked me not to," Bram said in warning, crossing his arms across his chest.

Even with the tension filling the room, I couldn't help the laugh that bubbled out of my mouth. I finally knew why the boys had begun crossing their arms when something pissed them off.

"What the hell are you laughing at?" Bram asked with a scowl.

"Okay, this is over," Shane stated, moving around the couch between Bram and me. "Hold her tight, baby."

I clutched Iris closer as Shane bent over and scooped her and me into his arms. He didn't flinch as Bram started ranting, just nodded at Alex—who was grinning—and carried us down the hall.

I glanced back toward my brothers as we reached my bedroom, and Alex had one hand on Bram's shoulder, his fingers gripping Bram's flannel shirt. He was saying something I couldn't hear, but whatever it was had Bram relaxing slightly and nodding.

"Your brother is insane," Shane mumbled as he kicked the door quietly closed behind us and set me on the bed.

"He's just worried about me," I replied, pulling off the irritating nursing cover I'd used when I was with my brothers.

"I'm not going to fucking hurt you," he rasped, dropping down next to me and running his hand over his head.

"You already have—that's worse in Bram's book."

His sad eyes met mine, and he barely nodded. "I'm sorry."

"Yeah, you've said that."

"I meant it."

"You always mean it, Shane," I said in exasperation as Iris finally stopped nursing with a small burp. I stood up and brought her to her bassinet, happy for a reason to step away from him.

"I'm trying, Katie." Shane's hands dropped to his lap.

"I'm not sure what you want from me." I stood in the middle of the room, my hands fisted at my sides.

"I just want you."

"Why?" I asked softly. "I already agreed to go back with you. You're getting what you wanted."

"Come here," he murmured.

"No."

He stood from the bed then, making my heart race.

"Why are we like this?" he asked, walking toward me until he'd stopped less than a foot away.

"I don't know what you mean."

"Yes you do."

"You fucked up," I whispered, my eyes filling with tears.

"I fucked up," he agreed, reaching out to cup the side of my neck in his large hand. "I won't do it again."

"That's what you said last time."

"Do you remember when you showed me your belly?" he asked, running his thumb up my throat. "You were just starting to get round, and you were nervous for me to see you."

I nodded, swallowing hard.

"I thought, *No one has ever been more beautiful than she is at this moment.*" He lifted his other hand to trace his fingers down the side of my face.

I scoffed. "I did my hair and put on makeup when I knew we'd be Skyping. I usually looked like shit."

"You got gussied up for me?" he asked with a small smile.

"You don't get it. That wasn't me. I don't wear makeup. I hate doing my hair, and usually I don't have time for that crap anyway." I tried to pull away, but the hand on my face dropped to wrap around my back and keep me close.

"I see you," he murmured, the smile never leaving his face. "You were even more gorgeous in the hospital after having Iris."

I startled. "What?" I hadn't seen him at the hospital.

A dark look crossed over his face, erasing his smile. "I got there as soon as I could, and you were sleeping. You were still a little bit sweaty—" I grimaced, remembering how gross I'd been.

"Your face was swollen, and you had these little red

dots on your cheeks." He reached up and ran a finger under my eyes. "You looked exhausted."

"I was."

"I've never seen a woman look more beautiful in my entire life."

"I looked disgusting," I argued.

"No. You looked like you'd just given birth to my daughter."

My heart raced, and I finally took a step back out of his arms. "What are you doing?"

"What do you mean?"

"You can't—I can't keep doing this with you," I cried quietly. "You have to stop doing this to me."

He looked at me in confusion, "Kate? What—"

"Get out of my room," I rasped, backing toward the bed. "I'll see you in the morning."

"What's wrong?" he asked, taking a step forward. "What did I do?"

"I'm going to California to be with the kids, but I think you're confused," I snapped, raising my hand to stop his forward momentum. "I'm not playing this fucked-up game with you anymore. I'm not some sort of fill-in wife for you—taking care of your house and handing out a random blow job. I'm not Rachel—"

"Don't bring her into this," he ordered, coming to an abrupt halt.

"Get out."

"Kate—"

"I'll see you in the morning, Shane," I said firmly,

staring at him until he spun on his heel and left the room.

I sagged onto the bed once he was gone, my hands shaking. A part of me felt good that I'd finally made a stand, but the rest of me was terrified that I'd made things worse between us. He was saying the right things, and God, he could be so sweet...but it never took long before he was making me feel like shit again, and I couldn't do that anymore.

Things had felt so simple while he'd been gone. He'd become my best friend, listening to my ramblings and flirting with me all the time, but that wasn't real life. I was almost thirty years old, and I had children to think of. Losing my mind over Shane was no longer an option.

* * *

After I'd kissed my parents and brothers good-bye at four a.m., we were on our way south. Thankfully, Uncle Mike, Aunt Ellie, and Trevor had said their good-byes the day before so we'd been able to leave without stopping by their house.

The kids were cranky, we were stuffed into the new rental van like sardines, and I knew before long Iris would be screaming. We were barely an hour into the drive, and I was already dreading the next two days of travel.

Thankfully, the van came with a built-in DVD system that would distract the kids for a while, but I knew that it wouldn't last. For children as busy as mine, sitting in a car for two days would be torture, especially when they'd made the drive less than a week before. I wasn't sure how Alex had survived the drive north.

"How're you feeling?" Shane asked softly, even though the kids were all wearing headphones.

"I'm fine." I stared out the window as the sun began to rise. I was already both bored and on edge, waiting for the baby to wake up.

"What's Iris's last name?" he said abruptly.

I twisted to look at him. His hands were tight on the wheel, but he kept glancing at me as he waited for my answer.

"I wasn't sure what you—" I mumbled.

"Evans?" he asked, his shoulders drooping.

"No," I replied softly. "Anderson."

He nodded, staring straight ahead as he swallowed hard. "Thank you."

"Iris Rachel Anderson."

"Good choice. She would have loved that," he said, rubbing his hand over the bottom half of his face.

"Probably not, seeing as how I fucked her husband," I replied drily. "Not sure she'd be crazy about that."

He choked out a laugh and looked at me like I was crazy. "I had a hard time with that at first," he said as he switched lanes, pulling onto the freeway. "Shit, the guilt was intense."

"Yeah, I remember." I turned to look back out the window.

"It took a long time for me to figure it out," he said before going silent.

I didn't want to play into it. I knew he was trying to draw me into conversation, and I wanted to ignore him, but I still asked. "Figure what out?"

"That Rachel doesn't give a shit," he said bluntly, checking the rearview mirror to make sure the kids were still occupied. "I miss her. Christ, sometimes when one of the kids does something funny, or Sage smiles, I think that I'll never stop missing her."

I nodded, pulling my sweatshirt over my suddenly freezing arms.

"But she's gone, Katie. She's never coming back. And she doesn't give two shits about what I'm doing now."

"Shane—" My voice stopped working. I didn't even know what to say. Did I agree with him? Mostly. I thought wherever Rachel was, she probably cared very much what Shane was doing, but not in the way he'd meant it. Rachel had loved Shane; she'd want him to be happy and safe. I didn't think jealousy was an emotion that followed you into the afterlife.

"Don't you think it was hard for me?" I finally asked, breaking the silence.

"I didn't know how you felt, Kate," he said seriously. "You never said a word."

"What could I have said, Shane?" I asked imploringly. "You didn't want anything to do with me. Should I have told you how bad I felt when you were already so intent on blaming me for everything?"

"I apologized for that."

"You may have apologized for being an ass, but that didn't mean that you were okay with the situation," I argued.

"What do you want me to say, Kate? Tell me, and I'll say it. I felt guilty. I hadn't been with anyone but Rachel in over ten years, and then suddenly I'm fucking you into a hotel mattress. I was a little overwhelmed."

"Yeah, well, join the club," I retorted. "I didn't treat you like shit."

"If I could go back and change things, I would," he said, sighing and leaning back into the seat. "I would have handled it better."

"I don't think either of us handled things very well."

"Don't, Kate."

"I was too busy reliving all that sexing in my head," I said with a satisfied hum.

"Can you be serious for a goddamn minute?"

"Who said I wasn't being serious?"

He scoffed and went silent. A few minutes later, Iris began to fuss.

* * *

"We're home," I told my mom, flopping onto the bench in the backyard. The trip back to California had taken three days of stopping every couple of hours for potty breaks, lunch breaks, and just-because breaks. It had been the longest three days of my life. "I'm never making that drive again."

"How are you feeling?" she asked with a chuckle. "How did the kids do?"

"They hated every second, and by the time we passed Six Flags, I was ready to jump out of the van while it was going eighty down the freeway."

"And Shane?"

"He was fine. Surprisingly patient. He just left to take the van back to the rental place."

"Did you two work anything out?"

"There's nothing to work out."

"Katherine," she said in warning.

"We're getting along, Mom. Okay?" I huffed and rocked Iris's car seat with my foot as she began to stir. "I'm too tired to worry about anything else at the moment."

"You two need to—"

"Mom!" I hissed, rubbing the tension from my neck. "Drop it."

"Fine," she grumbled. "I think Bram is ready to move to California."

"He's being a jackass."

"He's just worried about you."

"Why can't he be more like Alex?"

"Don't compare your brothers. That's not fair to either of them."

"Crap." I let my head fall back until my face was raised to the sky. "I know, it's just frustrating."

"Yeah, well he and Anita got into it right after you left."

"What? Why? Keller, stay out of the pool!"

"Who knows with those two? They're like oil and water. Alex finally threw Ani over his shoulder and carried her out of the house."

"Why didn't you stop them?"

"You know we've always tried to let you kids argue your own problems out."

"They're adults."

"All the more reason to leave them be," she murmured.

"Crap, Mom. I gotta go. Gunner just put something in his mouth." I stood from my seat and tossed my phone to the bench, yelling for Gunner to spit out whatever it was. Just as I reached him, he spit out a clod of dirt and started crying.

"Everything okay?" Shane asked, carrying Sage outside, her skinny legs wrapped around his waist.

"Yeah," I huffed, picking Gunner up. "Gunner put dirt in his mouth, and now he's regretting it."

I walked Gunner back toward the house, but stopped when Shane reached out with his free arm to stop me.

"It's almost bedtime," he said softly, wiping a frustrated tear from my cheek. "I'll do baths, okay?"

"I'm fine. I just need to—" I didn't want him stepping in. What the hell was I doing there if I wasn't taking care of the kids?

"I'll do baths, Katie," he said firmly, before yelling for the boys.

Iris chose that moment to wake up screaming, and I gave in without another word. I just needed one day to get my legs under me. I'd feel better by the morning.

* * *

"I'm sorry," I said, cringing as Shane stepped into my
room and closed the door behind him late that night. "I
don't know why she's doing this—she hasn't done this
before."

Tears were pouring down my cheeks as I paced back
and forth. Iris had been screaming for a full twenty minutes by then, but it felt like hours. I had no idea what
to do with her. I'd fed her, changed her diaper, and
wrapped her tightly just the way she liked it. There was
absolutely no reason for her to be so fussy.

"Did you get any sleep?" he asked, his voice so low I
nearly missed his words.

"Yeah, about an hour before she had to eat again. She
wouldn't let me put her in her bed so I just kept holding her," I said on a sob. I was so freaking tired.

"Come here," he said gently, reaching for Iris. "Have
you tried a binky?"

"I—she hasn't ever had one."

"Do you have any?" he asked, gently rocking Iris as
she screamed.

"I think maybe in her suitcase. My mom got her a
couple when we were at the hospital." I threw open
the suitcase and dug through it, finally pulling out a
couple of pacifiers in a plastic bag. "She even sterilized
them."

"Hand me one," he said quietly, reaching toward me.

It took a few minutes of him teasing Iris with the
binky before she sucked it into her mouth, and I

breathed a sigh of relief as the room grew silent. My eyes were scratchy and heavy from all the crying I'd been doing, and it took all I had not to reach up and rub at them like a little kid.

"Climb in bed," Shane crooned, looking at Iris but speaking to me.

I crawled onto the bed, sighing as I relaxed. A few moments later, Shane was cracking open the door and shutting off the light, leaving us in near darkness. I turned onto my side and curled my bottom arm under my pillow as he set Iris against the front of my body.

I stopped breathing when he walked around the bed and crawled in behind me.

"I know things with us aren't—" He sighed and scooted his body forward until he was spooning me. "I don't want to sleep without you anymore."

"This isn't a good idea," I whispered back, staring at the sliver of light coming through my bedroom door.

"Just sleep, baby," he said gently, smoothing my hair off my face and neck. "She'll be ready to eat again soon. Sleep for a little while."

I didn't think I'd be able to fall asleep with his warm body behind me, but it was only minutes before I was completely passed out.

"Shhh," I woke to hear Shane whispering near the end of my bed. "Daddy's going to just change your diaper so you're all clean before you eat. You don't want to eat your breakfast in wet drawers, do you?"

I opened my eyes slightly and looked down to see

Shane trying to wrangle Iris into a clean diaper. He wasn't having a very easy time of it as she squirmed and flexed her legs.

"Come on, sis. We can do this. I need your mama to be happy with me. Help me out a little, would you?"

I snorted, and Shane's head popped up. When he met my eyes, his face flushed. "How long have you been awake?"

"Not long," I rasped back, groggily. "My boobs are hard as rocks."

"Yeah, she slept for almost four hours. She must have worn herself out last night," Shane said, carrying Iris to me.

I fiddled with the little snap on the front of my tank top and blearily pulled down one side as Iris began to squawk. My eyes were still barely open as he laid her down next to me, and I startled as I felt a cool fingertip run over my nipple.

"They're darker," Shane said roughly as he turned Iris toward me.

"Like a bull's-eye," I mumbled, finally using one arm to situate Iris and get her nursing.

Shane barked out a quiet laugh, and I smiled. In the hazy place between sleep and wakefulness, everything was right in the world.

"She looks like you," he murmured, running his finger over Iris's cheek. "Her eyes and her nose."

"She's got your skin," I said back, closing my tired eyes. Four hours hadn't been enough sleep.

After a little while, I woke back up to Shane

disengaging Iris from my nipple and instructing me to turn over. After a little maneuvering, I was on my opposite side, and Iris was once again nursing.

"It's okay, baby," Shane said as I tried to keep my eyes open. "Just sleep."

"You'll stay?" I asked as I relaxed my head into the pillow.

"I'm not going anywhere," he answered as I fell back asleep with Iris's tiny little fingers digging into the skin of my breast.

* * *

"I'm awake," I mumbled as Sage came barreling into my room the next morning.

"Daddy's making breakfast," she told me excitedly, climbing onto the bed. "And Gunner pooped while he was sleeping. It got everywhere. So disgusting."

"Are you happy to be home, Sage the Rage?" I asked, pulling her closer and wrapping my arms around her.

"Yeah, now that you're here."

"Your dad was just trying to do what he thought was best," I said, giving her a squeeze. "You know that, right?"

"Yeah, but it sucked."

"I agree, kiddo."

"Hey, Auntie Kate?" she said softly.

"Yeah, princess?"

"Who's Iris's dad?"

My breath caught in my throat as I was blindsided

by her question. It had been months since any of the kids had mentioned Iris's dad, but I shouldn't have assumed I'd have more time. Sage was almost nine—she wouldn't be held off with bullshit much longer.

"I'm Iris's dad," Shane said cautiously from the doorway, holding the girl we'd been discussing. "But you probably figured that out, huh?"

He made his way into the room and sat down next to us.

"Yeah, I thought so," Sage said calmly. "You act like her dad."

"Well, I can't help that," Shane said with a small smile.

"Whatcha thinkin', Sage?" I asked after she'd been quiet for a few minutes.

"Are you going to get married?"

"No," I answered decisively before Shane could speak. His teeth snapped shut, and I could see the muscle in his jaw tensing.

"Can I tell Keller?"

"Uh, I guess so," I mumbled, becoming more uncomfortable by the second.

Sage scrambled off the bed and ran for the door before turning back with a weird look on her face. "So Iris is my sister."

"Yes," Shane replied firmly.

"Awesome," Sage said back, doing a little dance before running into the hallway.

"Keller's going to have questions," I mumbled, sitting up in bed.

"Probably."

"What will we tell him?" I asked, fidgeting.

Shane's eyes met mine. "That I'm Iris's dad and you're her mom. It's simple, Katie. He doesn't need any more than that."

"He's going to be confused," I argued.

"I think he'll understand far more than you give him credit for."

We went silent as we heard the sound of multiple little feet stomping up the stairs. Sage had obviously shared the news. I braced myself for the onslaught.

Chapter 15
Shane

I pushed myself harder as I ran past the gas station a few miles from our house, and cursed under my breath as one of my earbuds fell out of my ear.

I didn't have time to slow down as I pulled it back up. Kate was home with all the kids, and I'd hated the look she'd given me as I walked out the front door. She was exhausted—with good reason—and I knew she was dreading the fact that I had to be at work early the next morning. I'd taken as much time as I could, but duty called—at least for the next two weeks.

I had to go back in and get squared away before I could take my post-deployment leave. There was no getting around it, as much as I hated it. My commanding officer had been lenient as hell when I'd told him what was going on, but his patience only went so far.

My stomach clenched as I thought of what Kate

had been through in the last week—hell, the last few months. I'd been so caught up in my own shit—how *I* was feeling—I'd completely neglected the only woman who had ever loved me more than my foster mother.

Christ, when Bram had slid that video of Kate across the table, I'd honestly thought I was going to pass out. I'd been so horrible to her, treating her like she didn't matter when that was the farthest thing from the truth—and yet she'd still called for me. She'd needed me, and I'd been in San Diego, acting like a self-righteous douche. God, when I'd realized that Gunner was asking for marshmallows and not calling Kate "Mama," I'd wanted to sink through the floor in shame, but I'd thought it too late for me to change my course.

Bram asked me how I thought I'd make that right. I couldn't. I knew that there was no way to take back or make up for the shit I'd put her through. The agony on her face as she cried gave me nightmares.

I shook my head and turned around, working my way back toward the house. I couldn't change the past, but hell if I didn't want to be what Kate needed now. I wanted to make sure she was eating and getting enough rest. I wanted to take the boys outside so she could have a few moments to herself and cook breakfast so she didn't have to get out of bed.

For the first time in my life, I wanted to take on more so that she would have less to do.

It killed me that I'd never felt like that when it came

to Rachel. I'd come to the conclusion, sometime in my marriage, that because I'd been bringing home a paycheck and working outside the house, it was Rachel's responsibility to take care of our children. It wasn't as if I'd never helped—I had...when I had the time. But I hadn't made it a priority, and because she'd never spoken up, I hadn't realized how hard that must have been for her.

Or maybe it hadn't been as hard for Rachel as it was for Kate. Rachel had three children and a best friend who'd apparently dropped everything to help when she was feeling overwhelmed. Kate had five children and no one to depend on but an asshole that she didn't trust to help her. She watched me with suspicion every time I pitched in with the kids, and I was so ashamed that I pretended like I didn't see it.

I crawled into bed with her at night like a puppy begging for attention, ignoring the way she stiffened up each time until finally falling into an exhausted sleep.

Kate was the most forgiving person I'd ever met, and I felt nauseous when I remembered all the times she should have cut me from her life.

"What are you doing?" Rachel giggled as I rubbed my lips over her neck.

We were a few yards back from the bonfire the boys and I had built on the back edge of the property. For the first time in over a year, all of the Harris and Evans kids were home from various military bases and school, and we'd decided to celebrate with beer and a fire.

"Kissing you," I murmured, running my lips up her jaw. Shit, she was the hottest girl I'd ever seen, and I'd been fantasizing about getting into her pants since she'd arrived with Kate two days before. They'd been damn near connected at the hip until tonight, and as soon as Kate had run back to the house for their sweatshirts, I'd pounced.

"I thought you and Kate—" she murmured in protest, but completely contradicted herself by dropping her head back to give me better access to her neck.

"What about me and Kate?" I asked distractedly as I saw Anita and Kate coming through the trees. I was going to be pissed as hell if Katie had been telling this girl a bunch of lies.

"She talks about you all the time," Rachel said as I slid my hands down to her ass. "I thought maybe—"

I cut off her words as Kate and Anita reached the tree line a few feet from us. "There's nothing between Kate and me," I said against her mouth as Kate came to an abrupt stop and our eyes met. "She has a thing for me, but I've never been into her."

I pressed my lips against Rachel's, moaning when she slid her tongue into my mouth. My eyes never left Kate's—even as she stopped Anita from storming toward us.

Kate moved toward the fire with tears rolling down her face, and I closed my eyes relishing the way Rachel's hips had started rolling against mine.

As far as I knew, Kate had never said a bad word to Rachel about me. Within six months, I'd talked Rachel into moving to San Diego with me, and a few months after that we'd gotten married. I'd ignored

Kate when she'd moved down after us—a little worried that she'd come for me—but she'd never said a word. After the first couple of years, my wariness had turned to apathy, and the fact that Kate seemed to hang out with Rachel whenever I wasn't around had no longer bothered me.

If she'd planned on telling Rachel what a dick I'd been, I'd assumed she would have before the wedding.

I'd ignored her presence in our lives for years, tuned out every conversation when Rachel had tried to mention her, and pretended like she didn't even exist.

Looking back, I couldn't fathom how I'd done it. Kate fucking lit up a room. She was so happy and just fucking fun. I wasn't sure how I'd ignored her for so long.

I tried really hard not to compare her and Rachel. That wasn't a fair thing to do—but I couldn't help but notice the differences between the women.

Where Rachel was reserved, Kate was outgoing. Where Rachel was willing to sit with the kids through a Disney movie, Kate was there with snacks and all the makings of a blanket fort. Rachel never told me if something was wrong, instead preferring to work shit out herself or completely distance herself from me until I figured out what I'd done wrong and fixed it. Kate told me straight out if something was bothering her, and then moved on, almost too quickly for me to rectify anything.

What little relationship I had with Kate was so incredibly different from what I had with Rachel that I had a hard time keeping up. Kate just kept coming back. I loved that about her. She was so tenacious when she cared about someone.

I also hated that about her. I hated that I'd been such a fucking dick, and I hated that she'd *let* me.

For the past couple of nights when I'd lain down beside her, after she'd fallen asleep and I knew she couldn't hear me, I'd promised her that she'd never have to forgive me again if she could do it one last time.

I finally finished my run and walked the last quarter mile back to our house. Oddly, Miles's Jeep was parked in my driveway.

"I'm home," I called out as I opened the front door. I walked through the house when no one answered and found Kate and Miles sitting at the patio table laughing and watching the kids play.

My stomach turned, but as I reached for the handle of the sliding glass door, I paused. I smelled like ass.

I turned and ran up the stairs two at a time, throwing my clothes off as soon as I'd reached my room. After a fast shower, I threw on some basketball shorts and a T-shirt, not even bothering with boxers. I wanted to get outside and figure out what the fuck Kate had been laughing at.

As I hit the hallway, I heard Iris fussing in Kate's room. She'd left her in the fucking house?

"It's okay, princess," I called softly, walking through the open doorway to find Iris jerking her arms and legs furiously in her bassinet. "Did Mama leave you all alone in here?"

I picked her up out of bed and rubbed her back for a minute while she hiccuped.

"Daddy's here," I murmured against her bald head, rocking her from side to side. "Let's get that wet diaper off you."

I laid her on the bed and grabbed a diaper from the top of Kate's dresser, talking the whole time. "I don't know what your mommy was thinking, leaving my princess in here all alone," I crooned, my voice somehow keeping Iris calm. "She's outside with your brothers and sister and Daddy's friend Miles. He's a jackass. You stay away from him, okay?"

I smiled as Iris froze, like she was listening intently.

"Daddy was not very nice," I said, pulling her little pants down her legs and unbuttoning her onesie. "I wasn't even there when you were born, and I'm really sorry about that. But your mama came home with me anyway, so that means there's a chance, right? As long as Miles keeps his you-know-what in his pants."

Iris lifted her hand to her face and tried really hard to get it to her mouth, her eyes unfocused as I babbled.

"You're doing so good, princess. Look at you, not even crying while I change you. Such a big girl." I finished re-dressing her and pulled her to my chest. "You think your mama could love me again?" I asked, kissing her little cheek. "Probably not, huh? We'll just have to keep working at it so you can live with Daddy forever."

I sighed and grabbed the dirty diaper from the bed, leaving the room. I walked slowly down the stairs, relishing the few minutes I had Iris to myself. With so many people in the house and Iris connected to Kate's breast half the time, I hadn't had much time with her one-on-one.

I tossed the diaper in the trash and nonchalantly strolled outside with her, only to find Kate and Miles staring straight at me.

I froze, trying to figure out what they were staring at—I knew I'd put on pants—until Kate lifted her hand up.

Holding a fucking baby monitor.

Miles cleared his throat. "Congratulations, jackass," he said quietly, letting me know that they'd heard every word I said.

Son of a bitch. My face and neck suddenly felt like they were on fire.

* * *

"I wouldn't leave Iris in here by herself," Kate said softly that night as I crawled into bed behind her. "And I'd never take her away from you."

I didn't reply. What could I say?

"I can't be some sort of stand-in for Rachel," she whispered, making my heart sink to my stomach. "I'm not her. I don't want to be her." She sniffled, and I moved closer, silently wrapping my arm around her waist. "I want to be me."

"That's not what I'm doing, Katie," I murmured, pulling her back into my chest. "I just want a chance."

"A chance to what, Shane? A chance to sleep with

me? A chance for another blow job? I'm already the mom—I'm already doing that part. So what exactly do you want?"

"I want to be with you." I stumbled over my words, my thoughts becoming more jumbled the longer I tried to verbalize them.

I just wanted her. Even without the kids, I'd want her. The kids just made that bond a million times stronger. I wanted her to look at me the way she'd looked at me when we were stupid teenagers—like I could do anything. I wanted to see all the changes that carrying Iris had done to her body. I wanted to map her curves with my fingers and know when she was about to start her period because I'd been with her so long that I could recognize the signs. I wanted the little things and the big things.

But she'd never believe me if I tried to tell her that.

I'd pushed her aside for so long that there was no foundation to build on. Just a mess of shattered pieces that I'd crushed with a sledgehammer every time she'd grown closer than I was comfortable with.

I didn't know how to be with someone like Kate. She'd demand more from me than anyone ever had before, and that was terrifying. Because even though the history between us had proven that she wasn't going anywhere, I'd learned over the course of my life that people left.

"You want a housewife, and I'm convenient," she whispered, shaking her head against her pillow. "You don't even have to marry me. I'm already here. You know that Iris and I aren't going anywhere. Why search for anyone else when you've got a—"

"Don't finish that sentence," I growled, her words making my blood boil. "Easy? You're the least convenient person I've ever fucking met."

I pulled away from Kate and pushed her onto her back so I could climb on top of her, straddling her waist. I leaned down until our noses were almost touching.

"I don't know what I'm doing, Kate," I said softly, searching her eyes. "But I know that I want you. *Help me.*"

"I've been helping you since we were kids, Shane," she replied, with a weary shrug. "I just don't think I have anything left."

"You do," I whispered, leaning down on my elbows so I could brush my lips across hers. "You do. I know you do."

"I'm terrified that I'm going to wake up one day and you're going to take them again," she confessed in a shaky voice. "That you're going to decide you want someone else and there'll be no more room for me."

"No, Katie," I said harshly, gripping her head between my hands. "That won't happen."

"How can you know that?" she argued, her eyes filling with tears. "That's what you did less than two weeks ago."

My forehead dropped to hers, and I inhaled a shaky breath. "That wasn't what happened. There's no one but you, Kate."

She closed her eyes, and tears leaked out of the corners. "I can't trust you."

"I thought I was doing the right thing," I whispered frantically, kissing her face while she lay passively beneath me. "It wasn't you. It was me. I was being selfish. I wanted them with me, and I fucked everything up."

"That's the thing," she replied, defeat lacing her words. "You have that power. I have no rights when it comes to the kids, and at any point you could erase me as if I never existed."

"I wouldn't. I thought you'd follow behind us, Kate. *I swear.* I thought it was only for a little while until you could have Iris. I never planned—"

"I don't believe you."

Her words slapped me in the face. She still wasn't looking at me, and I hated that she was blocking me out that way. I was surrounding her, my body pressed against her from all sides, and she'd still found a way to keep herself distant.

"I'll prove it to you," I said resolutely.

Her eyes slowly opened, and I caught a glimpse of the Katie I'd used to know before her eyes once again took on the haunted look she'd had since Iris was born.

"Please do," she whispered back softly, her hand lifting to rest on my ribs. "I don't know what I'll do if you don't."

Both of us were breathing raggedly as I leaned down and pressed my lips to hers, tentatively sliding my tongue between her parted lips.

It was the first time I'd really kissed her in over six months, and within seconds I was hard as a rock. My mind knew that we would go no farther, but the rest of my body seemed to chant *Kate, Kate, Kate* as she slowly slid her hand up my chest and wrapped her fingers around the front of my throat. I wasn't sure why she did it, but the movement both turned me on and oddly centered me.

I finally pulled away as Iris began to fuss in her bed, and I immediately felt guilty for keeping Kate awake when she should have been sleeping. "I'll get her," I said, leaning back down to suck Kate's lip into my mouth one more time before crawling off the bed.

When I reached Iris, I couldn't help but glance back at Kate.

She was lying on her side again, a small sleepy smile on her face while she waited for me to bring her the baby. One half of her nursing tank top was already unsnapped and gaping at the top, and at some point while I was on top of her, the blankets had been pushed down past her hips, giving a glimpse of the flannel pajama bottoms she wore to bed and the soft belly above them.

I didn't care if it took the rest of my life to prove to her that I wasn't going anywhere—as long as she would let me roll over in the middle of the night and see her looking exactly the way she did then.

* * *

The next morning, I climbed out of bed before my alarm went off, anxious to get away from Kate.

She was killing me, and kissing her the night before had left me with an erection that would go down just enough for me to fall asleep and grow hard again as I started to dream. It was insane.

I made it into my old bedroom and stripped off my shorts in a hurry before sitting on the edge of the bed and fisting my erection.

Ah, God, I was so hard I ached.

I probably should have gone to the shower to take care of business, but I hadn't wanted to wait long enough for the water to heat up. I'd needed to come six hours before. I couldn't wait any longer.

I closed my eyes as I thought about the way Kate's body had grown more curvy and round since she'd had Iris, panting as I imagined fucking her tits like I had the first night we'd been together.

My breath caught and I held back a moan as my cock jerked.

"Shane, are you—"

I didn't see Kate come in but my eyes snapped open as she stuttered and clicked the door closed behind her.

"Oh, shit," she breathed, glancing down at my hand and then back up to my eyes, her face flushing.

I should have stopped. That would have been the decent thing to do after getting caught. But I couldn't force myself to stop pulling hard on my shaft—not when she was standing there in a white tank top that hid nothing, watching. Instead, I gripped myself harder and moved my hand faster, almost instantly feeling my balls draw up as her nipples hardened beneath her shirt and her hands fisted at her sides.

I watched her lick her lips, and just like that my

orgasm hit, tightening my leg and ass muscles as semen coated my hand.

If I hadn't been watching Kate's face, I would have missed the low noise she made and the way her eyes grew heated as she watched me move. Because as soon as I'd finished, she was fleeing back out the door and slamming it behind her.

Fuck.

Chapter 16

Kate

Time passes quickly when you're so busy you can barely see straight, and before I knew it I had a fourth grader, a kindergartner, a four-year-old, a two-year-old, and a two-month-old.

It was exhausting in the best possible way. As Iris got a little older, I felt more and more like my old self, and I'd even started getting reacquainted via email with my old business contacts. I thanked God every day that I'd saved up during Shane's deployment because the minute I'd gone on bed rest, I'd had to send emails to all my clients giving them the contact information for other web designers I trusted. I hadn't been able to work in months, and though I'd been frugal, my savings were getting low.

I wasn't sure that I was ready to go back to work yet—we were still trying to find our sea legs—but I knew that eventually we'd figure out a schedule and I'd have a little extra time on my hands.

I sang to Iris as I put her into her baby swing that I'd pulled into the kitchen, then spun on my heel to grab Gunner off the floor and dance him around the kitchen table. I was in a ridiculously good mood. I couldn't help it.

It was Friday night, homework was done, the big kids were playing on the Wii, Gunner had taken a three-hour nap that left him almost giddy, and I was ready to make homemade pizzas for my family as the sun shone through the kitchen window.

I sang, swaying Gunner from side to side as he giggled.

I got to the chorus right as Shane walked in the door from the garage, and I couldn't help but laugh as Gunner threw his hands straight up in the air and yelled, "Daddy!"

Shane smiled as I continued to sing, his eyes soft on my face. "Beautiful," he mouthed silently, never looking away from my face as the older kids stormed into the kitchen.

I blushed and broke eye contact, spinning Gunner around in a circle.

Shane and I seemed to be dancing around each other, pushing and pulling as we found our new normal. We'd never lived together before, which seemed odd when I thought about it. I'd given birth to his child and we'd been circling each other for a year, yet bumping into him in the bathroom each morning was new and a little embarrassing.

He was trying so hard to get back into my good

graces that it was a little bit endearing. He pitched in with the kids, and ran baths for me after the big kids were asleep, taking care of Iris so I could have a few minutes of quiet. He told me I was beautiful, sometimes when all I felt like was a big blob of human.

I loved that he was trying, but I couldn't help but feel like he'd missed what I was trying to tell him. I wasn't mad at him—not anymore. No, it went deeper than that. I loved Shane, I'd always loved him, even when I could have strangled him. But there was a bone-deep weariness inside me that I couldn't seem to shake.

It was as if, no matter how hard I tried, I couldn't get past the fear that he would leave me again and take the kids with him. I didn't think I'd survive it.

So I held him at arm's length, even though I saw how it wore on him. I couldn't let him bridge that distance no matter how much I wished he would.

We were at a stalemate, both aching for the same thing, but unable to reach it.

"Kids, in the living room while Auntie Kate makes dinner," Shane called out after the kids had told him all about their days. Poor Gavin had very little to contribute past the large spider he'd found on the outside wall of the house.

I set Gunner on his feet and watched him run clumsily after his brothers and sister before turning to look at Shane. "Pizza sound okay?"

"Pizza sounds great," he answered huskily, making my heart thump. "Come here."

I shook my head silently as his mouth pulled up in a small grin. He nodded back, taking a step toward me.

"I have to start dinner," I mumbled, frozen to the spot.

"You can wait ten minutes."

"The kids are—" He reached me before I could finish my sentence, and suddenly I was pulled tightly against his chest.

"Ouch," I hissed, pulling back.

"What's wrong?" he asked in confusion as I lifted my hands to cover my breasts.

"Iris hasn't wanted to eat in, like, three hours," I told him with a shake of my head. "I'm just a little...full."

"I'll be careful." He spun me around so we were both facing the kitchen window and began to sway from side to side. "I want to dance with my woman."

"Your woman?" I snorted.

"My baby-mama?" he asked with a small chuckle.

"That works." My breath caught as his arms shifted from my hips to wrap around the front of me.

"I love it when you sing to the kids," he whispered in my ear, making goose bumps pop out on my neck. "It's one of my favorite things."

"You have a list?" I asked breathily as his thumb began to sweep back and forth across the bottom of my breast.

"Mmhmm," he hummed before he began to sing softly in my ear.

"My voice leaves a lot to be desired," he said sheepishly after he'd finished singing the first verse, holding me tighter as I tried to turn and look at him. "Nothing like yours."

"I liked it."

"Liar." He chuckled, letting me go.

"I did," I insisted, spinning to face him.

"I'm going to go shower," he said uncomfortably, making me laugh.

"You blush like a little girl," I needled him, jumping when he took a step back toward me.

"I don't blush," he argued.

"Oh, yeah, you do. You turn red like a tomato."

I screeched as he moved for me and laughed hysterically as he chased me around the table.

"Get her!" Keller yelled, running into the room.

"Whoa!" Shane yelped, grabbing my hips and thrusting me behind him before Keller could barrel into me. "No roughhousing with Auntie Kate tonight, okay, bud?"

"Ah man!"

"I know. Dad shouldn't have chased her," Shane replied seriously, glancing over his shoulder to flash me a devious smile. "I'm going to shower. Why don't you see if there's anything you can help Auntie Kate with?"

Shane reached behind him and gave my hip a light swat before sauntering out of the kitchen. I stared at his ass until I couldn't see it anymore. *Shit.*

I shook my head and smiled down at Keller, who was watching me with a weird expression on his face.

* * *

"Holy shit," I moaned in the shower later that night. The kids were finally in their beds for the night, and Iris had passed out after nursing a little bit right after dinner. It had been hours since then, and when I'd talked to the advice nurse—who knew me by name after all the times I'd called about Gunner—she'd assured me that Iris could go longer than two hours between feedings.

Unfortunately, my breasts didn't get that memo. They were rock-hard and hurt so bad I was in tears. I'd pulled out my breast pump, took one look at it, and realized that that thing wasn't getting anywhere near the girls when they hurt so bad. According to the nurse, a warm shower was the next best thing, so I'd hopped in and let the hot water run down my body in an attempt to get them to express some milk and give me a little relief. It didn't seem to be helping.

"Kate?" Shane called, startling me. I hissed when one of my arms brushed the side of my breast. God, it was agony.

"Yeah?" I called out shakily.

"You've been in here awhile, baby. Everything okay?" His voice was getting closer.

"Yeah, I'll be out in a minute," I called back.

He must have heard something in my voice because, within seconds, he was pushing the curtain back a little and slipping his head inside the steamy shower. "What's wrong?"

I turned toward him and bit the inside of my cheek as his eyes widened.

"Jesus Christ!" he said. "What the fuck?"

"Iris isn't hungry," I sniffled. "They hurt so bad."

He popped back outside the curtain and, within moments, was climbing into the shower naked and staring at my breasts.

"Take a good look," I joked, pointing at the girls. "You'll never see them this perky again." The last word was almost a sob, I was so miserable.

"God, they look—"

"Hideous," I cut in, nodding. The blue veins in my breasts were vivid against the paleness of my skin. It looked like I'd drawn them on with a sharp crayon, giving them a slightly raised look.

"Painful," he corrected softly. "Did you talk to the nurse?"

"She said to take a hot shower," I answered in frustration, jerking back when he raised his hand to touch me. "It's obviously not working. You may want to leave while you can. I haven't shaved in—God, I don't even know—and pretty soon these babies are going to completely explode, leaving blood and milk spatter all over the bathroom."

"I'm pretty sure they won't explode," he said in horrified amusement.

"I don't think I'll even be able to get Iris latched at this point. They're going to stay this way forever." I shook my head. "And I'm getting this awful sense of déjà vu. Haven't we been here before?"

"Wrong shower," he replied seriously. "And last time you vomited on my feet."

"You're welcome," I said drily. "God, this is embarrassing."

"No, the vomit was embarrassing. This isn't."

"Equally embarrassing."

"Nope. Shit, you really haven't shaved," he mumbled, looking down.

"God, Shane! Get out!" I hissed, covering up my crotch with my hands and hissing as the insides of my arms pressed against the sides of my breasts.

"Quit that," he scolded, pulling my arms to the sides, his eyes never leaving me. "Your hair is redder here."

His fingers brushed against my pubic bone, and my stomach jumped.

"Focus, Dirk Diggler."

"I'm focused." His eyes snapped back up to mine. "What do we do?"

"I don't know! I've been in this fucking shower forever." I raised my wrinkled hand to his face. "My fingers may never recover."

He kissed my fingers, his eyes crinkling at the corners.

"Stay still," he murmured, lifting his hands to lightly run his fingers over my breasts. It didn't hurt exactly, but I still held my body tight and motionless—just in case.

"Ouch," he said softly, looking back up to meet my eyes.

"Is there something worse than ouch?"

"Motherfucking son of a bitch."

"Yeah, that pretty much covers it." I laughed a little.

His fingers slid off my breasts, and he leaned forward slowly to kiss me, wrapping his hands around my back as he did so. I so badly wanted to lean into him, but I knew that would be incredibly painful.

"Stay still," he reminded me against my lips, then pulled away.

Before I understood what he was doing, his mouth was on one of my nipples. I jerked, but his arms held me immobile as he sucked gently, once, then twice. When he finally pulled back, I watched his mouth turn up into a satisfied smirk. Then he moved to the other breast and did the same thing.

When he was done, I was leaking, and breast milk was running slowly down my torso, mixing in with the cooling water of the shower.

"Holy crap."

"I fixed it," he said proudly, lifting his hands to massage my breasts gently.

"Oh my God, it's starting to feel better already," I moaned, closing my eyes in relief. "Thank you. That was so weird, but *thank you*."

"Why was it weird?" he asked with a laugh, making my eyes pop open.

"You just sucked breast milk from my nipples."

"As opposed to sucking it from other places?" he asked, raising one eyebrow.

"Uh, no. Breast milk. In your mouth."

"And?"

"And what? Breast milk in your mouth!" The more I said it, the more my face reddened.

"Katie, I've had my face in your cunt," he replied bluntly, making my mouth drop open in shock. "I've pretty much had my face everywhere on your body. A little breast milk is nothing."

"What does it taste like?" I asked, sputtering.

"Sorta sweet," he said, tilting his head to the side. "Not like anything really."

"Huh."

"Feeling better?"

I reached up to rub at my breasts. "Yeah, damn. Way better," I breathed.

"Good."

He leaned down quickly and kissed me hard, his fingers sliding down my body until he'd reached the hair between my thighs.

"This is so fucking sexy," he murmured, sliding his hand more fully between my thighs. "Why the fuck is that so sexy?"

"Because you rarely ever see a woman with pubic hair?" I asked, trying to keep my balance as his fingers found my clit.

"You're so fucking ripe right now," he groaned, licking into my mouth. "God, I'm going to have to knock you up again when you're done nursing. I need more time with you like this."

"Slow your roll, turbo," I gasped, shivering as the water running over us went from cool to cold. "We have five children. No more."

He reached behind me and shut off the shower before I was done speaking, pulling his hands away to fling the shower curtain open.

"No more?" he asked quietly as he helped me out of the shower and started to dry me.

"God, I can't even think about more right now."

"So it's a maybe?"

"Can we get Iris past her first birthday? I'm still recovering from the birth here."

Shane blanched and glanced down quickly.

"No!" I blurted. "No, that's all healed up. Good to go."

He laughed. "That's good to know."

"I didn't mean—"

"Uh-huh."

"You wish," I said haughtily, pulling the bathroom door open while he still stood there soaking wet.

"Shit, Kate! Cold!"

I laughed and tiptoed out of Shane's room and into my own. I'd been using the shower in the master bathroom since I was pregnant with Iris, and I hadn't stopped even though Shane was back. It wasn't as if he ever slept in his room anyway—he ended up curled next to me in the guest room every night.

Iris was awake but thankfully not crying when I got back into my room. I closed the door firmly behind me, dropped my towel, and scooped her up, almost crying in thankfulness when she immediately turned her head and latched onto my nipple. Ah, bliss.

"Good girl, Iris," Shane said as he slipped into my room, closing the door behind him.

"She's not a dog," I retorted, rolling my eyes.

"Yeah, but she's emptying you out, which means you won't wake up in pain in a few...Goddamn, you look incredible right now," he breathed, staring.

"My hair's—"

"You're naked and nursing," he cut in. "You look like some sort of fertility goddess."

"Well...I *did* get pregnant after one night of sex. That's pretty fertile."

He snorted, shaking his head.

"My superpower is making babies."

"You *are* pretty damn good at that," he replied, lifting his eyebrows up and down as he lay down on the bed next to us.

"Shit," I laughed. "I walked right into that one."

"I'm happy," Shane announced, letting out a contented sigh as he rolled to his back. "Are you happy?"

"Yeah." I looked down at Iris, smiling as I saw the way she was staring up at me. "Beyond happy."

"I make you happy?" he asked softly.

"You and our kids."

"I'll always make you happy," he promised, reaching out to rest his hand on my thigh.

"Until you leave your stinky gym clothes on the floor in the bathroom," I replied ruefully.

"Except for then."

"I think I can live with that." I switched Iris to the other side and then put her back in bed. Thankfully she'd begun sleeping mostly through the night, which meant I'd get a full six hours of sleep before she woke me up again.

I walked toward the dresser, but Shane's husky voice stopped me in my tracks.

"Don't put any clothes on."

"That would be irresponsible," I whispered back awkwardly. "What if there's a fire?"

"I'll dress you before we go to sleep," he promised, sitting up on the bed.

"*You'll* dress me?"

"You'll be too tired to do it yourself," he said confidently, his eyes meeting mine before sliding back down my body.

My nipples grew tight at his words, and his eyes flared in response.

"Come here, Kate."

I moved toward him without conscious thought, and when he could reach me, he pulled me between his spread thighs.

"You want me?" he asked softly, running his hands up the outsides of my legs.

"I haven't shaved my legs," I answered, pushing at his hands. God, why did that shit only happen to me?

"Quit it, Kate," Shane ordered, lightly slapping my hands away so he could put his back on my thighs. "Quit worrying about your legs. They're fine. Soft."

I forced my hands down to my sides and met his eyes.

"Do you want me?" he asked again, his hands moving inward before sliding back to the outsides of my thighs.

"Yes," I whispered back, my heart racing. God, it had been forever since I'd had sex. The need for that connection almost overpowered my self-preservation. Shane had seen me at my worst—hell, he'd seen me in the mornings before I'd had a chance to brush my teeth—but he still wanted me. He knew all my secrets, and all my quirks. But I was still terrified to have sex with him.

I knew that once the line was crossed again, there would be no going back.

"Are you ready for me?" he asked, searching my eyes as his hands traced over the small pouch of my belly and curve of my waist.

"No," I answered, my eyes growing watery.

"It's okay, baby," he said gently, though I could hear the disappointment in his voice. "We've got all the time in the world."

"I'm sorry," I groaned, reaching out to rub my hands over his short hair. "I'm just—"

"Not ready," he finished with a nod.

"I'm being ridiculous."

"No, you're being cautious. I get it, Katiebear."

"What am I waiting for?" I asked under my breath as his hands slid around me and lightly over the curves of my ass.

"I don't know, baby," he replied seriously. "But you'll know it when it happens."

"I'm tired," I said wearily, dropping my hands back to my sides.

"Let's go to sleep then." He stood from the bed and gave me a light tap on the ass, moving around me to grab a nightgown and a pair of panties out of my dresser.

He dressed me gently and kissed my forehead. "I told you I'd dress you."

Once we were back in bed, he curled around me and fell asleep quickly, but I couldn't sleep for a long time. I felt like shit for turning him down yet again, but the thought of having sex with Shane caused this weird fluttery panic deep in my belly that I couldn't ignore.

I trusted my gut.

Chapter 17

Kate

"What the heck, Keller?" I yelled in frustration two weeks later, knowing that I should try keeping my voice down but unable to calm myself.

I was staring at a letter that he'd brought home from school, and I couldn't believe what I was reading.

My boy, my sweet sensitive boy who was protective of Gunner and Iris like they were his children, was a *bully* at school.

"What's going on?" I asked, tempering my voice a little.

He stood in front of me, his arms crossed over his chest—which incidentally was no longer cute anymore—and refused to say a word. Instead, he was glaring at me like he couldn't stand the sight of me. I didn't understand what was going on.

The first month of school had been hard for Keller. He didn't like being away from home all day, and he didn't seem to be making many friends in his class. But

I'd thought he was adjusting. He'd snapped out of the funk he'd been in and had gone back to being the playful daredevil we all knew and loved.

"Well?" I asked in exasperation, pointing and glaring at Sage and Gavin, who were trying to peek at us around the corner of the wall before looking back to Keller. "Your teacher says you've been being mean to the other kids. That you've been calling them names. Is that true?"

He scowled, his eyebrows pulling together.

"Answer me," I ordered.

After a few minutes of silence, I honestly had no idea what to do. I wanted to send him to his room, but I knew that wasn't really a punishment. Gavin and Keller had toys strewn from one end of the bedroom to the other. I'd essentially be sending him up to play.

"Fine," I mumbled, walking over to a kitchen chair and pulling it against the wall. "Sit."

He didn't move from his spot, and I finally had to take him forcibly by the hand and walk him to the chair, lifting his ridged body up until he was seated.

"You can stay there until you're ready to talk," I said in frustration.

I checked on Gunner, who was playing quietly on the floor, and Iris, who was drowsing in her swing, before sitting down at the table where I could check my email and watch Keller.

He didn't move. He just sat there staring across the kitchen.

For an hour.

Then two.

By the time Shane came home, I was almost in tears I was so frustrated. I didn't know what to do. I didn't want to make him keep sitting there, but I also didn't want him to outlast me.

"Daddy's home," Shane called as he pushed through the front door.

"Keller's in trouble!" Gavin called, his voice a little wobbly.

"Gavin! Shh," Sage scolded.

I couldn't see Shane but he must have acknowledged them somehow because they went quiet. Soon Shane was walking into the kitchen.

He took in Keller sitting in the kitchen chair then looked at me, raising his eyebrows. "How long has he been there?"

"A couple hours," I said in frustration.

He must have interpreted the tone of my voice wrong, because suddenly he was scowling.

"Up to your room, bud," he told Keller, turning to face him. "I'll be there in a minute."

Keller jumped up from his spot and raced out of the room, sending me a look of triumph as he went past. My jaw dropped in shock.

"What the fuck, Shane?" I hissed, standing up.

"Funny, that was going to be my question," he said back, unbuttoning his uniform. "Hours, Kate?"

"Are you kidding me right now?" I asked, my voice low.

"He's six years old, and he's been sitting on a wooden

kitchen chair for hours?" Shane asked derisively, pulling off his blouse. "A little excessive, don't you think?"

My heart raced as I watched him move around the kitchen, placing his wallet and watch on the counter before turning to face me. I couldn't speak. The words felt lodged in my throat.

"Don't do this again," he said, when I still hadn't answered him after a few moments. He moved to leave the kitchen, and I snapped.

"You fucking asshole," I seethed, tears filling my eyes. "He had the chance to get up. All he had to do was talk to me."

"What?"

"I can't believe you." I shook my head, closing my laptop and sliding it under my arm. "Keller was still there because he was being stubborn as hell. All he had to do was say one word about why his teacher sent a note home from school saying that Keller was being a bully."

"What the hell?" Shane asked, his head jerking back.

"Yeah, that was my thought," I replied. I set my laptop in a cupboard above the counter where the kids couldn't reach it and grabbed my keys. "I'm going to the store. I just fed Iris, so she should be fine for a while."

"Kate," Shane called, but I didn't pause as I moved through the living room, telling the kids good-bye as I went. I was so livid that I had to get out of there before I said something I didn't mean.

* * *

I took my time at the grocery store. I took a *long-ass time* at the grocery store.

By the time I got home, it was after the kids' bedtime, and I was sure that Shane had had to heat up some breast milk I'd stored for Iris in the fridge. I'd been gone for hours.

My anger had turned to frustration, which had then turned to hurt. I wanted to say that I couldn't believe Shane had immediately acted like I was being a heartless bitch for disciplining Keller but I couldn't. He'd made his views clear on that a long time ago, and because we'd never had another run-in, I'd let myself forget about it.

It was a hard fall back to reality.

I backed my SUV into the driveway and popped the hatch before getting out. The thought of carrying in all the groceries I bought made my shoulders slump, but I grabbed a huge package of toilet paper and two gallons of milk on my way inside anyway.

I hated grocery shopping with the kids, but I couldn't deny how much easier it was when they helped me unload the car.

"Hey," Shane called out, shutting off the television as I passed through the living room.

"Hey," I answered, setting the milk on the counter and the toilet paper on the floor before turning right back around. "There's a ton of groceries in the car."

He nodded and followed me outside, grabbing half the contents of my trunk in one go. We moved silently around each other, putting things away. I was too tired to even converse with him in any type of normal manner.

After we finished putting everything away in their proper places, I turned and walked up to my room without a word. For the first time ever, I locked the door behind me. If the kids needed something in the night, Shane could take care of it.

I stripped to my T-shirt and underwear before checking on Iris, who was sleeping peacefully. Then I crawled between the sheets.

I was just...melancholy. That was the best word for it. We'd been functioning so well for so long that I'd grown complacent with the way things were. I hadn't even thought twice when I'd sat Keller on that chair. I had hated it, but shit—all he'd had to do was speak up. My stomach sank as I thought about how he'd been acting at school. Was there something going on with him? He'd seemed fine up until I'd asked him about the note from his teacher. Had I missed something? What was I doing wrong?

The doorknob rattled, and I glanced that way before closing my eyes and pulling the comforter higher on my shoulders. I just wanted to go to sleep and start fresh in the morning. Everything looked better in the morning.

Within minutes, I heard another sound at the door, and I watched in disbelief as it swung open, the light from the hallway outlining Shane's bare torso.

"You don't get to do that," he said quietly, walking forward and closing the door until only a crack of light remained. "You sleep with me—even when you're pissed."

"I didn't want to sleep with you," I replied flatly, lying unmoving beneath the blankets. If he thought I was going to just ignore the shit he'd done that evening, he was sadly mistaken.

"When you're pissed, you don't get to walk away anymore." He circled the bed and lay down behind me, a few inches separating our bodies.

I snorted.

"I thought you were in this with me, Kate," he said quietly, frustration lacing every word.

"Yeah, well, so did I."

"What's that supposed to mean?" He rolled to his side and leaned up on one elbow to see my face.

"I'd forgotten that you didn't want me to discipline the kids," I answered bitterly. "No problem, boss."

"Don't. Don't do that. I'm trying to fucking talk to you."

"You probably should have done that before you made me feel like shit," I said, silently cursing the way my voice wobbled. "I didn't want to make him stay there, Shane. But if I'd let him down, he would have known that he could pull that shit again."

"I didn't know—"

"You didn't ask. You just came in and made me look like the bad guy—once again overruling anything I fucking said. I thought we'd moved past that shit. So stupid."

"I'm sorry!" he growled. "But you don't help the

situation when you just walk away. You were gone for hours, Kate!"

"Well, I needed a fucking minute to breathe."

"I could have used some help with our six-year-old who was completely fucking silent the entire time I tried to talk to him." His voice rose as he jerked up in bed, and suddenly Iris's wails filled the room.

"I'll get her," he grumbled, throwing the blankets back before I could climb off the bed.

His voice changed to a soothing croon as he laid her on the bed and changed her diaper, and I had a lump in my throat the size of Texas by the time he handed her to me and lay back down—turning his back to me.

"He didn't say anything when you tried to talk to him?" I asked after a few minutes of silence.

"Nope. Just stared at me like I was an asshole," he answered flatly.

"God, I wonder what the heck is going on with him?" Iris slipped off my breast, her mouth slack. I guessed she wasn't hungry, just pissed that her dad had woken her up.

I laid her back in her bed and crawled in next to Shane, facing his back. I wanted to reach out and touch him but I was still so mad—so disillusioned by his attitude when he got home.

"Sometimes I say shit before I think about it," he said quietly, his voice apologetic. "But I figure it out, and I apologize. I can't apologize to you when you're not here, Katie."

I chewed on the inside of my cheek as my eyes

watered and my nose started to run. "I need you to back me up with the kids, Shane. No exceptions."

He didn't turn around. "I will. It's instinct for me to step in—I have a hard time stopping myself. Especially when it comes to the kids. The shit I saw in foster care—"

The meaning behind his words hit me like a sledge-hammer, and I clenched my fists so hard that my nails bit into my skin. I moved forward and wrapped my arm around his waist, molding myself to his back.

"I trust you, Katie. I don't know why I jump to con-clusions—"

"I get it," I murmured, kissing his back. "I'm sorry I left."

"Please don't do that anymore." The ache in his words made my breath catch.

"I won't," I promised, kissing his back again.

"I'm beat," he finally said, lifting his hand to cover mine against his belly. "Let's figure out the Keller stuff in the morning."

I nodded and closed my eyes, breathing in the scent of the man in front of me.

* * *

Keller was grounded off all electronics indefinitely, but he was still refusing to talk to me or Shane about what was going on. I didn't know what to do with him.

For a while, things went back to normal.

Then one day while I was folding laundry on the couch, the doorbell rang.

Keller and Sage were still at school, Gunner and Iris were napping—Lord, how I loved nap time—and Gavin was sitting at the coffee table coloring quietly. I hopped off the couch and practically sprinted to the door, afraid that whoever was there would ring the bell again and wake up the babies, ruining the few moments of quiet I'd come to relish.

"What the heck?" I exclaimed happily as my cousin Henry wrapped his arms around me and spun me in a circle.

"Hey, Katiebear!" he said, grinning broadly.

"What the heck are you guys doing here?"

I looked past him to see Bram, Anita, and Trevor standing around with bags spread at their feet.

"Came to celebrate your dirty thirty," Anita announced, stepping forward to shove Henry out of the way so she could hug me. "Now where is my beautiful niece?" She pushed by me into the house, and I had to let her go because Bram and then Trevor were hugging me hello.

"I can't believe you guys are here," I called, grabbing Anita's bag before Bram pulled it from my arms. "This is so awesome. Come in."

The guys followed me into the house just as Anita came down the stairs carrying Iris. "She was awake," Anita told me happily, making faces at the baby.

"You're so full of shit," I laughed, giddy at my unexpected company.

"Uncle Bram! Uncle Trev!" Gavin yelled, hopping from his spot on the floor.

"Hey, little man," Bram said softly, pulling Gavin into his arms.

I looked around the crowded entryway, so excited I didn't know what to do with myself. My favorite people in the entire world were all in one place. If Alex had come with them, it would have been completely perfect.

"Alex wanted to come, but he didn't have any leave." Henry read my mind, wrapping his arm around my shoulder. "Now, do you have beer in this house, or is it all apple juice and breast milk?"

I punched him lightly in the chest and dragged him toward the kitchen.

I couldn't wait for Keller and Sage to get off the bus that afternoon.

"What time does Shane get home?" Trevor asked as the entire group migrated to the kitchen table.

I ignored Bram's scowl as I passed out the last of the beer in our fridge. I wasn't even sure how long the stuff had been in there. Shane and I rarely drank. "He usually gets home between four thirty and five," I answered. "Was he in on this?"

"Hell no," Bram grumbled, setting Gavin on his feet as he picked a spot at the table.

"Oh, man. He's going to be stoked," I exclaimed, clapping my hands together.

"Doubtful."

"Can it, Bram," I scolded, but there was little heat in my voice. I couldn't believe they were all there, sitting in my kitchen and bantering back and forth. I freaking loved it.

"So what's the plan for your birthday?" Henry asked, kicking back in his seat. "Any good bars around here?"

"I have no idea." I chuckled. "I don't get out much, and I lived in Carlsbad before."

"Well, we'll find one. Karaoke bar?" Anita asked, grinning.

"Not happening." Trevor scowled.

"Bawk!"

"Real mature, Ani."

We sat around the table for the next two hours as Gunner woke up and the boys ran around like chickens with their heads cut off. We rarely had anyone but the Camden family or Miles over for dinner. I wasn't sure the kitchen had ever held so many people at one time.

Sage and Keller were equally excited when they clamored off the bus to see their aunties and uncles waiting for them on the front porch. I sighed in happiness as Keller wrestled around with Trevor and Bram in the front yard, his giggles echoing throughout the neighborhood.

We'd needed this, and I hadn't realized how badly until I saw how happy the kids were.

Anita and Henry brought Sage with them to the store for supplies that afternoon. By the time Shane got home that night, I had a huge pot of spaghetti simmering on the stove and my face hurt from smiling.

"What the hell?" Shane asked, laughing as he came in the front door. His eyes immediately found mine across the room. "We've been overrun."

"Hey, man!" Henry called, climbing off the couch. "Long time no see."

"How the hell did you get here?" Shane asked in amazement as they wrapped their arms around each other and did the weird back-patting thing guys did.

"Had some time, decided to take it and come visit my favorite cousin," Henry answered with a smile. "Trying to get stationed out here. We'll see how it goes."

"Kate would fucking love that," Shane said with a nod.

The noise in the room grew with everyone talking over each other, and I relaxed into my brother's side on the couch. I was so incredibly happy I could have screamed with it.

* * *

"You're staying here?" I asked everyone, looking around to where they were lying on the floor and couches.

"I told them it was a bad idea," Anita called out from where she was resting her head on Trevor's belly. They looked like a giant T covering half the living room floor. "No one listens to me."

"We don't have that many beds," I said softly, looking over to where Henry and Shane were talking shop across the room.

"Couch!" Bram and Trevor yelled at the same time, locking in their places to sleep for the night.

"Nice, guys," Anita grumbled. "Real fucking gentlemen."

"I can sleep anywhere," Henry piped up with a chuckle. "The floor's going to feel like a fucking feather bed."

"Ani can sleep in my room," Shane said, tipping his beer bottle toward her.

"The fuck?" Bram growled, looking between Shane and me.

"I'm not gonna sleep in there with her, asshole," Shane scoffed, a snarky smile crossing his face. "We don't use that room anyway."

Ani's eyebrows lifted up and down when I glanced at her, and I shook my head in annoyance. My excitement over their visit was slowly losing steam.

The kids still had school in the morning, and after staying up well past their bedtime that night, they were going to be complete terrors in the morning. How the hell was I going to get them ready to go when I had people sleeping on every available surface in the house?

"We're gonna head up," Shane announced suddenly, seeing the panic on my face. "I'll show you where to sleep, Ani."

Everyone agreed it was time to hit the sack and began moving quietly around the house getting ready for bed. Thankfully, we had blankets and pillows for everyone, and before long the lights were turned off and Shane, Ani, and I were moving up the stairs.

"You don't sleep in the master bedroom?" Anita asked quietly as I brought her into Shane's room while he checked on the kids.

"No," I answered simply. "I have my own room."

"Which it sounds like Shane sleeps in?"

"Yeah."

"That's weird," she mused, closing the door so she could change into some pajamas.

"I'm not sleeping in here," I mumbled, going into the bathroom to brush my teeth.

"Oh, yeah," she said, following in behind me. "I wouldn't want to sleep in Rachel's room, either."

I put some toothpaste on my brush and stuffed it into my mouth without answering. I didn't know what to say. Shane had taken away anything that had belonged to Rachel long before his deployment, and the room looked like it had always been exclusively his... but I'd been in there with Rachel more times than I could count.

"It's not like it's a big deal or anything," I mumbled around the white foam in my mouth. "It's just never come up—and I'm sure as hell not broaching that subject. I guess if he wanted me in here, he would have asked by now."

"So, what, you're just going to leave the master bedroom empty? That doesn't make much sense."

"Hell, I don't know." I spit and rinsed my mouth with water from the tap.

"Things are good with you guys now?" Ani asked, following my lead and spitting out her toothpaste.

"I guess."

"What do you mean?"

"Kate, you ready for bed?" Shane asked, poking his head in the door.

"Yeah." I turned to Ani and gave her a tight hug. "I'm so glad you're here."

"Me too."

Shane opened the door wide so I could pass by him, then followed me into my room.

"I can't believe they're all here," I whispered with a smile, meeting Shane's eyes as I pulled my yoga pants down my legs.

"I can't believe they're all staying at our house," Shane snickered, pulling his T-shirt over his head. "I thought Bram's head was going to explode when I told Ani she could take my bed."

"You did that on purpose." I rolled my eyes.

"Hell yeah, I did. God, your brother's such a dick."

Iris stirred, and we both froze, our eyes snapping to the crib wedged in between the bed and the wall. Her arms jerked before she went limp again, and as soon as she was still, we climbed gingerly into bed, lying down to face each other.

"He's just protective," I whispered as Shane pulled me into him.

"He's in my fucking house," he replied incredulously.

"Yeah, bad form." I chuckled silently, reaching up to rub one hand over his short hair. He'd just gotten another haircut, and I loved the way it felt against my palms.

"I love this tank top," Shane said out of nowhere, his nostrils flaring.

"What?" I looked down at the nursing tank top I was wearing. I had, like, four of them, and I wore them all the time so they were getting a little ragged looking.

"Just one little tug..." He slid his finger underneath the small snap by my collarbone.

My breath caught as I watched his face, his finger snapping and unsnapping the strap. We'd been riding a fine line, sometimes crawling into bed practically vibrating with sexual tension—but we still hadn't had sex. Shane was beyond ready, but I was still putting him off.

He finally left the snap undone and glanced up at my face as his fingers pulled the fabric down.

"What are you doing?" I whispered breathlessly.

"I've been watching you all night," he said softly. "So gorgeous. Smiling and laughing—and you've been using your nursing cover so I haven't even gotten a glimpse—"

The fabric caught on my nipple and finally fell beneath my breast. "Ah, there it is," Shane breathed, his fingers ghosting up and over my nipple.

"I think this probably has more to do with the beer you were drinking," I replied, swallowing hard.

Shane chose that moment to lean down and wrap his lips around my nipple, making my hips jerk forward. He groaned deep in his throat, sucking slightly to pull my nipple into a sharp point as he reached down to pull my leg over his.

My neck arched as his hand slid down between us, and I gasped as his fingers slid over my inner thigh. *I should've wore pants to bed*, I thought as his fingers tunneled under the fabric of my underwear. *I'm playing with fire.*

"This isn't a good idea," I tried to say as his fingers brushed over my entrance.

"Fantastic idea," Shane mumbled around my breast. "Look how wet you are. Just let me—" He stopped speaking as a finger slid inside me, making both of us groan.

"Shit," I gasped, rolling my hips. It had been so freaking long that it felt like my entire body was going to burst into flames from just that small point of contact.

"There you go," he whispered back, lifting his head to catch my lips with his as he added another finger.

He slid his tongue into my mouth as I began to shake, and I kissed him back until I finally couldn't concentrate on both his mouth and his hand at the same time.

"Harder," I ordered, clenching my teeth so hard it was a wonder I didn't shatter them.

"Goddamn," he groaned, sucking on my shoulder as I got closer and closer to the edge.

My hands were frantic as I tried to touch all of his torso at once, the nails of one hand digging into the forearm between us as it flexed over and over. His fingers were curled up inside me, and every time he jerked his hand up, his palm rubbed over my swollen clit.

I came hard, my mouth at his throat as I tried not to make any noise.

"I can't—" I began as his fingers finally slid out of my

underwear, his wet hand coming to rest gently on my lower belly.

"I know, baby," he said, breathing hard. "Fuck. That was all I wanted."

I stared at him incredulously, and he chuckled before groaning. "I wasn't expecting anything else."

"Well, now I really feel like an asshole," I mumbled, making him snort.

"After all this waiting, I'm not going to fuck you with our house full of family," he said with a shake of his head. "Bad timing."

"Well what was this?" I asked as he pulled away, climbing off the bed to grab a baby wipe to clean his hands.

"I knew I could keep you quiet but no way would I be able to," he told me with a wicked smile, crawling back up the bed on his hands and knees.

"I am pretty good at the sexing," I replied seriously, relaxing my body into the bed as I nodded.

His face showed surprise for a moment before he began laughing loudly, falling to his side on the bed.

I watched him, giggling at the way he clutched at his belly. "You are," he agreed through chuckles.

I couldn't even be frustrated as Iris woke up and started babbling from her crib.

I couldn't remember the last time I'd had such an awesome day.

Chapter 18
Shane

Kate was practically bouncing around the house when I got home from work on Friday afternoon. She and Anita were deciding on what they were going to wear when we went out for her birthday that night.

She actually didn't turn thirty until Monday, but with everyone's jobs, it made more sense for the group—whom Ellie and Liz had aptly but unoriginally referred to as "the kids" even though all of us had been adults for a while—to visit for the weekend.

Kate had been worried about a babysitter after the initial excitement over their visit waned a little, but I'd promised her I'd take care of it. Trevor had pulled me aside and let me know that Kate's surprises weren't quite over yet.

Katie was sitting at the kitchen table with Anita, makeup spread out in front of them, when excited shouts filled the front of the house.

"What?" Kate asked in confusion, her entire face lighting up as the new arrivals came into her view.

"Holy crap," she yelled, coming to her feet.

"Happy birthday," Liz called, raising her hands and shaking them from side to side.

"I can't believe this!" Kate pulled her mom into a hug and shot me a huge smile over her shoulder.

She was looking at me like I'd cured some disease, even though I'd had nothing to do with any of it. I didn't care—I'd take credit for it if she was going to look at me like that.

Kate made the rounds, giving out hugs to my foster dad, Dan, Ellie, and Mike while she chattered happily.

"Hey, son," Mike said, making his way to where I was leaning against the counter. "Missed you."

"Missed you, too," I told him, going in for a hug. "How long are you staying?"

"Oh, just until Sunday," he assured me, giving me a wink. "Ellie and Liz are staying a bit longer, though. Wanted some extra time after everyone left."

"Are you guys staying here?" Katie called out nervously over the noise.

"Why the hell would we do that when we can stay in a hotel room with room service?" her dad asked quietly, laughing.

"Well, everyone else is staying here—"

"Abraham!" Liz scolded, turning to glare at her son. "Your sister has her hands full already."

"We're only here a couple of days," Bram grumbled.

"I tried to tell him," Anita tattled.

"Good grief," Ellie snapped, making her way toward me. "We didn't raise you guys to act like a bunch of locusts. Bring it on in," she ordered as she reached me, lifting her arms.

"Hey, Mom," I said softly, leaning down to hug her.

"How you doing?"

"Good," I answered with a nod.

"Yeah?"

I glanced at Kate laughing with her dad across the room and smiled. "Yeah."

* * *

Later that night, we piled into Kate's SUV while Anita and Henry bitched about having to sit in the very back. I didn't know why they bothered; as the youngest they'd pretty much always been bullied into getting the last piece of pizza or the worst seats in the car.

"Karaoke!" Anita yelled once I was pulling out of the driveway.

"Do you know a karaoke bar around here?" Kate asked excitedly, turning to face me.

"That's where you want to go?" I asked, reaching out to take her hand in mine.

We didn't do public displays of affection normally. Kate was too nervous for that kind of shit—like it mattered in the long run what people thought about our relationship. So I was surprised when she turned her hand and laced her fingers through mine.

"Yeah!"

"Okay, I know of one. Here—" I pulled my phone out of my pocket. "Call Miles and tell him where we're going."

"I'm having the best time," she said, scrolling through my phone.

"We've barely left the house." I laughed.

"It doesn't matter." She smiled, lifting the phone to her ear. "It's already the best birthday ever."

* * *

Trevor agreed to be the designated driver, and by the time I was a few beers in, I knew that had been a bad idea.

The girls were happy, singing 1980s pop songs every time their names were called. Between their turns, which happened about every half hour, they danced and laughed throughout the bar.

My eyes followed Kate around the room as she had fun, but the longer we stayed and the more alcohol we consumed, the more the mood at the table shifted.

Miles sat next to me, watching Anita as she shook her ass, completely oblivious to the man sitting next to him watching Miles.

"So, you and Katie," Henry said jovially over the noise of the crowd. "Did not see that coming."

"Yep," I murmured back as Bram's eyes moved from Miles to me.

"How the hell did that happen?"

I glanced at Kate, laughing at something Anita said, and ignored the question. I wasn't going to get into the story surrounded by a hundred strangers in a bar. It wasn't any of Henry's business anyway.

"He fucked her," Bram said nastily after an awkward silence. "Got drunk and knocked her up."

"Shut the fuck up, Abraham," I growled, refusing to look his way.

"It's the truth," he chuckled drunkenly. "On the anniversary of Rachel's death, no less. Good timing, that."

Kate glanced at me, and her eyes widened as I stood abruptly from the table.

"Shut your fucking mouth," I said to the asshole across the table.

"Come on, Bram, knock it off," Trevor said quietly as Bram jumped to his feet.

"Wonder how long you'd been waiting," Bram mused, looking me up and down. "Must have been a while since you'd gotten your dick wet. Some good luck that Kate was right there in your house—ready and willing to scratch your itch."

I launched myself over the table, slamming Bram into the floor with the entire weight of my body. "You know nothing," I said, punching him in the mouth. "Keep your fucking mouth shut!"

He jerked his body, throwing me off, and soon we were rolling all over the floor, taking down chairs and tables as we fought.

It couldn't have lasted more than a few minutes, but by the time Miles pulled me off a bloody Abraham, Kate was sobbing.

"Out," a bouncer yelled as he reached us.

"Yeah, man, we're going," Trevor assured him,

nodding to Henry, who was holding Bram from behind in a bear hug.

Miles pushed at me as I tried to move toward Kate. "Not the place, man. Wait until we get outside," he warned quietly, ushering me out of the bar.

I wiped the blood from beneath my nose with the back of my hand and followed as Anita escorted Kate out ahead of us. They were speaking quietly while Kate brushed the tears off her face.

"Miles, you got Shane?" Trevor asked as we got outside.

"Oh, hell no," I mumbled, moving toward Kate's SUV.

"You are sure as shit not getting into the car with Bram right now," Trevor told me, shaking his head.

"The fuck, Trev? Did you hear the shit he was saying?" I asked, turning my head to meet his eyes.

"I heard him. Dumb fuck has been itching for a fight since we got here." Trevor rubbed the back of his neck. "I'm not putting the two of you in a confined space with Anita and Kate, man. Not happening."

"Fine." I glanced toward the SUV and met Kate's sad eyes, sighing. *What a great fucking birthday.* "Let's go, Miles."

We climbed into Miles's truck and followed the rest of the group back to my house.

"He's staying at your place?" Miles asked, shaking his head.

"Yeah. They all are."

"What's his deal with you?"

"He fucking hates me. The shit that went down with Kate wasn't good. I fucked up big time—"

"I don't need to know details," Miles cut in.

"Yeah, well, neither did Bram, but apparently he knows more than I realized."

We pulled up to the curb outside my house, and I swung my door open. "Thanks for the ride."

"You need me to stay?" Miles asked as Bram stumbled out of the SUV ahead of us.

"Nah, his brothers will keep him in line, and their parents are in the house with the kids."

"Are you sure?"

"Yeah, even Bram wouldn't start shit with the kids there."

I waved as I walked toward the front of the house, coming to a stop outside the passenger-side door of Kate's SUV. She was passed out, her head tilted back against the seat.

"You want to carry her in?" Trevor asked quietly as Anita and Henry walked a stumbling Bram inside.

"Yeah, I'll get her."

I opened the door and unbuckled Katie, sliding my arms under her so I could lift her up.

"Bram's going to feel like shit in the morning," Trevor told me, shutting the car door after I'd pulled Kate out.

"He ruined her fucking birthday," I snarled, situating Kate more solidly against my chest as she wrapped her arms around my neck. "He needs to get a handle on his shit. Kate and I are fine—why the fuck does he have to keep bringing that shit up?"

I walked toward the house and slid in sideways while Dan held the door open.

"Looks like she had a good time," he said quietly.

"Yeah, until your son lost his fucking mind."

"What happened?"

I shook my head and walked Kate up the stairs to bed. She didn't stir again as I pulled her hands from around my neck, and I didn't bother doing anything but unsnapping her bra and pulling her jeans and shoes off. She was out for the night.

I grabbed a wet washcloth and cleaned my face off as I checked on each of the kids. I always made the rounds at night, making sure each of them was safe and sleeping before I crawled into bed. Half the time one of the boys was on the floor when I checked on them, and I had to re-tuck them into their beds.

I could hear the murmur of voices as I shut Sage's door, so I walked back downstairs.

Bram was passed out on the floor of the living room, a pillow stuffed under his head. I wanted to kick him, but didn't.

"Coffee?" Ellie asked as I moved into the kitchen.

"Yeah, thanks."

Everyone was gathered around the kitchen table, with Trevor and Henry seated at the bar stools next to the counter.

"You okay?" Dan asked, glancing from my face to the bloody washcloth in my hand.

"Yeah, I'm fine," I huffed, finding an empty seat and sinking into it with a grunt. Bram had knocked me into

the legs of a table, and I could already feel bruises forming on my lower back.

"What the hell happened?" Liz asked, her eyebrows
drawing together. "You two just started throwing
punches?"

I shook my head, thanking Ellie for the cup of coffee
she placed on the table in front of me.

"Bram was running his mouth," Henry spit out furiously, turning to look at me. "I'm sorry I brought it
up, dude. I had no idea it was going to cause such a shit
storm."

"Not your fault, Hen."

"I thought Kate was going to jump in between you
two," Anita said quietly, her eyes tired and rimmed with
smudged makeup. "God, Bram is such a dick sometimes."

"I shouldn't have hit him," I said, my stomach
clenching as I thought of the conversation I'd have with
Kate when she woke up.

"If you didn't, I would have," Trevor said. "And I'm
not even drunk."

The conversation was steered to the girls' musical tal-
ents and the songs they'd sung, and before long Ellie,
Dan, and Liz were leaving as the rest of the group got
their beds ready.

"Why're you staying?" I asked Mike, after he'd kissed
Ellie good-bye and come back into the kitchen.

"Gonna keep an eye on Bram," he said, patting my
back as he passed me. "Dan has trouble sleeping when
he's not in his own bed, so it was better for him to go
with Liz."

"I couldn't believe that shit tonight," I groaned, slouching down in my chair. "He picked a fight and I stepped right into it."

"Now that your mother's gone, why don't you tell me what he said?"

"It wasn't as much what he said, as how he said it," I told my dad, clenching my hand into a fist. My knuckles were torn. "He made some comment about getting my dick wet and how Kate was just waiting to take care of it."

"Jesus Christ," Mike snapped in disgust.

"The rest of the shit I would have ignored. He was drunk and being an asshole, but he made Kate sound pathetic." I met my dad's eyes. "She's not fucking pathetic."

"Don't need to convince me of that."

"I fucked up bad with Kate—I know that. But just because she puts up with my shit doesn't mean that she's some fucking doormat."

"She loves you," Mike said quietly. "Love can overlook a lot of things."

"We've been doing good."

"Oh, yeah?"

"Yeah. I think she's starting to trust me again. I've been trying really hard to make up for the shit before."

"Seems to be working. I got an earful about the sleeping arrangements earlier."

My face reddened, and Mike chuckled. "No reason to be embarrassed."

"I'm not talking about this with you."

"Trust takes time, son," Mike informed me with a small smile. "You just keep doing what you're doing and things will all work out."

"Did you and Mom ever—"

"Hell, I was far worse than you," he said seriously. "But that's not a subject I'm ever discussing with my sons."

I grimaced when I thought of ever discussing my past with Kate with any of my kids. "Fair enough."

"You better go up and get some sleep. I'm just gonna work on my crossword puzzle for a while."

* * *

I woke up with Kate tucked in tight against me the next morning, just as someone pushed open our bedroom door.

"I'm just going to grab Iris," Liz whispered softly, tiptoeing to the edge of the bed. "So you and Katie can get some more sleep."

"Thanks, Liz," I murmured as she lifted the smiling baby out of her crib.

She closed the door behind her when she left, and the noise woke Kate just enough that her hips twitched against my morning erection. *Shit.*

The mornings were always the hardest for me, no pun intended. Kate had no idea how she moved against me before she'd completely wake up. I knew without a doubt that I could have her so hot before she'd finally gotten her wits about her that she'd let me do whatever I wanted ... but I didn't want to start out that way.

She wanted to wait—for whatever reason—and I

wanted her to come to me when she was ready. Fucking her before she trusted me fully again would feel fantastic in the moment, but the lasting effects would not be pretty. She wasn't sure yet, and sex wasn't going to make up her mind.

Sex made things infinitely better, but it didn't fix anything. We'd still be right where we started even if I was fucking her into the mattress every day.

Christ, I needed to stop thinking about sliding into her while she tilted her hips against me.

"God, my head hurts," Kate rasped, finally waking up fully. "Too much booze."

I kissed the side of her neck as she raised her hand to cover her eyes.

"You had quite a bit," I agreed softly. "How's your stomach?"

"Oddly enough, I have an iron stomach when your spawn isn't growing inside me."

I knew the exact moment that she remembered the events of the night before because her entire body went rigid against me.

"What was the fight about?" she whispered, reaching down to grab my arm as I tried to move away.

"Just stupid shit," I said, relaxing back into her body. "Abraham's a mean drunk."

"Not usually," she argued, her voice calm. "You know I'm going to hear about it when we go downstairs. Wouldn't you rather I heard it from you?"

"I'd rather you didn't hear it at all," I grumbled, pressing my face into her hair.

"It was about me, huh?"

"Not specifically," I hedged, not willing to hurt her feelings. "It was about past shit with me and you that he can't seem to let go."

"I figured." She sighed. "I'll talk to him."

"Don't," I ordered, scooting back so she'd lie flat and I could see her face. "Me and you are good, right? You don't have to defend me to him."

She opened her mouth to argue, and I covered it with my palm. She looked so cute as her makeup raccoon eyes widened in surprise.

"You don't have to talk about our relationship to anyone but me," I told her, taking my hand away so I could kiss her lips. "It's no one's business but ours."

"Do you think he'll apologize?" she asked hoarsely, clearing her throat.

"Doesn't matter one way or the other—only thing that matters is us, right? He'll come around eventually or he'll learn to keep his mouth shut."

She wrapped her arms around my torso and pulled me down on top of her, digging her fingers into the skin of my back.

"I'm sorry your birthday was ruined, baby," I mumbled into her mouth as I kissed her.

"Are you kidding? I had a great time for the first two hours. I'd call that a success," she retorted with a huge smile.

"Parents are taking care of the kids this morning," I whispered suggestively, wiggling my eyebrows at her.

"Oh yeah?"

I rocked my hips down once and ground them into hers before pulling back and dropping one hip to the bed at her side. "You wanna curl back up with me and actually sleep in for once?"

Her mouth dropped open in surprise at my words, and she giggled, shaking the entire bed. "Oh yeah," she whispered, giving me a sultry smile.

We slept until ten a.m., and it was fucking fantastic.

* * *

I watched Kate and Bram as they talked quietly across the driveway. Everyone was heading out in a few hours to go home, and even though Kate had treated Bram like normal for the rest of the weekend, I'd known that she was going to corner him at some point.

Even though I'd asked her not to.

I wasn't pissed about it, though. That was her brother—they had a relationship completely separate from mine and Kate's. If she needed to clear the air between them, I was all for it. I didn't want her worrying about that shit, and I knew she had been.

Bram reached up and smoothed Kate's hair down while they talked, and every once in a while one of them would nod as if agreeing with the other. Their little powwow didn't last long: About fifteen minutes later, Kate was grinning at Bram as he rubbed at the back of his neck uncomfortably. He turned to walk away and said something over his shoulder, making Kate laugh loudly.

Before Bram knew what was happening, Kate was hopping onto his back—almost knocking him to the ground—and giving him what looked like a really painful noogie while laughing hysterically.

Whatever reservations I'd had completely vanished.

I loved her.

Chapter 19

Kate

Hey, Katie?" Aunt Ellie called from the back door. "The school just called. They said you need to come get Keller."

My head snapped up from where I'd been spraying off the patio furniture. "Is he okay?"

"Yeah, sounds like he got into trouble."

"Fuck," I hissed and stomped to the side of the house to turn off the hose.

"You want me to go with you?" my mom called as I jogged up the stairs. I was in cutoff shorts and a pair of Crocs—no way was I leaving the house that way.

"No!" I called back down to her as I reached my room. "I'll just go pick him up."

It didn't take long for me to get to Keller and Sage's school, and by the time I'd pulled into the parking lot, I was both furious . . . and embarrassed. I wasn't sure what Keller had done yet, but if they'd moved from sending notes home to sending the kid home, I figured it must be pretty bad.

When I reached the office, I found Keller sitting all alone in one of the chairs against the wall, his face covered in dirt and smeared with tears.

"Auntie Kate!" he gasped, jumping up and running toward me. He wrapped his arms around my hips and buried his face against my waist just as a tall woman came out of the principal's office.

"Hi, I'm Susan McCauley," she introduced herself, reaching out to shake my hand. "I work as a counselor here at the school."

"Kate Evans," I replied, letting go of her hand so I could drape it over Keller's shoulders. "What happened?"

"Is Keller's dad going to be here soon?" she asked, rudely ignoring my question as she looked past my shoulder. "I'd really feel more comfortable talking to Keller's parent."

I felt like I'd been slapped in the face; I was so shocked by her tone. What the hell?

"Keller's dad is at work," I answered flatly.

"Well, it's very important that he comes in to speak with me. Can you please call him and ask him to come in? It seems we don't have his phone number in our records."

"He can probably come in after work," I hedged, grinding my teeth.

"Office hours end at four, so that's not really going to work out unless he can get here before then."

"Are you new?" I asked bluntly, in awe of her audacity.

"I've been here for a few months. Why?"

"Word to the wise, most of these kids have parents in the military. Most of the time they can't just leave in the middle of the workday."

She grew flustered as I stared at her, then straightened her shoulders. She had to have been younger than I was, but she held herself like someone much older.

"Well, what time would work for him?" she ground out, giving me an insincere smile.

"Probably around five," I answered, lifting Keller into my arms. "Are we done?"

I signed Keller out quickly, trying to juggle his heavy body and my oversized purse, and within a few minutes we were in the car and headed back toward the house.

"What happened, bud?" I asked, glancing at Keller in the rearview mirror.

"I got in a fight," he mumbled, meeting my eyes.

The mask of indifference he'd been wearing for the past few months anytime he was in trouble slowly disappeared off his face, and he burst into tears.

"Why the heck would you do that?" I asked gently, pulling onto the freeway.

"Nathan called me Little Orphan Annie," he bit out, swiping a hand over his face angrily.

"Well, that's ridiculous," I stated. "You're not an orphan. Orphans don't have parents."

"And I'm not a girl!"

"That's also true," I said, trying not to laugh at the disgust on his face. "But you can't get in fights, little man, because then you get in trouble."

"Daddy's gonna be mad at me," he replied softly, making my heart ache.

We were silent for the rest of the drive. When we finally reached the house, Keller jumped from his seat and crawled out of the car, running inside as I pulled my cell phone from my purse.

"Hello?" Shane answered after a few rings.

"Hey, so I just picked up Keller from school..."

"Shit." He sighed. "What happened—is he okay?"

"Yeah, he's fine. According to Keller, he got into a fight because some little snot called him Little Orphan Annie."

"Well, that's not much of an insult."

"It is when you're six."

"What did the office say? Is he suspended or something?"

"I don't know—they wouldn't fucking talk to me," I answered in exasperation, frustrated all over again by that snotty counselor.

"What? Why?"

"The counselor wanted to talk to *you*."

"But you were already there."

"She wants you to go in after work and talk to her."

"Fuck. I won't be off work until after four."

I climbed out of the car as my mom stepped out onto the front porch. "Yeah, she said she'd wait."

"Okay, then I'll meet you there at like four thirty. Shit, I have to go. See you in a few hours."

The phone disconnected, and I dropped my arm down to my side. I guessed I was going to have to deal with Snots McCauley again that afternoon.

* * *

"Hey, beautiful," Shane called, opening my door as I put the car in park. "How was the rest of your day?"

"Eh. Keller spent most of the day playing Legos with Aunt Ellie. The poor kid looked like he was waiting on the executioner; he's so terrified about seeing you."

"I don't know why—you're way more scary," he said, putting a hand on the small of my back to lead me inside the school.

"Hello, Mr. Anderson. I'm Susan McCauley, the counselor here."

"Nice to meet you," Shane replied politely, reaching out to shake her hand.

"Why don't you come on into my office?" she said, waving her arm toward a door to the right.

Shane gently pushed me forward, and Susan barely looked at me as we passed her. Fun times.

"I asked you to come to see me because it seems Keller has been having some behavioral issues for most of the school year."

"What?" I asked in confusion. "We only got one note."

"At first it was name-calling, but today it progressed into actual physical violence," Susan said to Shane, completely ignoring me. "We have a no-tolerance rule. That's why we sent Keller home with Ms. Evans. But I wanted to speak to you one-on-one so we could work together to help Keller."

"From what Keller said, some boy was calling him names—"

"That's the story I heard, too," Susan said with a nod. "But we really can't excuse violence because of a little name-calling."

"Keller has scratches all over his arms. Did you send the other kid home, too?" I asked, clenching my hands in my lap. The woman acted like a robot—I didn't understand how she was supposed to be a counselor for little kids.

"Ms. Evans, please let me speak to Mr. Anderson," Snotty McCauley chastised, glancing at me briefly before turning her eyes back to Shane.

He made a sound of disbelief in his throat, looking over at me in surprise.

"Kate has just as much to say here as I do," Shane defended, his brows pulling together.

"In situations like these, I find it more beneficial if I speak directly to the child's parents, Mr. Anderson," she said simply. "I meant no disrespect."

"She's his mother," Shane argued, making my breath catch. "I'm not sure why you'd have an issue talking to her."

"Oh." Susan looked thrown for a moment and glanced down to shuffle through some papers on her desk. "Keller called her aunt when she picked him up earlier, and I was under the impression that Keller and Sage's mother had died in a car accident two years ago."

The breath left my chest at her nonchalant mention of Rachel's accident. When she looked back up from her desk, her eyes widened at the looks on our faces.

"Yes, she did," Shane agreed softly. "But Kate has been taking care of Keller since he was born. She's his mother in every sense of the word."

Susan sputtered for a moment, then seemed to get her nerves under control. "I hadn't realized," she said flatly, before wrinkling her nose as if she smelled something bad. "Well, sometimes untraditional home lives can be the root of behavioral issues. Perhaps Keller—"

"Yeah, we're done here," Shane said in disgust, shaking his head as he stood and pulled me up beside him. "Have the office call Kate tomorrow and let us know when Keller can come back to school."

"Mr. Anderson!" Susan called as Shane opened her office door. "We really haven't settled on any plan of attack—"

"Keller's *mother* and I will deal with any behavior issues he has," Shane said, turning to face her. "You've been condescending and rude since the moment we walked into the school—and I shouldn't have even had to come in here when you could have talked to Kate earlier. I'm not sure what your deal is, but I sure as shit hope that you treat the kids in your care better than you treat their concerned parents."

He grabbed my hand and pulled me to my car so fast I was practically running to keep up with him.

"That fucking bitch!" he mumbled, taking the keys from my hand so he could unlock the car for me. "Could you believe that shit?"

"She was like that when I picked Keller up."

"Why the hell didn't you warn me?"

I shrugged and reached up to give him a small peck on the mouth. "You took care of it."

I climbed inside the car and started it up as he shut the door.

"I'll follow you," he mouthed through the window before walking over to his truck.

My hands were shaking from adrenaline as we pulled out of the parking lot, and I took a deep breath to try to calm my nerves. I'd always hated confrontation. I didn't like it when people were mad at me, and knowing that someone disliked me made my skin crawl. I think that may have been why I was such a people pleaser as a kid.

We'd had so many other children in and out of our house growing up—children with behavioral issues that made Keller's look like nothing—that I'd learned early how to avoid any type of conflict. When it couldn't be avoided, my brothers had always stepped in, first Alex with his charm, and if that didn't work, then Bram with his fists.

When I'd become an adult and entered the business world, I'd learned to deal with my fear. But emailing back and forth with a disgruntled client wasn't anything like dealing with someone's dislike to my face.

I'd felt frozen inside that little office, my face burning with mortification. I'd never done anything to that woman, but she'd seemed to dislike me anyway. She'd made me feel small until Shane spoke up. His words had soothed me the way nothing else could have.

He'd given me a sense of validation that he'd never given me before.

I looked up to my mirror to check on the truck behind me and caught sight of him singing along to the radio, sunglasses covering his eyes. That small piece of something I'd been waiting for suddenly clicked into place.

Tenderness filled me as I pulled off the freeway and into a small gas station parking lot.

He'd barely stopped the truck before I was out of my car and making my way to his door.

"What's up?" he asked, opening it as I reached him.

I stepped up onto the running board and pulled his face to mine, kissing him hard as he fumbled to turn off the truck.

"I love you," I whispered into his mouth.

One hand gripped my ass as he groaned, and suddenly the other was pulling the lever under his seat so it slid backward, giving him room to pull me into his lap. I scrambled up to straddle him, and we both moaned as our lower halves met.

"What's this about?" he asked, gripping my hair so he could tilt my head and press his lips to my neck. "Fuck, ignore me," he gasped against my skin. "I don't even care."

I laughed breathlessly, pulling away from him, and looked down into his dilated eyes. "You're *so* getting lucky tonight," I said, grinding my hips down against him.

"I'm lucky every night," he replied softly, pulling my head back down so he could kiss me again.

* * *

"Naked," Shane demanded as he entered our room that night after his shower.

"Damn, you're bossy," I teased back, pulling my hair into a ponytail.

We'd driven home that evening flushed and turned on, but by the time we'd talked to Keller and had dinner with the kids and our mothers, the tension between us had calmed considerably.

It was still there, just under the surface, but life and family had overshadowed it for a little while.

"If you're not naked in the next fifteen seconds, I'm going to bend you over the bed and fuck you with your clothes still on," he replied, dropping the towel from his waist. "I'm not picky at this point."

I laughed softly and pushed my pants down my hips as he stared.

"I shaved my legs," I said with a grin, pulling off my shirt. "It's your lucky day."

"It sure as hell is," he breathed, looking up and down my body.

"Do you think our moms knew something was up and that's why they took Iris in with them for the night?" I asked as he moved toward me.

"I am not talking about Ellie and Liz with you when you're completely naked and we haven't had sex in over a year," he mumbled, gripping my hips to push me backward onto the bed. "The only thing you get to say is *Fuck me harder, Shane*, or *I forgot how huge your dick is*."

I laughed as he climbed on top of me. "You could pray, too. An *Oh God!* wouldn't go amiss."

"You're so big," I whispered huskily, a small smile on my face. "Oh Shane, however will you fit?"

"Yes. Go with that," he muttered distractedly, leaning down to press his lips to mine.

I practically bubbled over with happiness as he came down on his elbows and slipped his tongue into my mouth.

"Mmm, you taste like garlic bread," I mumbled as he pulled away slightly.

"Shit." He burst out laughing and dropped his head to my shoulder, his entire body shaking with mirth.

"What?" I asked, pushing at him. "I *like* garlic bread!" My words only made him laugh harder, and soon I was giggling because the sound was so infectious.

"Will I *ever* feel cool around you?" he asked with a wide smile, once he could finally catch his breath. "I'm using all my good moves, and you're commenting on my garlic breath."

"Those were your best moves?" I asked stupidly, making him bark out another laugh. "I mean, *of course* those were good moves. Awesome moves—"

"I am so in love with you," he said, cutting off my rambling.

"That's good," I mumbled, my eyes wide.

"Really good," he confirmed, pulling me up the bed until he could move between my thighs.

"I love you, too."

"I know."

"So do you think—"

"No more talking, Kate," he ordered, kissing me hard.

Within seconds I wouldn't have been able to speak anyway because he was leaning on one elbow and using his other hand to tweak my nipples into hard, little points.

My hips rolled against his, and I pulled my knees up high, urging him closer. His skin was hot under my palms as I traced the ridges of muscles on his back and arms.

"God, you're so sexy," he rasped, pulling his mouth from mine to move down my neck. His lips reached my nipple, making me gasp, and he chuckled darky as he slid his fingers between my legs. I jerked against his hand as he slid his fingers inside, his thumb rubbing my clit in little circles.

"Fuck," I gasped, groaning when he pulled his hand away.

"Next time," he gasped, his breathing rough, "I'll take my time."

He knelt up between my legs and grabbed my thighs with both hands, draping them over his so I was tilted with my hips a bit higher than my head. "This time, I can't wait." He met my eyes as he reached between us to position his cock at my entrance. "And I want to watch."

He looked back down as he snapped his hips forward, and my back completely arched off the bed at the feeling of him thrusting inside me.

He paused when he'd bottomed out, and his chest heaved as his hands tightened on my thighs. "Birth control?"

"Got an IUD," I snapped, trying to work my hips against his strong grip. "We're good."

"Thank God." He pulled back and thrust forward again a few times before stopping.

"What the fuck, Shane?" I asked in annoyance, leaning up on my elbows.

"Need you closer," he mumbled, reaching under me to pull me up against his chest. "Oh fuck," he groaned as he slid a bit deeper inside. "Yeah."

I reached up, wrapping my hand around the front of his throat, and felt him swallow hard against my palm as his eyes met mine. He began to move, and I countered him, rolling my hips slightly so my clit would rub against his pubic bone with every thrust of his hips. "Fuck me harder, Shane," I said with a small smile, repeating his words from earlier. "I forgot how huge your dick was."

He smiled wide and thrust harder.

Before long, I was scratching the hell out of his back as I came. "Oh God," I mumbled, my breath catching.

Sweat was dripping down his temples when he lay me back down a few seconds later, and he completely ignored the racket he was making while he jerked his hips forward over and over, slamming my bed into the wall behind us until he finally came with a deep, satisfied groan.

"Holy hell," he mumbled, dropping like a stone on top of me.

"Really good moves," I replied blearily, closing my eyes as he chuckled.

* * *

Hours later, we were still awake, talking quietly about anything and everything from our favorite sexual positions to stories from our childhoods.

"I'm pretty sure, if our moms didn't know before, they know what we were doing now," I said with a groan as Shane traced his fingers over a couple of stretch marks on my belly.

"We got a little loud at the end," he agreed, leaning down to run his lips over my belly button.

"We? What *we*, kemosabe? That was all you. I was quiet."

"Yeah yeah."

"Man, I'm going to have to start working out," I grumbled. "My legs are sore as shit."

"Thighs or calves?" he asked, sitting up.

"Yes," I answered, making him smile.

He reached out and began to massage my legs, starting with my thighs.

"We should sell the house," he said after a quiet few minutes.

"What?" I leaned up on my elbows to look at him.

"We're not using the master bedroom." He glanced at me before looking back at what he was doing to my legs. "We should have a house that's ours."

"Are you sure? I mean, I know that you don't want to use that room, but—"

"Is that what you thought?" he asked, looking at me in surprise. "I don't care what room we're in. But at the beginning, I was sneaking in here at night and praying you wouldn't kick my ass out. I wasn't going to push it by asking you to switch rooms."

"Oh," I responded quietly.

"Everything I have is yours, Katie, okay? I don't have any hang-ups about that shit."

"I don't know. It's just a little weird." I shrugged uncomfortably. "It probably shouldn't bother me."

"But it does."

I nodded, giving him a half smile.

"So we should get our own house," he said, switching legs. "It'll probably take a while to sell this one though."

"I'm not in any hurry," I assured him.

We grew quiet, both lost in our own thoughts.

I'd gotten past the feeling of being Rachel's substitute—my relationship with Shane had very little to do with her—but sometimes I still felt funny when I went through their bedroom to use the shower or found something she'd bought in the back of a closet. I figured that kind of stuff would pass with time, but I wasn't quite there yet.

"Sometimes I think I would have always found my way back to you," Shane said quietly as he stretched out next to me. "Which makes me feel like shit."

"There's no reason to think like that," I whispered, sliding my hand up his bare chest and around his neck.

"I wouldn't trade Iris for Rachel," he said softly. "I wouldn't trade Iris for anything."

"Shane," I said, my throat clogged with emotion, "if

Rachel hadn't died, you wouldn't even know Iris. Making those kind of comparisons is pointless. Don't do that."

"I love you. I love our life. I don't think I could go back," he said hoarsely.

"That's not even an option, so stop it."

He closed his eyes tight, and I slid my hand to the front of his throat as he swallowed.

"Why do you do that?" he asked, opening his eyes again slowly as he reached up to grip my wrist.

My face heated as I rubbed my thumb up and down the side of his neck, clearing my throat. "When you first came to Aunt Ellie and Uncle Mike's, you were so quiet," I told him, meeting his emotion-filled eyes. "I could usually read people, but you—I couldn't tell what you were thinking. I watched you, you know?"

He nodded, smiling slightly.

"Well, I finally noticed that if you were upset, or mad, or even happy, you swallowed hard. Just once sometimes, but it always happened. I learned to watch for that."

"Weird," he whispered.

"I knew what you were doing when I caught you kissing Rachel because your faces were so close together, but for a second you raised your head, and I saw you swallow hard."

"That was such a shitty thing to do."

"Yeah, you were such a little asshole," I agreed, running my hand down his chest to pinch his nipple.

"Ow!" he yelped, catching my hand and bringing it back to his neck.

"I put my hand on your throat"—I followed the words with the movement—"because even if you're not saying anything, I can physically feel your emotion. It's a million times better when I know that emotion's for me."

"Marry me," he whispered hoarsely, searching my eyes as he placed his hand over mine and I felt his Adam's apple bob. "Be my wife."

"Yes."

Epilogue

Shane

Tell me again why you're wearing all that junk on your face," I said to my girl, switching lanes so I could pull off the freeway.

"Because Auntie Kate said I could!" Sage replied, glancing over at me. "Since it's a special night."

Kate had adopted the kids less than a month after we'd married, and the little boys started calling her "Mom" right away—probably because Iris did. Keller had taken a little longer to feel comfortable with the idea, but he'd eventually started doing it, too. Sage, though—well, she remembered her mom clearly, and when she continued to call Kate "Auntie Kate" long after the adoption, we hadn't mentioned it. That was her decision. It didn't matter what she called Kate; their bond was set in stone.

"I don't know why you need makeup on to go to a coffeehouse," I grumbled. "It's dark in there anyway."

"Because I'm a girl and girls wear makeup," she said, losing patience with me.

"Not at thirteen."

"Can you just drop it? Geez, Dad!"

"Fine," I said, pulling my truck into the parking lot already filled with cars.

I hopped out of the truck and walked around the hood to help Sage out. She hated when I did shit like that, but I couldn't help myself. She was my little girl, and I was hoping that, if I continued to open doors for her and make sure I walked on the outside of the sidewalk, she'd remember that when she started dating and had to decide which boys she'd spend her time with.

"You're such a dork," she told me as I crooked my elbow for her to grasp.

"You think I'm awesome, don't lie," I retorted, opening the front door and ushering her inside.

We found a table off to the side of the room, and I smiled as I watched Sage glance around us at all the teenagers. She was quite a bit younger than most of them, and I knew she was feeling a little nervous about being there with her dad.

"Hey, guys, can I get you anything to drink?" a young kid in an apron asked us right after we'd sat down, flipping his bangs off his forehead as he stared at Sage.

"Can I have a hot chocolate?" Sage asked softly, blushing.

Oh hell no.

"Black coffee," I barked, making the kid jump.

"Uh, sure thing," he mumbled, backing up a step before spinning around.

"Seriously, Dad?" Sage hissed, glancing around us.

"What?" I knew exactly what. I'd been a jackass, but I wasn't about to explain that that boy had been checking out my *thirteen-year-old* daughter right in front of me. Better that she had no idea about the effect she had on the opposite sex.

"Hey, San Diego," a familiar voice called out over the speakers. "How you guys doing tonight?"

The room filled with cheers, and Sage's face lit up as she looked past me toward the stage.

"Aren't you guys sweet?" Kate rasped with a short chuckle. "I love coming in to play for you. You're good for my ego."

The crowd grew even louder, and I couldn't stop the smile that spread across my face.

"If you're new to our little open-mike night, there's a coffee can being passed around. Who's got it?" She paused. "Okay, see the boy in the yellow shirt? Raise your hand, Colby. There, that guy. When you get ahold of that coffee can, drop in a few dollars if you can and pass it on."

The crowd clapped, and she chuckled again over the sound system.

The clear notes of a single guitar came through the speakers, and I watched Sage freeze as the entire room went silent. Even the baristas behind the counter stopped what they were doing to watch the stage as Kate began to sing.

My eyes were glued to Sage as the sound of Kate's voice hit me the way it always did.

Even after five years together, she still took my breath away when she sang. She was incredible. My eyes finally left Sage's enraptured face, and I turned to see Kate in a flowing red flowered dress, her lips and eyes painted dark. She knew exactly what she was doing, and the kids around the room freaking loved her.

She hadn't sung in public for quite a while after Iris was born, but a little more than a year ago she'd mentioned that she wanted that creative outlet again. I'd supported her wholeheartedly.

There was something about her self-confidence onstage that just did it for me, and I was willing to pay a couple of girls in our new neighborhood to watch the kids for an hour or two so I could take her for a night out once or twice a month.

When we'd moved from Oceanside almost a year after Iris was born, Kate had been nervous that the kids would never make any friends and we'd never be able to find a babysitter again. Fortunately, she'd been wrong on both counts, and our small cul-de-sac was filled with families with both little kids and teenagers. It was pretty much the best neighborhood we could have chosen.

We could go out once a week, even if it was just for a quick dinner, and sometimes we were even able to catch a movie afterward. But my favorite nights—by far—were the ones I watched my wife on stage. Kate loved performing, especially for charity, and I loved watching her have fun. It was a win-win.

"Pretty cool, huh?" I asked Sage, smiling as she

waved off the kid who brought our drinks when he
stepped between her and the stage.

"Shh, Dad! She's been practicing this Ella Henderson
song *forever*. She's completely slowed down the tempo. I
wanna hear!"

"Sorry," I mumbled, laughing a little.

Sage wasn't particularly talented when it came to playing instruments—that was where Gunner excelled—but
she had a really good ear. I didn't understand most of
what she and Kate discussed, but apparently Sage could
understand music composition better than most people
twice her age. Kate was begging me to let her get Sage
a turntable and a mixer, but I was dragging my feet...I
liked the way my wife tried to talk me into things.

Kate moved on to another song without a break, and
Sage bounced in her seat a little, bumping the table so
our drinks spilled. She didn't even notice as I used some
napkins to clean up the mess.

"Hey, you two in the corner!" Kate called into the
mike when I'd finally gotten the mess cleaned up.
"Aren't you a little old for her?"

The crowd laughed as they figured out who Kate was
talking about, and Sage dropped her blushing face into
her hands—completely mortified.

Kate was smiling so brightly that she looked giddy.
"That's my little girl, right there. Isn't she gorgeous?"

Sage's face popped up in astonishment, and the crowd
laughed and cheered quietly.

"I wanna know who the guy is!" a girl called out from
across the room, making everyone laugh.

"Eh, that's just my husband," Kate answered flatly, causing the crowd to snicker.

She met my eyes across the room, smiling brightly, and slid her hand behind her guitar where I knew she hid a slight roundness. We weren't telling anyone she was pregnant yet, instead taking a little time just for us to relish the news in secret. It would be our last baby, and we wanted to enjoy the intimacy of her first few months without having to share it.

My wife winked and blew me a kiss, then grinned before looking away—starting in on the next song as if she hadn't just made my stomach drop.

I glanced around me and rubbed my hand over my face, forcing myself not to walk up there and pull her off the stool like some kind of caveman. I was trying not to imagine taking her home to bed so she could wrap those dark red lips around my cock.

As she sang the chorus of the new song, Kate's eyes found mine again and her smile widened. She knew exactly what she'd done, and she found it hilarious.

She was going to pay for that shit later.

Bram and Anita may be like oil and water, but the sparks they generate prove that opposites attract. When life throws them a curve, however, a no-strings relationship may no longer be enough...

Please turn the page for a preview from

A Change of Heart.

Chapter 2

Anita

I was distracting myself. It was stupid. I knew that I shouldn't be following Bram through the streets of downtown Portland, but when he'd left the house in such a hurry, I'd been curious.

Okay, I'd been *dying* to know where he was going.

Bram wasn't exactly social. I could count on one hand the number of friends he had, and he'd never brought a woman home. Sure, I'd seen him leaving with chicks from one of the local bars—but he never actually introduced them to us. So where was he going at nine o'clock on a Friday night?

I let the question roll over and over in my brain, taking my mind off the things I actually *should* be worrying about, as Bram parallel-parked across from a dive bar. What the hell? There wasn't much else on the street so I knew that was where he must be headed, but why?

Pulling around the corner, I parked in the smallest parking spot ever made and jogged toward the entrance of the bar. Bram had already gone inside, and when I glanced at the patrons smoking near the entrance, I groaned and looked down at myself. My jeans and flannel shirt were perfect for dinner at the Evans house, but I was going to stick out like a sore thumb if I tried to go inside.

I stepped quickly back around the corner as I unbuttoned my top, making a homeless guy down the street wolf whistle. Jesus. Keeping one eye on the man sitting on the sidewalk, I pulled the shirt down my shoulders and tied it around my waist, leaving me in a black cami. That should work. I bent at the waist and scrubbed my fingers through my short, dark hair, then rose back up as I reached inside my nose and pulled down my septum piercing so it was visible. The retainer was easily hidden when I was around Dan and Liz, and I didn't think either of them even knew I'd gotten it pierced. I loved it—I thought it looked badass, but my foster parents really wouldn't and I didn't want to deal with their kind but scolding comments about my "pretty face." I'd gotten enough of that when I'd dyed my hair blue my sophomore year in college.

Rifling through my bag, I pulled out a deep-purple lip crayon and used a rearview mirror to color in my lips and smooth my crazy hair a little. Perfect. I walked back around the building and made my way to the door as I slid my tongue ring in and twisted the ball on the end a few times to secure it.

The hipsters at the door ignored me as I walked past, acting like their damn clove cigarettes held the answers to the universe, and I couldn't help but snort as I stepped inside. Acting like you don't care doesn't make you look cool; it just makes it look like you're trying too hard. I could practically feel their bespectacled gazes on my flannel-covered ass. *Take a good look, guys.*

"Welcome to open-mike night," a guy called into a microphone as I bellied up to the bar and slid my ass onto a stool. "For those of you who're new here—the rules are simple. We don't want to hear your song about the melting glaciers in Alaska or the time you drove your VW bus to the Grand Canyon. Covers only, folks. You sing an original song, we'll boo your ass off the stage."

The crowd laughed, and my lips twitched as I looked at the guy on a small stage across the room. He was tall and lanky with a short beard and a shirt that said, BEER ME. Good looking, if you were into skinny guys.

"Got a friend starting us off tonight while you pussies get up the courage to sign in. Abraham?" the guy called, looking off to the darkened side of the stage.

My mouth dropped open as Bram stepped on stage, a worn guitar dangling from his hand. What in fucking fuck?

"Hefeweizen," I called, glancing at the pretty, tattooed bartender who was leaning across the bartop next to me. "A shot of tequila, too, please."

She nodded and pulled her eyes away from Bram to get my drinks.

"Hello, Portland," Bram said softly, making my stomach do a weird somersault. "Haven't been on stage in a while, so you'll have to bear with me."

"Yeah, 'cause you're an asshole," the tall, skinny guy called out.

"Yeah, yeah. I'm here now," Bram grumbled, making the crowd chuckle. "Can I sing, or are you gonna keep running your mouth?"

"By all means," Tall Skinny Guy replied, throwing his arms out.

"First song, you might not know—"

"No originals!" Tall Skinny Guy yelled as the bartender slid my drinks over the counter.

Bram went completely still and turned his head slowly toward the side of the stage while the crowd snickered.

"Fine. Fine. Go ahead," Tall Skinny Guy said over the crowd.

"Jesus." Bram shook his head. "And I worried I'd be late."

I couldn't help but smile at the way the crowd was eating Bram up. He was working them—Bram who rarely got along with anyone and walked around with a permanent scowl—and held the crowded bar in the palm of his hand.

"Like I said, you might not recognize this one—but it's not one of mine so Jay can shut the fuck up and let me do it," Bram said, leaning into the mike with a small smile on his face as he settled himself more comfortably on the bar stool he was perched on. "This is 'Thief and a Liar' by Jeffrey Martin."

By the noise of the crowd, I guessed they knew who he was talking about—but I'd never heard of him.

The minute Bram began to play, my heart began thumping hard in my chest. I couldn't tell if it was nervousness or excitement. When his voice came through the speakers again, I think I stopped breathing.

He sang, his voice a little raspy but seriously good, and I spun away, taking the shot fast before chasing it with my beer. My hands were shaking as I pulled the orange off the rim of my glass and dropped it into the glass. I wanted to turn back around and see him, but for the first time since I'd walked into the bar, I felt weird about the way I'd followed him.

It was odd. I was watching Bram do something that he'd obviously not wanted us to know about, but I was the one who felt naked.

After a few moments, I turned back around holding my beer in front of me just so I'd have something to do with my hands...and met Bram's eyes from across the room.

Oh God, I'd thought that the dim spotlight on him would hide me from view, but when I'd sat at the bar, the lights behind it had illuminated me.

"*I am a thief and a liar of the very worst kind. Oh, I sell to the broken and I rob them blind. I will build you a house with my own two hands, and then burn it to the ground as quick as I can.*" Bram's voice didn't falter, not even when he raised his eyebrows as if to say, *I caught you.*

I swallowed hard and glanced away, bringing my beer to my lips like nothing was wrong as I slid slowly off the stool. I wondered if I'd make it out the doors without him catching me. Part of me thought that he'd ignore my departure and keep going, but the other part of me knew that if I took one step away from my bar stool, he'd be calling me out over the damn speaker system.

As Bram strummed the last chord of the song, the crowd burst out in applause, and he smiled wide, glancing around in front of him.

"Damn, you guys have a lot of energy. I've been up since four a.m. I think it's past my bedtime," he said jokingly as he scratched at his beard. "You want one more?"

Whistling and cheering came through the room, and I wondered how often he came to this bar to sing. The people seemed to know him, or at least recognize him.

"All right. One more." He repositioned on his stool. "Pretty sure you'll know this one. This is 'First' by Cold War Kids."

Bram's eyes came back to me, and I fumbled with my empty beer glass, setting it on the bartop behind me.

He crooned into the mike, slowing down the familiar song.

Holy shit. He was going to kill me.

I stood frozen through the entire song, and Bram's eyes never left me. When he was done, he climbed off the stool, and I calculated my distance from the front door as I pulled a twenty-dollar bill out of my purse and threw it on the bar.

I took one step toward freedom, my eyes on Bram, when his head slowly shook from side to side warning me to stay put.

"Your turn to entertain me," Bram said, leaning down toward the microphone. The crowd cheered, but his words were for me.

"We'll entertain you," a tall girl called out, her arm wrapped around her much shorter friend as they swayed. The entire bar erupted in laughter, and the girl's face dropped as her eyes went wide. She was drunk, but apparently not drunk enough to ignore the fact that she'd just made an ass out of herself.

Bram's eyes went soft as he glanced over, then he leaned back into the mike again and nodded toward me. "Sorry, beautiful, but my girl's waiting for me at the bar."

My mouth dropped open and my stomach flipped as he moved toward me, but before he'd made it through half of the crowd, I'd snapped it shut again and was crossing my arms over my chest. He better have been talking about some other woman at the bar. If he thought I was playing along with his bullshit announcement, he was sadly mistaken.

"You di—" The words weren't even out of my mouth before his hand was wrapped lightly around the front of my throat, his fingers and thumb resting at the bottom of my jaw.

"Hey baby," he murmured, leaning in without any warning and kissing me gently.

I'd been expecting something different. Something punishing. Hard. Maybe a bite. I think that was why, when he went to move away, my mouth followed his.

It was instinct. Nothing more. But the soft brush of lips hadn't been enough.

Bram made a surprised noise in his throat when my arms dropped and wrapped around him. Our eyes met for a split second before he groaned and pushed me back against the bar.

Then his mouth was on mine again, and there was nothing soft about it. He pulled at my bottom lip, and I opened my mouth, my breath hitching as his tongue slid inside. Holy shit, Bram could kiss.

I forgot where we were. I forgot who he was. Hell, I forgot who I was.

Nothing mattered except our points of contact. His hips pressing against my waist, his hard back beneath my palms, one of his hands at my throat and the other setting his guitar on the bar behind me so he could slide his fingers through the short hair at the back of my head.

"I'll put this in the back room," the tall guy's voice said teasingly from behind me, I assumed talking about the guitar.

Bram nodded, still kissing me, and then his hand was on my ass, lifting me as I jumped up and wrapped my legs around his waist.

Oh God, that was so much better. I ground against him as he stepped away from the bar and pulled his mouth from mine. His hand moved around to the back of my head, and he shoved my face into his neck as he moved through the bar.

Shit. What the fuck were we doing? I held on tight, my face burning in embarrassment even though it was hidden, and my pussy rubbing against his dick with every step he took.

We were both breathing heavy when we hit the cool

night air, and I shivered as he asked me where I was parked.

"Around the corner," I rasped, making him shudder as my lips rubbed against his skin.

He strode down the pavement, never letting me down until we'd rounded the corner and were shadowed by the tall building.

"What the fuck are you doing here?" he asked as he dropped me to my feet.

"What the hell was that?" I snapped back, stumbling a little as I lost my balance.

"If I wanted you here, I would have fucking invited you." He ignored my question, scowling as he gripped my arm to make sure I didn't fall over.

"I didn't know you could sing like that."

"Who do you think taught Katie?" My foster sister Kate was incredible on the guitar, and she'd had a kick-ass voice for as long as I'd known her. I'd never wondered how she'd learned; it had just always been true.

"Oh," I mumbled, sidestepping him.

"Did you follow me?" he asked incredulously, moving back in front of me. "What the fuck is wrong with you?"

"With me? Yeah, *I'm* the one who fucked up tonight. Right," I said back sarcastically. "You just kissed me!"

"That's the way you want to play it?" he murmured, shaking his head as he scratched at his beard. "Sure. I was getting the barflies off my back and used you to do it, but the rest of that shit was you."

"Me?" I screeched, making the homeless guy down the street start yelling about waking him up.

"Shut the fuck up," Bram yelled back at the guy, making him go silent.

"I didn't do shit!" I hissed, my hands fisting at my sides.

"That wasn't you, grabbing me and pulling me into you—giving me fuck-me eyes?"

"Fuck-me eyes?" I screeched again.

"You're still fucking doing it!" Bram yelled back, leaning down.

We both went silent for a long moment, glaring at each other.

I'm not sure which one of us moved first, but all of a sudden, Bram's mouth was back on mine, and he was pushing me against the brick wall of the building behind me.

"When the fuck did you get a tongue ring?" he gasped into my mouth as he slid one of his thighs between mine, lifting my body slightly as he pressed up.

"A couple years ago," I moaned and rocked against him.

"I've never seen it." His hands moved over my torso, reaching up to grip my breasts through my cami.

"I know." I slid my hands under his T-shirt and dug my fingers into the warm skin at his sides.

A familiar wolf whistle came from down the street, making us pause.

"Keys," he mumbled before pressing his mouth to mine again. "Keys. Now."

I fumbled with the purse hanging over my shoulder and pulled my lips from his as I found the keys to my SUV.

The second Bram heard them jingle, he was stepping back and grabbing them. Without a word, he took my hand and walked me over to my car. When we reached it, he paused and turned his head to look at me.

I held my breath as he clicked the remote, unlocking the driver's-side door.

Then he clicked it again, unlocking the rest, and opened up the door to the backseat. He stood there, not moving, letting me make the decision. I could have snatched the keys out of his hand and moved around to the front of my SUV. That would have been smarter.

Instead, I slid past him and climbed into the backseat.

I was making a really bad decision. I knew that. I think we both knew that. Nothing good could come from messing around with Bram. At best, things would be even more awkward between us later. At worst, we'd actually hate each other instead of the halfhearted bickering we'd been doing before.

But I didn't care.

About the Author

When Nicole Jacquelyn was eight and asked what she wanted to be when she grew up, she told people she wanted to be a mom. When she was twelve, her answer changed to author. Her dreams stayed constant. First, she became a mom, and then during her senior year of college—with one daughter in first grade and the other in preschool—she sat down and wrote a story.